BOLD IN HONOR

Knights Of Honor

Book Six

Alexa Aston

Books from Dragonblade Publishing

Knights of Honor Series by Alexa Aston
Word of Honor
Marked By Honor
Code of Honor
Journey to Honor
Heart of Honor
Bold in Honor

Legends of Love Series by Avril Borthiry
The Wishing Well
Isolated Hearts
Sentinel

The Lost Lords Series by Chasity Bowlin
The Lost Lord of Castle Black
The Vanishing of Lord Vale

By Elizabeth Ellen Carter
Captive of the Corsairs, *Heart of the Corsairs Series*
Revenge of the Corsairs, *Heart of the Corsairs Series*
Dark Heart

Knight Everlasting Series by Cassidy Cayman
Endearing
Enchanted

Midnight Meetings Series by Gina Conkle
Meet a Rogue at Midnight, book 4

Second Chance Series by Jessica Jefferson
Second Chance Marquess

Imperial Season Series by Mary Lancaster
Vienna Waltz
Vienna Woods
Vienna Dawn

Blackhaven Brides Series by Mary Lancaster
The Wicked Baron
The Wicked Lady
The Wicked Rebel
The Wicked Husband

Highland Loves Series by Melissa Limoges
My Reckless Love

Clash of the Tartans Series by Anna Markland
Kilty Secrets
Kilted at the Altar

Queen of Thieves Series by Andy Peloquin
Child of the Night Guild
Thief of the Night Guild

Dark Gardens Series by Meara Platt
Garden of Shadows
Garden of Light
Garden of Dragons
Garden of Destiny

Rulers of the Sky Series by Paula Quinn
Scorched
Ember
White Hot

Highlands Forever Series by Violetta Rand
Unbreakable

Viking's Fury Series by Violetta Rand
Love's Fury
Desire's Fury
Passion's Fury

Also from Violetta Rand
Viking Hearts

The Sons of Scotland Series by Victoria Vane
Virtue

Dry Bayou Brides Series by Lynn Winchester
The Shepherd's Daughter
The Seamstress
The Widow

TABLE OF CONTENTS

PROLOGUE

ANCEL DE MONTFORT made Old Davy's cottage his last stop of the day. The oldest tenant on Kinwick lands had died the previous week. At the end of his life, Davy had gone blind and usually doffed his clothes when the weather turned warm, complaining that they irritated his skin. Ancel remembered how he and his twin sister, Alys, had been frightened of Davy when they were young children but as Ancel grew older, he had learned to respect the irascible serf. Davy grew mellow during his last years and Ancel enjoyed visiting with him each time he returned home to Kinwick on summer break from fostering at Winterbourne.

He checked the inside of the cottage and found it in good condition. The sparse furnishings included a table and two chairs that the next tenant could use. Davy's bed had been a pallet on the floor near the fire. The threadbare blanket could be tossed away with the old straw. Ancel went outside and examined the walls and roof of the structure and found it needed some new thatching in one spot. That could wait until early autumn, after the harvesting had been completed. He wondered who his mother had in mind to receive the vacant cottage. Merryn de Montfort was always matchmaking among their workers and soldiers and he had no doubt the cottage would soon have new occupants.

Ancel remounted his horse and wound his way through the forest until he reached the main road which led to the keep. He'd enjoyed his day, visiting with various farmers as he helped work the hay harvest.

Tomorrow, he'd spend time with other serfs involved with the June shearing. His father had emphasized that Ancel must get out on the estate frequently and learn everyone's name, as well as what tasks occurred throughout the year on Kinwick lands. One day, he would become the new earl upon his father's death and Ancel wanted to be every bit the man his father was. Geoffrey de Montfort not only had a reputation as one of England's greatest warriors but he was a fair liege lord, involved with every aspect of his estate.

As Ancel approached the castle, he saw in the center of the lane a bedraggled young man. The stranger had almost reached the closed gates. Ancel spurred Storm on, curious as to who this visitor was.

"I demand to see Lord Geoffrey de Montfort at once," the man said, shielding his eyes from the bright sunlight as he looked up.

"And what might your business with Lord Geoffrey be?" called down the gatekeeper.

The filthy stranger hollered back, "I have a very important missive from the king for the baron. 'Tis something Lord Geoffrey must read at once and act upon."

"And where is this missive?" Ancel asked as he drew up his horse beside the man. "I am Ancel de Montfort, Lord Geoffrey's eldest son."

The messenger looked at him warily before he pulled a small, rolled up parchment partly from his shirt. "I'm to put this in Lord Geoffrey's hands. No others," he insisted.

"Usually, a messenger sent from the king is riding a horse," Ancel noted, his eyes skimming their visitor's shabby appearance. "And he has the king's banner so that all may recognize where he comes from. You have neither." He didn't add that the king's man would have been dressed in a much better quality of clothing. This stranger, who looked close to Ancel's age, wore attire that was more suitable for a servant in the royal kitchens.

The young man's mouth set stubbornly but his eyes darted about nervously. Finally, he said, "Please, my lord. I swore to the king I would see that Lord Geoffrey read this. The king needs him. If your father reads it, he'll understand why."

Ancel studied the stranger before him. Despite the unusual circumstances, for some reason he found this messenger to be credible. He wondered why the king might have sent such an unusual courier but the answer could lie within the missive itself.

"Open the gates," Ancel called up. "I'll escort our visitor to his destination."

"Oh, thank you, my lord," the man said with relief.

As the gates swung open, Ancel told him, "Go directly to the keep and wait at the foot of the steps. I'll drop my horse at the stables and meet you. We'll go together to see my father."

"Aye, my lord."

Ancel rode straight to the stables and left his mount with a groom. The young man supposedly sent from King Edward had drawn Ancel's curiosity. He hadn't seen the king in several years now. The monarch had made it a habit to call on the de Montforts every few years by directing the royal court's progress toward Kinwick, but the sovereign's health in recent years had been poor and prevented him from traveling across his kingdom as he'd done each summer for decades.

Ancel rounded the corner and saw the messenger nervously pacing at the foot of the steps leading up to the keep. He visibly relaxed as Ancel came toward him.

"Thank you again, my lord, for seeing me inside the gates. And for granting me an audience with your father. The king was insistent that his missive reach Lord Geoffrey as soon as possible." He paused. "I know I am not the kind of man the king usually sends but he had his reasons for me coming all the same."

"Come." He motioned for the man to follow him. As they mounted the stairs, he asked, "What's your name?"

The courier hesitated.

Ancel laughed. "Surely, you can share your name with me."

"I suppose so," he said reluctantly. "I am Jupp."

"See, that wasn't so hard," Ancel teased.

Jupp scowled. "The king told me to be wary. To trust no one till I reached Lord Geoffrey's estate."

"I see." Ancel found himself even more intrigued as he led the man inside the keep. He spotted Tilda carrying a tray with food and drink on it.

"Is that for Mother and Father?" Ancel asked her.

"It is, my lord."

"Are they in the solar together?"

"Aye." She eyed the scruffy messenger beside him with disdain.

Ancel took the tray from the trusted servant. "I'll see they get it." He nodded at the stranger. "This is a messenger from the king. Would you see that clean clothes are found for him? He'll need something to eat and drink, as well, once he's met with Father." He glanced back at the bedraggled young man. "And a bath, I think, before we send him back on his way to London."

Tilda frowned. "I've never seen a royal messenger that looked like this one and we've had plenty of them over the years." She paused. "And we don't just go giving baths to strangers, you know."

The opinionated servant had always had a soft spot for Ancel, so he gave her an engaging smile. "Please, Tilda."

"Oh, all right," she said begrudgingly. "But he needs to wash the grime from his face and hands before he meets with Lord Geoffrey. Lady Merryn will be appalled at his appearance as it is," Tilda declared.

"That's a good idea," Ancel agreed.

"But my lord," protested Jupp. "I need to deliver the king's message."

He shook his head. "You heard Tilda. Her word is law inside the keep, Jupp. Clean your hands and face thoroughly and then she will deliver you to the solar to meet with my parents. I will see you in a few minutes." He looked at the servant. "Tilda, Jupp is all yours."

Ancel climbed the stairs and went to the end of the corridor. He pushed opened the door to the solar, balancing the tray in one hand, and then closed it from the other side.

His mother's face lit with a smile. She put her sewing aside. "This is a surprise. I was expecting Tilda to bring us refreshment, not my handsome son."

Ancel set the tray on the table and kissed her cheek. "Are you making something new for Wyatt and Philippa?"

She smiled. "I am. They'll grow so fast. Alys has so much on her hands since she gave birth to twins this spring. This is a small way that I can be helpful to her."

His father laughed. "Your mother would move to Brentwood without a second thought if your sister asked her to."

"Geoffrey, I would never leave you. You know that. But if Alys does have need of me, I might go and spend a few weeks again with her and Kit and the little ones. Besides, weren't you the one saying the minute we returned to Kinwick last week that you couldn't wait to see your grandchildren again?"

He shrugged. "It's not every day that twins are born. And they are our first grandchildren, my love. I know we are both eager to spend more time with them."

"I look forward to meeting my new niece and nephew," Ancel said. "Mayhap when Mother is done sewing these clothes and blankets for them, I can escort her to Brentwood." He sighed. "It's funny to think of Alys as a mother now."

"Well, she's always mothered your brothers and sister since they are younger than the two of you," his father pointed out. "Alys has a nurturing spirit."

Ancel laughed. "Hal and Edward both think they're too old to be coddled by her anymore but I know Nan still enjoys the attention she gets from Alys."

His mother asked, "How did you find Old Davy's cottage?"

"It's in very good shape. The roof could stand a little work but it can wait till we do repairs to the other cottages come autumn."

Her eyes lit up. "I'm glad to hear that. We may have need of it very soon."

His father groaned. "Don't tell me you've gone and decided to marry off another of my soldiers, Merryn."

She shrugged. "If you don't want to know, then I won't tell you."

He laughed and turned to Ancel. "Be glad she hasn't married you off yet, Son."

Merryn clucked her tongue. "I would do no such thing, Geoffrey. You know our family believes in love matches. I'd never pick a mate for Ancel. He needs to be free to find a wife of his own choosing."

Ancel laughed. "And I have no desire to marry for several years, Mother. But I have other news." He paused. "A messenger arrived from the king just minutes ago."

"I want to see the missive at once," his father demanded. "Where is it?"

"The courier doesn't look like a usual messenger, Father. Jupp was on foot when I came upon him and covered in filth. I believe he actually walked all the way here from London by his appearance."

"Not on horseback? That's odd. Where is he?" Geoffrey asked.

"He should be here any moment. Tilda had him wash up before he came to see you."

A knock sounded at the door.

"That should be him now."

Ancel retrieved Jupp from the hallway. He saw his mother's eyes widen at the young man's tattered appearance.

"My lord. My lady." Jupp bowed awkwardly and swallowed hard. "I bring you a missive from the king. He asked that I see it placed in your hands." He removed the small scroll from under his muddy gypon and handed it to Geoffrey.

His father took it and frowned. "What? There's no seal on this. How can I believe this is from King Edward, much less take it seriously?"

Jupp implored, "You must, my lord. The king is counting on you. He didn't call for wax and his seal because he wanted no one to know he sent it to you."

Geoffrey handed the parchment to Ancel. "Here. You read it. Tell me if it's worth my time," he said dismissively.

Ancel sat at the table and unrolled the scroll. The first thing that surprised him was the number of blotches on it. He'd seen missives the king had sent to his parents and those letters were beautifully written with no ink spots upon them. He scanned it without reading it and saw numerous misspellings.

"Why did a child write this?" he quizzed the messenger, who shuffled uncomfortably.

"Because he couldn't trust his secretary," the young man blurted out. "The king said he could trust no one."

Ancel saw that statement got his father's attention.

Geoffrey wheeled to face the messenger and asked, "What has happened at court that would lead to such secrecy?"

"The Black Prince is dead," Jupp revealed. "He summoned the king and the Duke of Lancaster to his bedside as he lay dying. The Black Prince had both his father and brother swear an oath that they would recognize Richard as the next king. And King Edward will ask Parliament to do the same."

Although Richard was the son of the Black Prince and should be next in line as heir to the throne with his father's death, Ancel knew there was always the possibility that John of Gaunt, the Duke of Lancaster, would try to seize power once King Edward passed. As the king's second oldest son, Lancaster might feel he would make for a better monarch than a small boy. England had been stable for decades, thanks to King Edward's long rule. A nine-year-old boy was hardly a replacement for a king who'd sat on the throne for almost fifty years.

"When did this happen?" his father asked.

"Prince Edward died last week on the eighth of June. King Edward knows that the duke has spies everywhere. The king asks to see you in person, Lord Geoffrey, and he didn't want his son to know you'd been summoned to court by him." Jupp paused. "I'm only a servant in the royal household. The king told me that you'd find a place for me at Kinwick. He said by the time I reached you, his son's spies would know I was missing. That I've been gone. If I return?" Jupp shuddered.

Geoffrey looked to Ancel. "Read the missive aloud."

To Lord Gefrey de Monford —

Grandfather says to tell yu that these are his words, my lord, but I am writting them down for him. I am Richard, son of Edward of Wood-

7

stock, known as the Black Prince of Englund.

Lord Gefrey, I have need of yu. My helth is fayling and I must see yu at once. Bring yur oldest sun when yu come. I warn yu—there's danger evrywhere.

Pleas keep Jupp at Kynwyk. He's a good workur and will serv yu well.

Hurry, my lord.

Sorry, Lord Gefrey. I'm not the best speller in Englysh. My Latin is beter.

Ancel glanced to his father. "That's all there is."

He watched a look pass between his parents. They had been married long enough that they could communicate without words. His mother nodded but Ancel saw her eyes mist with tears.

His father took his wife's hand and pressed a kiss to her fingers. "We must go, my love. Our king has need of us."

"I understand," she said softly.

He looked to Ancel. "Will you ride with me?"

"Of course, Father." Ancel could barely contain his excitement. Intrigue at court? Going on a mission with his father to see the king? He'd never been part of anything like this.

Geoffrey took the scroll and held it to the flame of the candle sitting on the table. The parchment caught fire and began burning. Ancel realized that his father was intentionally destroying any evidence of the king's command.

Geoffrey dropped the burning paper in the fireplace and looked at the messenger. "Lady Merryn will find you a place at Kinwick, Jupp. You can work the land or help with the horses."

"Does your blacksmith have need of someone?" Jupp asked. "I was training to be a smithy before my father died. That's when I went to work with my mother in the royal kitchens."

"We can arrange that," Merryn said.

Geoffrey turned to Ancel. "Find Gilbert. Tell him I want twenty of our best men to go with us to London," he told his son.

THEY ARRIVED IN London at night after riding for two days at a quick pace. Ancel had never been in the city, much less at any of the royal residences. He'd only heard Alys describe them from her time spent in service fostering with Queen Philippa. Leaving their men outside the Palace of Westminster, he and his father moved through a myriad of long hallways and cut through many groups of people collected in small clumps. Ancel couldn't believe the size of the magnificent rooms, much less the sumptuous tapestries and luxurious furniture and tiled floors. He'd thought Kinwick a beautiful place but the king's palace left him speechless.

Finally, they stopped near where a small group of men gathered. Their clothing and bearing told him they were some of the most important men at court. His father motioned one of them over.

"Lord Geoffrey," the balding man exclaimed. "I didn't know you were in London. Did you hear of the Black Prince's death? Such a shame. Edward of Woodstock would have made a most excellent king for England."

"I did hear the news. I would like to offer my condolences to the king, as well as speak to him regarding other matters. Can you arrange an appointment with him? As soon as possible, since I'm only passing through London."

The man hesitated. "That might prove difficult, my lord. The king's schedule is quite full." He thought a moment. "It will probably be a good two months before you'll be able to see him."

"That's not acceptable," his father said evenly.

Ancel shivered inwardly. He knew that tone. He'd tried pushing the boundaries with his father when he was younger. Geoffrey de Montfort tolerated nonsense from no one. This nobleman would do well to beware.

"I see." The court official frowned and glanced around surreptitiously. "I must confide in you, my lord. The king is actually quite ill. Mayhap you would like to meet with the royal council instead? I can consult with the Duke of Lancaster to see when they might be able to accommodate you. If you'll come back tomorrow afternoon, I can let you know."

"Thank you, my lord. We'll see you then."

Ancel wondered why his father agreed to putting off being seen but he knew he would soon learn why as his father marched from the room and down a hallway. Ancel kept pace with him as they continued down several corridors and found an empty chamber.

"I doubted we'd be able to see the king," his father confided. "The Duke of Lancaster will have him insulated since the Black Prince's death. Especially if the king is also ailing."

Ancel suggested, "Remember when Kit and Lady Thea sought an audience with the king? Kit said they spoke to him the first thing in the morning, before he'd even broken his fast."

His father grinned. "It's worth a try. We'll stay inside the palace and try to see him before most noblemen begin to stir. The guards on duty won't question me if I appear since I've come to the king's rooms many times before."

They found a bench and leaned their backs against the wall so each could take a turn at getting a couple of hours of sleep. Then, before servants even began stirring, they made their way down a maze of hallways to the king's chambers. Ancel saw members of the royal guard standing at the door as they approached.

"The king is expecting us," Geoffrey said easily. "And how are you, Manfred? It's been some time since I've seen you."

Ancel listened with one ear as his father made conversation with one of the soldiers on duty. What drew his interest instead was a small boy that slinked along in the shadows. Ancel made eye contact with the child and the boy motioned to him.

"Is that Lord Geoffrey?" the boy whispered when Ancel came to stand beside him.

"Aye. How did you know?" Ancel asked.

But he didn't receive an answer. His father caught his eye and waved him over. They entered the royal rooms. Just as the guard began to close the door, the boy scurried in behind them without a word from the guards. He ran ahead through another door and then poked his head out and indicated for them to hurry.

As they entered the royal bedchamber, Ancel was again astonished by its size and opulence. A servant lay on a pallet next to the king's bed.

"Open the curtains!" a deep voice commanded. Ancel recognized it as that of King Edward.

The portly servant scrambled to his feet and pushed the bed curtains aside.

"Leave us."

"But sire—"

"I said leave. Bring me some bread and ale. And not a word to anyone. Do you understand?" The king's stern look would have frightened a grown man.

"Aye, sire." The servant fled the room without a backward glance. The young boy closed the door once the servant departed.

"You came." Edward looked old and tired to Ancel, nothing like the tall, vigorous figure he remembered from half a score ago.

Geoffrey bowed to the king. "I did, sire, and I've brought with me Ancel, my eldest son, as you requested."

Ancel also bowed and said, "And we've brought someone with us."

He saw a fond smile appear on the king's face as the old man patted the bed. The boy rushed over and climbed up next to the king, taking his hand.

"This is Richard of Bordeaux, my grandson. He's my heir now. I want everything to go smoothly for him since my time draw nears."

"Grandfather, you aren't going to—"

"Nay, Richard," the monarch said sternly. "We've spoken of this. 'Tis best to be prepared." He looked at Geoffrey and Ancel. "Though my son, John, promised his brother that he would see Richard on the throne upon my death, John always was a greedy boy—and a greedier man, amassing land and wealth. Thank the heavens that Parliament acknowledged yesterday that Richard will follow me when I'm gone. So for now, John will try to rule through the boy. I know what that's like."

Ancel understood what the king spoke of. Edward had been crowned at fourteen when the queen and her lover, Roger Mortimer, deposed Edward's father. Mortimer ruled England through Edward for three years until Edward led his own coup against Mortimer and seized complete control of the throne. So the king had experience and was looking out for his grandson.

"My son will try his best to maneuver around the royal council once I'm gone. They can only keep him at bay for so long. Lancaster has a powerful personality and friends in many places."

Geoffrey asked, "So what do you ask of me, your majesty? Do you wish me to remain in London and take a place on the council to ensure that young Richard here keeps his throne once you pass?"

The king grunted. "Nay. I know you wouldn't, though I've asked you to sit on the council several times over the years. I can't blame you, Lord Geoffrey. London and the royal court aren't the same place since my beloved Philippa's death."

Edward pushed aside the covers and swung bony legs over the side of the bed till his feet touched the floor. "I have a different favor to ask of you, my lord. Actually, more one your own boy can provide."

Suddenly, Ancel felt the king's intense gaze upon him. Ancel saw steely resolve in the old monarch's eyes.

"I need someone to look after my grandson. Someone to protect him. A man willing to give his life to do so. I've trusted Geoffrey de Montfort for many years." The king eyed Ancel carefully. "You're so much like your father. Will you come to London? Will you watch over my Richard and keep him safe?"

Ancel glanced to the young boy who still held his grandfather's hand. A boy of only nine. One who'd recently lost his father. Ancel remembered the first six years of his life when he didn't have a father, thanks to Geoffrey being imprisoned by an enemy. Ancel had been lonely and unsure throughout that time.

Richard looked at Ancel hopefully and he knew his decision had been made. Without hesitation, he said, "It would be my pleasure, sire."

"Teach him all you know, Ancel de Montfort. He'll have tutors for his education. They'll deal with his atrocious spelling and appalling penmanship. But you? You will guide him in other things a man should know. Swordplay and weaponry. Military strategy. How to treat his horse and how to treat a woman. Teach him about the important things in life—honor, duty, respect. How to be a good man. And most important of all? Keep him safe from the dangerous men who walk these halls. Help Richard mature. Help him become the man he needs to be to rule this kingdom. Can you do that?'

"I accept, sire. I will do my best to help shape him into becoming Richard the Second, King of England."

With those words, Ancel knew his life had changed forever.

CHAPTER I

London—June, 1381

A NCEL SAW THE billowing clouds of black smoke in the distance. Moments later, the wind blew the acrid smell his way. It invaded his nostrils and left a harsh taste in his mouth.

London was burning?

He spurred Storm on, covering ground more quickly than he had in the past week. He hadn't wanted to leave the king but Richard had insisted that Ancel ride north to Scotland to be his eyes and ears. A bulk of the royal forces had been scattered along the border because of the rampant rumors of an impending Scottish invasion. The king wanted a show of force in the north to prevent any type of rebellion from taking place. Since other English troops were still stationed on the continent, it left the monarch with only a few hundred men at his disposal.

That left London vulnerable. But who had attacked the city?

Ancel remembered his promise to Richard's grandfather and how he'd pledged to keep King Edward's grandson safe from harm.

What if Richard was already dead—and the Duke of Lancaster had finally seized the throne?

Ancel pushed that thought aside. He wouldn't let worry cloud his judgment. He'd make his way to the king. Find out what had taken place in London. Then do whatever it took to protect the young royal.

Even if it meant giving his life.

Richard had matured in the five years since Ancel had come to court. At ten and four, the young king was already as tall as any grown man. He was also intelligent and well read. Unfortunately, he still had a tendency to stammer when he became agitated but Ancel believed once Richard took on more responsibility, he would begin to have faith in his own abilities and leave his nerves behind.

The harsh smell from the fire irritated his nose and throat as he drew close to the city. Ancel saw hundreds of people on the road headed in his direction and more pouring through the gates. He wondered how many had lost their homes in the fires—and who was responsible for the setting of the flames. He maneuvered his horse through the disheveled crowd. Londoners carried their possessions in their hands and wore lost looks on their faces as they shuffled en masse.

Ancel rode over the bridge. Either no one alive was left on duty or the soldiers had abandoned their posts when the chaos broke out. As he galloped through the streets, the scope of the destruction stunned him.

He came to Savoy Palace, home of the Duke of Lancaster—or what had been the duke's home. Embers still smoldered around the little that remained of the structure. The best Ancel could tell, the blaze here had occurred in the last day or two. He traveled further and found the entire legal district of the Temple also in ruins. Remnants of burnt law books lay scattered in the streets, their pages floating in the wind.

Then scores of dead bodies came into view. Some by themselves, others piled together. A quick assessment told him these weren't men who'd perished in the flames.

They'd been murdered.

He spun his horse around. Bodies lay in every direction. Not all were connected with the government. By their dress, he recognized several of the dead to be Flemish in origin. A deep prejudice ran against the Flemish weavers who'd practiced their trade in London for decades, invited there by King Edward and Queen Philippa. Had a group from the English weavers' guilds killed these artisans? Even if they had, who'd murdered the rest and set fire to the city?

Ancel saw a man picking his way through the dead and called out to him. "What happened here?"

The man tucked something shiny inside his gypon before he looked up. "'Twas the rebels. They did it all."

"What rebels?" Ancel demanded. "I've been gone from London the past month."

"Them from Kent and Essex way. They've set fires across the city. They're killing anyone associated with the royal government. Their mob marched in over London Bridge two days ago. No one dared to stop them. A lot of townsfolk even joined in. They stormed Westminster Gaol and Newgate Prison. Freed everyone imprisoned there."

Ancel's mind reeled with this information. He knew how unpopular Lancaster's taxation policies had been. The duke's poll tax instigated just before King Edward's death had been revised twice and Ancel knew common folk were at their breaking point, giving up coin and livestock to pay the heavy burden to the royal treasury.

"Is there any news of the king?" he asked, almost afraid to hear the response.

The man shrugged. "I heard he's locked himself up safe in the Tower but that could be a rumor."

Ancel thanked the man and turned Storm in the direction of the Tower. He reached the grounds minutes later only to find it in shambles. People running in every direction. Screaming. Looting. It was a city gone mad. His eye caught a large mass of men moving toward Tower Hill, so he followed them at a discreet distance. Shock reverberated through him as he recognized the Lord Chancellor and Lord High Treasurer being dragged before a jeering crowd by armed rebels. Sudbury looked terrified, while Hales seemed numb to everything going on around him.

Both men were forced to their knees and beheaded within seconds. Bile rose in Ancel's throat. He wouldn't allow the king to suffer such a punishment.

He wheeled his horse and spurred it back toward the White Tower, where the monarch kept rooms.

"Sir Ancel! Sir Ancel!"

He spied a member of the royal council rushing toward him on foot.

"Help me!" the nobleman cried as he reached Ancel.

"Where is the king?" Ancel asked, his heart beating frantically.

"He's gone," the man panted. "To Mile End in east London. To meet the rebels."

Ancel didn't wait for further information. He galloped away from the Tower, ignoring the pleas of the royal councilor to rescue him. Reaching the king was paramount. He pushed his horse hard, hoping to come across Richard before the young man came in contact with the rebels. If these men were burning London to the ground and beheading royal councilors, he couldn't imagine what they might do with the king.

Ancel cursed the Duke of Lancaster and his group of friends that had inserted themselves into every aspect of royal life. Lancaster managed the throne and his taxation policies had caused this unholy mess. Ancel knew the time drew near for Richard to assert his authority and force his uncle aside.

If he lived long enough.

Cresting a hill, Ancel saw thousands of peasants gathered, as far as he could see. He spied the king's banner and rode straight toward it, yelling for those in front of him to get out of his way. Ancel made it through the throng and caught sight of the king. A lump formed in his throat. He'd grown to love Richard as a brother and would shield him from any harm.

"Sir Ancel!" the king called.

Ancel jumped from his horse and hurried toward the monarch. He gave a quick bow and asked, "Are you all right, sire?"

"Aye." The king motioned for Ancel to come close as he turned aside from the small guard that surrounded them.

"How is the border?" Richard asked. "Has it held?"

Ancel felt a moment of pride in the young boy who'd become a young man. Surrounded by thousands of his angry subjects, he still thought as a king despite the danger that encircled him.

"The Scottish border is secure, sire. I will share reports from the various commanders I spoke with when the time is right. But what's happened here?"

The king's mouth flattened in displeasure. "'Tis Uncle's taxes. These men are calling for me to hand over my uncle, two archbishops, and key members of my royal council."

Ancel glanced around. "I don't see Lancaster present."

Richard snorted. "Funny how Uncle has made himself scarce these past few days. I don't plan to hand anyone over but they have a charter they want me to sign."

He frowned. "What else do these peasants want?"

The king held up a sheaf of papers in his hands. "I'd just finished reading this when you arrived. It calls for the abolition of serfdom and wants me to grant a general amnesty for the rebels." Richard gave him an earnest look. "I can do both in good faith, Sir Ancel. These men have told me that they support me and the monarchy. They simply wish to rid the royal council and courts of the corrupt officials within them." He hesitated. "Do you think this a good course of action?"

Ancel had often given the boy king advice but this went beyond anything that had ever been asked of him. He chose his words carefully, knowing what Richard did and said today might influence the course of England's future.

"I agree that you shouldn't hand over anyone to these rebels, your majesty, no matter what they demand." Ancel decided now wasn't the time to tell the king of what he'd witnessed happening at the Tower. They needed to deal with the situation in front of them. "I do think abolishing serfdom would be a wise move on your part. The Black Death's killed half our workers. Serfs have been able to bargain for higher wages due to the lack of manpower. Your action would give them the chance to leave the land they're tied to and travel where they wish. It would allow them to negotiate fair wages for their labor."

Richard nodded in agreement. "And the amnesty they wish for?"

"You could say that is coming without guaranteeing exactly who would receive it."

The king's eyes narrowed in thought. "I like that. It's a good plan, Sir Ancel. I knew I could look to you for wise advice." He gripped the parchment in his hand. "Come, join me. Let us meet with these rebels."

Ancel watched as the king walked proudly to where the leaders of the rebellion awaited him. The royal guard followed Richard. Ancel hurried to take a place near the king.

The monarch held the parchment high above his head. His voice rang out loud and strong.

"Good people, I choose not to hand over any of the officials you seek. Instead, it is my solemn vow to personally see that justice will be meted out to those who deserve it."

Before the crowd could grumble in discontent, he quickly added, "What I will sign, here and now, will be an order that will forever abolish serfdom in all of England. Riders will be sent immediately to every corner of the land. Englishmen will be able to negotiate fair pay for a good day's labor. And I plan to grant general pardons to most men involved in the rebellion of this past week."

A rousing cheer went up at the king's words. Richard called for a quill and ink and quickly signed his name to some of the papers. He handed these over to the leadership of the rebellion, who seemed stunned that the monarch had accommodated their wishes so easily.

Ancel took a few steps that closed the gap between him and the king. He leaned and whispered into Richard's ear, "We should leave with all haste, sire, while they are happy—and before they decide to press you on the issue of your uncle and royal council members."

"Good thinking, Sir Ancel." The king moved rapidly away from the center of Mile End to where his horse awaited him, along with almost two hundred soldiers.

Before he could mount the animal, Ancel told him, "You cannot return to the Tower, sire. I was there earlier when I rode in from Scotland." He didn't want to say anything more until they were safely away.

"Then we'll go to Blackfriars," Richard decided. "And I want to hear everything, Sir Ancel. About Scotland." He paused. "And whatever's happened at the Tower."

CHAPTER 2

Highfield

MARGERY ORMOND SAT silently breaking her fast as Lord Umfrey Vivers bitterly complained about the recent peasants' revolt to his younger son. As always, Gervase agreed with everything his father said.

She couldn't blame the serfs—at least, not the ones who toiled at Highfield. Her stepfather was a cruel man who lashed out in rage over the smallest problem or mistake. She knew from their grumblings that the estate's tenants were underpaid and overworked. Many had deserted Highfield and joined in Wat Tyler's revolt as he led rebels from Kent and Essex to London to meet with the king a fortnight ago. Now Tyler was dead and the rebellion seemed to be collapsing without his leadership.

Margery wished *she* could rebel.

From the time she and her mother had arrived at Lord Umfrey's manor house, she'd been told how grateful she should be that she had a roof over her head and food for her belly and clean clothes to wear. Lord Umfrey had married her mother after Margery's father killed himself and left his family with huge debts. Her mother constantly emphasized how gracious the baron had been to take them in when they had nothing, for once the debts had been paid, naught remained.

Gracious was the last word Margery would use to describe her stepfather—or her two stepbrothers. Thurstan was a year older than she and Gervase a year younger. The boys had been unkind to her from the day she arrived at Highfield, taunting her about her father's gambling and how he'd killed himself and now lay in unconsecrated ground. Their harsh words turned to vicious actions as they would pinch her. Push her. Yank her hair. Spit on her food. They hid her hairbrush and ruined her shoes. She'd soon learned that tattling to her mother didn't help matters. By then, Marian Vivers was totally under her husband's thumb and wouldn't hear a word against him or his unruly sons.

Margery was thrilled when both boys finally left the manor to foster, only returning a few times a year. She thought she, too, would be allowed to foster with another family and escape the oppressive atmosphere at Highfield but her new stepfather said that Highfield was already a new place for her. She could learn as much here as from any other nobleman's family, so she might as well stay put and help her mother run the household. But each year that passed brought Margery more misery—which is why she wished she could rebel.

But where would she go? As a woman, she had no say in her future. Frankly, she had no future. She could see wasting the rest of her life waiting upon her stepfather and then Thurstan, once he inherited the title and lands.

"At least London's mayor and Standish did the right thing by running a sword through Wat Tyler," Lord Umfrey proclaimed to a nodding Gervase. "But rebellion continues in Hertfordshire. Suffolk. Cambridgeshire. Looting. Destruction. And the king was foolish enough to grant pardons to most of the rebels, with their sticks and axes and old swords still in their hands."

"Then they should be returning to the fields to work," Thurstan said, a smug look on his brutish face. "'Tis where they belong. I hope things will get back to the way they should be."

"But some of our people left and followed these rebels." Lord Umfrey snorted. "Until they trickle back, look what I'm forced to do. I've been sending my soldiers out to the fields to work the harvest since I'm short on labor. Already, five of them have left my service. They told me farm work was beneath them. That they'd find another liege lord who respected their soldiering skills and would give them just pay."

Margery knew her stepfather barely paid his soldiers more than he did his serfs. She didn't blame anyone that left. She only wished she could leave with them.

She rose to slip away. Lord Umfrey wouldn't wish for his tirade about the peasants' revolt to be interrupted. She'd learn to speak only when spoken to when in his presence. Margery went past the wooden screens that blocked the kitchen from the great hall and quickly assembled food and drink for her mother's meal. Now, though, she must cross the great hall again and she dreaded drawing her stepfather's attention. Her fingers clutched the tray, hoping he wouldn't notice her. She had much work to accomplish today and didn't want to be pulled away from it.

"Margery!" he called from the dais across the room.

Reluctantly, she came toward him. She kept her expression neutral but she could feel Thurstan's eyes raking over her. Ever since he'd come home the previous month, she grown more uncomfortable with his blatant stares in her direction. She'd made sure never to be alone with him.

"What do you plan to accomplish today?"

It didn't surprise her that Lord Umfrey asked this. Though he did very little himself, he always insisted that his stepdaughter remain busy throughout the day and well into the night. She couldn't remember the last idle moment she'd had. It seemed the man even begrudged the sleep she stole every night.

She raised the tray in her hands. "First, I will help Mother break her fast and bathe and dress her for the day. Then I need to—"

"My men haven't had time to polish their armor, what with them having to play at being farmers. I need for you to do it for them. All of it. At once," he barked.

She wanted to bark back that if he had a page or two, it would be their job to polish armor—not hers. But no families sent their sons or daughters to foster with Umfrey Vivers. Margery could only imagine what other nobleman said about her stepfather and his uncontrollable temper.

"Aye, my lord," she said meekly, because that's what she always said. No matter what he requested, she never questioned his authority. Her mother had told Margery since she was five years old that her duty was to see to her stepfather's every wish. Margery never spoke out or disagreed with Lord Umfrey. She never drew attention to herself. Instead, she strove to remain patient and calm as her mother wished her to do. On the rare occasions when Margery had complained when the two of them were alone, her mother had reminded her daughter that women didn't fight battles. They must do as they're asked.

Or told. Her stepfather never asked. He only issued orders to her and he expected them to be followed without question.

She bowed her head briefly to hide the rage that would be revealed if Lord Umfrey looked her in the eye. Slowly, she gained control of her emotions.

Raising her head, she added, "I will do so, my lord, as soon as I've attended to Mother." Margery walked to the stairs that sat next to the buttery, not wanting to contemplate how many hours over the next few days would be wasted shining the armor of Highfield's soldiers.

She climbed the stairs and started down the small corridor which held only two rooms. One belonged to her stepbrothers; the other, Margery shared with her mother. She balanced the tray against her hip and opened the door. Before she could walk in, a creak in the floorboards behind her had her whip around.

Thurstan had followed her.

He stepped close to her. Margery backed into the doorframe, relieved that she held the tray between them. He loomed over her, his eyes roaming her face and then dropping to her breasts. Thurstan grabbed a hold of her wrist. His other hand stroked her cheek.

Bile rose in her throat. She was afraid of him and always had been—and he knew it. But the light in his eyes now caused a new kind of fear within her. It coiled in her belly and sat like a cold lump. Margery was afraid she would drop the tray and then have no barrier between them.

"You've grown into a beautiful woman, little sister," Thurstan said softly, his tone meant to intimidate her.

"I'm not your sister," she snapped. "And you've never treated me as one."

He grinned as his fingers took her chin in hand. "No, you aren't. But you could be something else to me." His words hung in the air.

Margery knew what he meant. It made her sick to think about it.

"Get away from me," she hissed, not wanting her mother to over-hear their conversation.

Thurstan tightened his fingers on her wrist. "You always thought you were too good for us. Right from the start. That pert little nose stuck high in the air. It's about time that I took it down a notch or two," he warned. "All the way down to my cock, *little sister.*"

"And if you do, then I'll bite it off," she cautioned. "Make all the threats you want, Thurstan—but be prepared to pay the price."

"Margery?" her mother called, her voice faint.

"Coming, Mother." She jerked her head, freeing it from his fingers. "Release me before you cause a scene."

His face grew red. He squeezed her wrist till she thought her bones would shatter. "Say what you want, you silly, little bitch. But I'll be waiting for you sometime when you least suspect it. Gervase, too. I wouldn't want him to lose out on the fun."

Thurstan released her wrist and strode away.

Margery stood frozen for a moment. She didn't trust her trembling legs to support her if she tried to walk. She leaned against the wall and took a deep breath, composing herself, then she entered the bedcham-ber and kicked the door shut with her foot.

"Good morning, Mother." She was pleased that her voice didn't betray the hysteria that she strove to tamp down and banish.

"Hello, dear," her mother whispered. Then the coughing began.

Margery placed the tray on a nearby table and helped Marian to sit up. She propped several pillows behind her mother and handed her a clean cloth. More coughing ensued. When the cloth came away,

Margery saw it was stained with blood. Each morning, she prayed her mother would recover from the lingering illness she suffered from but, in her heart, Margery knew that her mother's time was limited. She grew weaker by the day.

"Let's get some of this broth in you," Margery suggested as she brought the small bowl to her mother's lips.

After a sip, her mother frowned and pushed it away. "I can't."

"You must. Mother. You're wasting away."

"So be it. I feel my life ebbing away. I haven't the strength to do anything about it."

Margery resigned herself to the fact that the day was approaching when she would awaken and find her mother dead in the bed next to her.

What would become of her then?

For five years, Margery had acted in her mother's stead. She'd taken over the duties of running the household as her mother grew more and more ill. Her stepfather had insisted that his wife move out of the solar because Lady Marian disturbed his rest, so Margery shared a bedchamber with her mother. She took sole care of Marian and did many physical tasks inside the manor house since her stepfather was so tight with his coin that he hired as few servants as possible.

When her mother passed away, Margery would be even more trapped. Her father had gambled away the promised bridal price and her betrothal had been broken once it became known that he'd taken his life. She was already one and twenty but her stepfather had proclaimed that he needed his stepdaughter here at Highfield to run his household and refused to arrange a marriage for her. She knew once her mother was gone, Lord Umfrey would never consider finding her a husband. Margery would never be able to have children of her own. She would die in this gloomy place, miserable and alone. So much for accepting her fate and being a docile daughter all these years.

"Is there any news?"

Her mother asked that each day. Margery would tell her about different tasks she'd accomplished or what had been plucked from the garden. She might share if a new babe had been born on the estate or if a couple had wed. But she'd kept quiet about the uprising surrounding them and how it had affected London and Highfield. She didn't see the need to worry a woman whose whole world had been reduced to inside these four walls.

"Not really," she said breezily. "Though I'm to polish armor today. I won't be able to spend as much time with you as I usually do. Lord Umfrey expects me to drop everything when he has a request."

Her mother patted her hand. "You're such a good girl, Margery."

She brushed her mother's hair and bathed her face before dressing Marian in fresh clothes. Those actions alone tired her mother, so she decided to let the woman sleep. Before she could even slip from the room, Marian already snored softly.

Margery returned the untouched tray to the kitchen and then headed for the armory. She spent the entire morning polishing armor, humming softly to herself as she tried not to worry about how far behind she would fall in all her other tasks. Gradually, her fingers began to cramp. She decided it must be time for the noon meal. Since they had no cook, she and Sarah had been preparing a lighter meal because it was harvest time and the workers were eating out in the fields. The heavier cooking would be done this afternoon for the evening meal. Still, Margery needed to make sure she helped Sarah deliver the food to the hungry harvesters. Lord Umfrey's soldiers were already cranky enough by having to work as common laborers. She didn't want them complaining to their liege lord about a delay in receiving their food.

Putting aside her cleaning rags, she flexed her fingers and then rotated her wrists. Her neck and back ached from bending over all morning. She glanced around and was pleased at how burnished the completed armor looked so far. If she worked as quickly for the remainder of the day, she might finish before the evening meal tomorrow.

Margery couldn't shake the odd feeling that came over her as she started toward the great hall. She couldn't put her finger on it.

Then she realized that it was too quiet inside the manor house. She rushed to the great hall and found it empty, so she hurried to the kitchen. No one was there. Dread filled her. Sarah and their few servants should have already prepared the baskets so they could take the meal to the fields. Yet not a soul was in sight, nor had she passed anyone on her way here.

Where could everyone be?

Then she knew. She'd caught bits and pieces of conversations that died down when she came across various servants inside the keep this past week but she'd heard enough to realize that Wat Tyler's rebellion wasn't yet done. Margery had listened as her stepfather told his two sons of how noblemen had been killed and their keeps burned as the Kent and Essex rebels marched to London. How the peasants had set fires that raged across the city. She hadn't wanted to think anything like that could happen at Highfield, even though it was in Essex. They'd seen no signs of trouble at Highfield.

That should have been a sign in and of itself, she realized, being lulled into complacency. And if anyone deserved the wrath of the serfs, it would be her stepfather and his two spoiled sons. Their harsh ways with their tenants might be the downfall of them all.

Margery ran to her bedchamber and found her mother still dozing, so she shook her awake.

"We must leave Highfield at once," she said calmly, though her insides churned.

A puzzled look crossed her mother's face. "What? Leave? Why?"

Quickly, she explained what had happened in the last two weeks and saw the dawning horror on her mother's face.

"And now I can't find anyone inside the manor house," Margery revealed. "I'm afraid our servants may have joined with the other peasants in this rebellion. They may be trying to make another stand against the king's men." Margery took her mother's cold hands in hers. "I'm afraid for our safety, Mother. We can't stay here. The people hate Lord Umfrey with a passion. All of them. They might set fire to the manor house with us in it."

"Fetch my casket. It's in the bottom of the chest."

Margery flung the chest open and dug until she found the casket. She hadn't seen it in years.

"Bring it to me."

She did as her mother asked, wondering why this was so important when they were pressed for time.

"There are only a few jewels in here. They belonged to my mother. When I married, my father passed them along to me. They were pieces your father didn't know about or he'd have gambled them away or sold them. Lord Umfrey gave me none in all these years, so you'll have to make do with what's left."

Margery opened the casket and found an amethyst ring and a pearl necklace. She quickly tucked both of them into her pocket.

"Lift the bottom out," her mother commanded, her voice stronger than Margery had heard it in months.

She tugged at it until her nail could get under the false bottom. When she pulled it up, she discovered a silver pendant that she'd never seen before. Margery removed it from the casket and held it up by the chain, intrigued with its unusual design and inlay of garnets.

Her mother's face softened. A beautiful smile came to her lips, making her look years younger. She reached for the necklace and Margery placed it in her hands.

"Oh, I haven't seen this in so long." She shook her head, her lips moving silently.

Suddenly, the door flew open. Sarah, Margery's favorite servant and only friend, rushed in and slammed it. She had some bunched up brown wool in her hands and quickly shook it out. Margery recognized it as one of Sarah's unadorned kirtles.

"They're coming," she gasped. "We've got to hide you both. They'll kill you. They've already attacked the soldiers in the field." Tears spilled down Sarah's cheeks. "Those poor men. They didn't know it was coming. Suddenly, scythes being swung left and right. Blood everywhere. It was horrible."

Margery clasped her mother's hand. Her mind reeled, trying to think about places they could hide without being discovered.

Sarah came toward her. "Quick, my lady. Put this on over what you're wearing. If you manage to get away from here, you might be able to pass as a serf. At least for a little while."

The servant held the gown up and slipped it over Margery's head as she said, "The Wycliffe preachers have stirred up the crowds. The rumor is that the pardons will be revoked. It's started the uprising again." Sarah cast her eyes downward. "You know the baron and the Crown constantly squeeze us for more money, my lady. The people are tired of it. They're tired of everything."

"But Margery and I have done nothing wrong," her mother proclaimed weakly. "We haven't hurt a soul."

Sarah shook her head. "You are nobility, Baroness. 'Tis all they'll see."

"I must tell you about the pendant, Margery. About your father." Marian wheezed and then began coughing uncontrollably.

Margery thumped her mother's back, hoping to get the coughing to cease.

Then a thought struck her fast as lightning. A place to hide. Somewhere no one would find them. She'd seen the boys go into it years ago. A secret passage in the solar, hidden behind a tapestry. They'd chided her, warning her not to enter behind them. She could still hear Thurstan's stinging words.

"It's not for girls. It's only for us. For real Vivers. You and your mother will never be Vivers as we are. You're a stupid girl whose stupid father killed himself. You'll never be one of us."

No, Margery remained an Ormond. She'd persevered in being a good girl and hadn't explored the passageway though she wished now that she had. At least she knew where it was located, even if she had no idea where it went.

Sarah placed a cloak around Margery's shoulders. "You can pull the hood over your hair and face, my lady. That might help disguise who you are since your cloak is so plain." The servant fastened the cords as she spoke.

So her stepfather's penury in supplying her with cloth to make her cloak might come in handy after all.

"Come, Mother. I know of a place in the solar where we can hide. It may lead away from the manor house."

Her mother shook her head in sorrow. "I can't leave, child. I wouldn't last the day. I can barely walk, much less run and hide. You must go without me."

"No," Margery said, tears blurring her vision. "I won't leave you."

"You must." Her mother held out the silver pendant. "Put this on. It's yours now. It comes from your father. He wanted you to have it when you were old enough." She shook her head. "I should have told you sooner. And now there's not enough time," she fretted.

"I know everything I'd ever need to know about my father. He gambled away our home and his lands. He lost everything of value. He took the cowardly way out and killed himself."

"Nay," her mother said, another coughing fit preventing her from speaking. Marian took Margery's hand and dropped the pendant in her palm, closing her fist over it. Finally, her mother wheezed, "Lord Joseph Ormond wasn't your true father, Margery. My—" More coughing erupted, with blood spilling from her mother's mouth and dribbling down her chin.

Margery wanted to stay and ask what her mother meant. Her father wasn't her father?

Then who was?

But Sarah tugged urgently on her hand. "Come, my lady, or it may be too late."

Margery let Sarah pull her toward the door. She paused when they reached it, wanting to turn back and kiss her mother goodbye. Her mother still coughed harshly, the blood more profuse now. She fell back into her pillows, spent, her eyes closed.

"Now!" Sarah insisted.

They raced down the stairs and across the empty great hall toward the second staircase that led to the solar. As they approached the stairs, Margery could hear angry shouts in the distance.

"They're coming," Sarah warned. "You need to go by yourself, my lady. Hide. Do whatever you must to survive."

"Won't you come with me?" Margery pleaded.

"Nay. You go. Stay hidden away. I'll try to come to you at nightfall if I can find you." Sarah took off running toward the kitchen.

Margery pulled the cloak about her and ran up the stairs. She could hear the voices now.

"Find the baron!"

"Find the bloody bastard!"

"And his sons!"

"And kill them all!"

"There he is!"

Margery dashed into the solar, blood rushing in her ears so loudly that she couldn't hear. She ran into the bedchamber, straight to the tapestry, as she brought the necklace over her head to free her hands. She lifted the tapestry and felt along the stone wall, pushing high, low, in the middle, frantically searching. She didn't even know what she was looking for. It had been so many years ago that she'd seen Thurstan and Gervase playing here.

Where was it?

Was she wrong? Had she dreamt it? Suddenly, a large stone popped back, swinging as if it were on some kind of hinge. Memories flooded her. She remembered the boys dropping to the ground and crawling through. Margery did the same now.

It was like a half-door, low to the ground. She climbed through it, pulling her cloak away from the opening, and dropped to her knees in order to push the stone back into place.

Now, she was in total darkness. The passageway smelled musty and damp. Margery ran her fingers along the hidden door and discovered a bar. She pushed and heard it snap into place. Relief washed through her. Then she heard steps on the other side as if someone had run into the solar. Had the mob already arrived?

She held her breath as tapping sounded on the other side of the doorway. A groan occurred as if someone had triggered the secret stone but the door didn't move, thanks to the bar holding it in place.

"Bloody Christ! Who's in there?" a panicked voice demanded.

It was Lord Umfrey.

CHAPTER 3

MARGERY'S HANDS FLEW to her mouth to keep any sound from escaping.

"God's Bones! Open up! They're almost here," the baron pleaded, his voice cracking in despair.

Dare she open the secret passage and admit her stepfather? Was there time?

With trembling fingers, she reached out in the dark and located the bar. Before she could slide it, a muffled noise thundered on the other side of the stone wall. Angry shouts followed and she knew the peasants had arrived. She snatched her hands back and wrapped them tightly around her as she crouched on her knees in the dirt. Fear paralyzed her. Even if Margery had wanted to help her stepfather, she couldn't move.

A surge of voices filled her head, as many people began to bellow. Margery could pick out Umfrey Vivers. At first, the noblemen shouted boldly at the mob. Then their voices swelled in volume and number. She could hear him begging them.

And then screaming . . .

She cupped her hands over her ears, trying to block out the sound. Tears leaked from her eyes and fell into the dirt as she leaned over and pushed her forehead hard against the ground. A blood-curdling shriek shattered the air, traveling through the thick wall that separated her from certain death. Margery sobbed silently, her body heaving as terror filled every fiber of her being.

Then the unearthly cry abruptly ended. Shuffling sounded again.

The throng withdrew from the bedchamber and the solar. An eerie silence reigned.

Margery remained where she was, her arms curling about her head. Her entire body trembled in fear. She didn't know how much time had passed since the darkness was so disorienting.

Then she knew she had to act. She'd left her mother alone and helpless while she cowered like a gutless weakling. Her mother's life might depend upon it. Margery had to go back or she would never be able to live with herself.

Gradually, she pushed herself to an upright position and reached out to explore her surroundings. All she felt was the dirt beneath her and the cold stone walls of the secret passage around her. She was afraid to exit her hiding place where she had entered in case anyone remained in the solar and decided she would push onward to see where the hidden route led her.

After she took two steps, she stumbled, pitching to her knees. Her hands came to rest upon something. Running her hands along it and feeling smooth wood, Margery determined it was a large chest. She tried to open it and found it locked. It piqued her curiosity but she could always return later and examine it with the light from a candle. For now, she would press onward.

Though she was of average height, she had to stoop as she made her way through the narrow passage. Both hands ran across the walls on either side of her as she inched her way along. In the dark, she had no idea of the direction she took and she came across no other doors in which to exit. Surely, the concealed path wouldn't lead to a dead end.

Then she came to a widening of the corridor and found she was faced with a choice. Should she go to the left or the right? Margery was left-handed and chose to go that way. Using the walls as her guide, her fingers finally brushed against something that was similar to the slide she had thrown across the door when she first entered the passageway. With trepidation, she took a deep breath and decided to push the bar aside to see where she might be.

Then, suddenly, voices startled her. She dropped her hands to her sides and leaned her ear against the half-door.

"Who are you? Why are you here?"

Her heart tore in two as she recognized her mother's voice. The path had led her to the other side of the manor house as she had hoped.

And her mother wasn't alone.

"We want what's due us," a resentful voice cried. Margery recognized it as belonging to their carpenter and her stomach twisted.

"I have nothing," Marian said. "If you are from Highfield, then you know I've been ill for many years. Whatever could I have done to wrong you?"

"All nobility has wronged us," another man called out.

Margery bit her lip. She was too frightened to open the door at this point.

"When did I or my daughter ever mistreat any of you?"

It surprised her how calm her mother seemed. For a moment, she sounded like the Lady Marian of former times, assured and in control of any situation.

"Where are your jewels?" demanded a woman, her tone harsh. "Your casket?"

Margery could hear objects being tossed about. She assumed the peasants confronting her mother rooted through her chest.

"There's nothing here," the same woman said. "Lord Umfrey probably took it."

"My husband treated me worse than you," Marian revealed. "There are no jewels from him. No rich clothing. He never gave me any boon in all the years of our marriage."

Deep coughs erupted and Margery knew her mother was spent. The brief interlude of standing up to the unruly group had taken its toll on her.

"You lie," the woman proclaimed, her raspy, grating words full of spite.

A groan erupted, eerie and long, then nothing.

What had happened?

But Margery knew. Either these people had snuffed out her mother's life or she had finally passed from what ailed her. Margery's resolve strengthened as she promised herself that she would find justice for her mother—no matter how long it took.

"You! Where is Lady Margery?"

Margery tensed. Sarah must be in the room.

"I don't know," her trusted friend said. "Lord Umfrey had Lady Margery polishing armor in the armory. Mayhap, she's still there."

Margery sent a silent prayer to the Blessed Virgin that Sarah wouldn't be caught in her lie and punished by these bloodthirsty peasants.

She could hear footsteps retreating from the bedchamber and bided her time. When several minutes passed, she decided it was safe to leave her hiding place for a few moments. As quietly as she could, Margery pushed the bar away and then eased open the door and nudged a stone away similar to the one in the solar's bedchamber. A tapestry blocked the way, which was why her attention had never been drawn to it before, though it must have been as concealed as the panel in the solar had been. She wondered if her stepbrothers even knew this bedchamber could be accessed from the hidden passageway. Something told her they didn't—else they might have used it to visit her during the night.

Climbing out, she stepped into the room where she had slept for many years and forced herself to move toward the bed that she shared with her mother.

Shock reverberated through her as she saw Marian slumped against the pillows, her throat cut, blood soaking the bedclothes. Margery knelt and forced herself to stare at the image, burning it into her soul.

Taking her mother's cold hand, she pressed it against her cheek and whispered, "You were very brave, Mother. You stood up to them. I am so proud of you." She placed a kiss on the dead woman's forehead, the tinny scent of blood filling her nostrils. Rising, she promised, "They will pay. Of that, you can be certain."

With new resolve, Margery took the candle from the table next to the bed and returned to the wall. Lifting aside the tapestry, she bent and set the candle inside the passage and then climbed inside again. She secreted herself once more, though this time she now had a source of faint light. Making her way back more quickly than before, she arrived at the fork and took the other branch this time. Her legs trembled as she followed it to its end.

Who would have dreamt the serfs of England would rise up as they did and kill anyone of noble birth without rhyme or reason?

Though she had sympathized with them in the beginning, murdering her innocent, helpless mother had changed everything.

Slumping to the ground, Margery set the candle down beside her and leaned against the wall. She would bide her time and wait till nightfall before she revealed herself.

MARGERY OPENED HER eyes, unsure of where she was. Darkness surrounded her. Her hands fell from her lap and brushed against dirt.

The secret passageway.

Everything came back to her in an instant. She bit back the scream that threatened to erupt. She must have fallen asleep and wondered how much time had passed.

Listening to her surroundings, no noise came. She remembered that she'd reached the end of the hidden path that wound through the manor. The candle must have gone out. Gathering her courage, she removed the bolt from the half-door and pushed at it. It didn't budge. Margery supposed it could have been many years since the entrance had been opened. She threw her shoulder into it and still made no progress. Finally, she sat facing it and brought her feet to the entrance to kick against it. That did the trick.

As she crawled out of the space, a cool breeze greeted her. Night had fallen. From somewhere, faint laughter carried on the wind. In the distance, she saw light and believed something burned. Replacing the door so it would remain unnoticed by anyone who might pass by,

Margery kept close to the walls along the manor house in order to hide in the shadows.

Footsteps caused her to pause and hold her breath.

"They all got what they deserved," a man said.

"The baron thought he was so grand," a woman cackled. "He ain't much to look at now, is he?"

"The bastard always had a heavy hand in punishing his serfs," the man added. "It's a good thing he finally got a taste of what he doled out."

The voices faded as the pair's footsteps receded. Margery waited and heard no one else coming, so she continued to skirt the building until she came to a corner. She forced herself to venture beyond the house now and sneaked across the empty bailey. As she passed the training yard, she tripped over something and hit the ground hard with her hands and knees, skinning them. Turning, she realized that she'd stumbled on a body. The wind blew a cloud against the sky, allowing moonlight to shine down and expose the face of a knight she recognized. His vacant eyes stared up into the sky.

Quickly, she averted her gaze only to see a few other bodies littering the yard. Her stomach lurched and, without warning, vomit spewed from her mouth. She hoped these men hadn't suffered long as she rose to her feet and made her way to the stables. Though she'd never been on a horse in her life, she wanted the quickest way to escape all of the death that surrounded Highfield. She wanted to ride away and be anywhere but here. She realized she had no idea how to saddle one of the beasts, much less climb upon one and control it enough to flee, but no other idea of escape came to her. Margery only hoped she could figure out what to do.

Crossing to the stables, she came across no one before she arrived. Ducking inside, she lit a lantern to guide her way as she walked along the line of stalls. No horses remained in the entire building. Margery didn't know if they'd been stolen or set free.

She supposed she would have to walk. But where? She had lived at Highfield ever since she was five years of age. At one and twenty, she had never left the estate in all these years. Even though she knew the names of a few of their neighbors, they also could have suffered the same fate as her mother had at the hands of the revolting peasants.

Should she make her way to London? Would it be the haven she needed from all of the violence she'd seen today? Rumors had reached Highfield that Wat Tyler had led many of those in rebellion toward London but Margery wasn't certain if the mobs had actually reached the great city. Not knowing if she could even find her way to London, she thought the best plan was to set out on foot and stop at the first convent she came to along the way. Though she had no religious calling, surely the nuns would give her sanctuary until the madness ended. If they didn't, she had no idea where to turn.

Leaving the stables, she decided to exit through the postern gate, hoping no one was there, and seek the road that lay past the wheat fields. The thought of wheat made her stomach gurgle. Hours had passed since she'd last eaten this morning but she was afraid to reenter the keep to search for food in case she came across more angry serfs.

The bright moonlight continued to light her way as she hurried across the bailey. Thanks to it, she saw the still body lying in her path. As she skirted it, Margery halted in her tracks.

Clothing she was all too familiar with draped the dead man in the dirt. He'd been disemboweled. Both legs protruded at odd angles. Scattered fingers lay in the dust surrounding him. A dark pool of blood oozed from beneath him. Worst of all, Umfrey Vivers' corpse was headless.

No one deserved this kind of torture, not even her cruel stepfather. Margery retched again but nothing came up. Then she heard the hum of many voices carried on the wind and she knew it wasn't safe to linger. The sound came from the direction of the postern gate, so she abandoned that route of escape and rushed back to the stables to hide in its shadows.

She watched as a group of people carrying torches traveled through the open area. Horror numbed her as she spied the baron's head impaled on a spike that bobbed up and down in the midst of the assembled group. They passed by, not seeing her, most looking up at the nobleman's face, the last moments of terror emblazed upon it. They continued marching and singing to the front gates and Margery knew they would mount the head at the entrance for all who passed by to see it as some twisted lesson.

Thoughts of fleeing tonight died within her. She would never be able to get past the out of control mob. The safest place to hide to prevent being discovered would be inside the secret walkway. Hurrying back toward the keep, she hoped everyone would be celebrating the baron's death, and she was right. The great hall was empty, its fire burned down to embers.

Margery rushed into the kitchen and grabbed a basket, throwing a small round of cheese, a half-loaf of bread, and two pears into it. She slinked up the stairs and back to the bedchamber she'd shared with her mother. She hadn't bolted the secret door there as she had the one in the solar. Guilt flooded her at what had happened to Lord Umfrey due to her refusal to admit him.

She deliberately kept her eyes away from the bed where her mother's lifeless body lay and went to the tapestry that concealed the entry to the hidden passage. Entering it, she secured the bar behind her so no one could follow her that way. Once more, she crouched as she felt her way without the use of a candle and took the right fork until she reached the end where she'd recently exited. Using her hands, they roamed until they found the bar and slid it into place.

Now, she was locked in for the night. Margery slid her back against the wall until she sat in the dirt again and devoured the food she'd brought with her. Only after she'd eaten it all did she regret not saving any for whatever journey she embarked upon tomorrow. She hoped she could leave in daylight before anyone stirred. Being out in the dark tonight had frightened her.

Curling into a tight ball, Margery wrapped her cloak about her and fell into a fitful sleep.

CHAPTER 4

A NCEL AWOKE FROM the nightmare, sweat dripping from his body. He sat up and gazed around the armed camp. Darkness still hung over the earth. Dawn would not occur for several more hours. He lay down again, his mind whirling with the events of the last two weeks.

The plot to end the rebellion had taken longer than any of them had thought possible. The day after Ancel had returned to the horrors in London, he accompanied the king to a meeting with Wat Tyler and his rebel force, which numbered in the thousands. The Essex rebels, satisfied with the charter King Richard signed, had dispersed for the most part—but Tyler wanted more.

Much more. And it had cost Tyler his life.

The rebel leader had greeted the king with a familiarity that didn't sit well with the noblemen and soldiers gathered at Smithfield. Wat Tyler had addressed the monarch as *"Brother"* and offered promises of friendship between the two of them. Then Tyler demanded in rapid succession the end of the tithe system, abolition of the bishops, a redistribution of wealth, and equality for all before the law. The peasant rounded out his list of demands with insisting on the freedom to kill animals in the royal forests and then calmly requested refreshments be brought to him.

Before a shocked Richard could reply, William Walworth waved about his sword, trying to intimidate the brash peasant. Tyler attacked London's angry mayor and Walworth repeatedly stabbed the rebel, aided by a royal squire.

Ancel thought for sure that carnage would break out immediately and drew his own sword but, somehow, the fast-thinking monarch defused the situation. Riding to the middle of the gathered rebellion, he shouted for the mob to follow him and he led them to Clerkenwell Fields in central London. A bold move by the boy king but it worked. The mass followed him without question and Walworth somehow managed to gather the city's militia and disperse the poorly-equipped peasants after they arrived. By the end of the day, the London rebellion had collapsed—and Wat Tyler's head adorned a pole.

Skirmishes had popped up outside the city and into the countryside north and east of London and the king had led his troops against them ever since. Richard had confided to Ancel that he never meant to honor the pledge he'd signed, only doing so to buy time so that he could regroup his army. The king's superior army had pushed the dwindling force of ill-equipped Essex rebels closer together until the entire group fled to the woods northeast of the town of Billericay. Come dawn, the attack would begin.

Ancel would never be able to fall back asleep at this point. He rose and walked to the west, where he could stretch his legs while feeding his belly, then he would prepare his mind for the battle ahead.

As he reached the fire where a huge cauldron of stew simmered constantly, he spotted a familiar figure scooping food into a bowl.

"Greetings, my lord," he said to Thomas of Woodstock, the Earl of Buckingham. Buckingham and Sir Thomas Percy had been chosen to lead the king's forces against the rebels.

"Ah, de Montfort. Couldn't sleep?" Buckingham handed the steaming bowl to Ancel and retrieved another one for himself.

"Nay, my lord." He brought the bowl to his lips and tilted it, tasting venison and onions.

"I never do the night before battle," the nobleman confided. "I'm on edge and can never relax." He turned the wooden bowl up and slurped some of the stew from it.

"Do you think it will end tomorrow?" Ancel asked. "This rebellion against the Crown?"

"Here in Essex? Aye, I do," Buckingham confirmed. "More peasants have run off every day and the ones we've trapped are weak and hungry, not to mention lacking weapons and training." He eyed Ancel carefully. "But you are close to the king, so I know you have heard that the movement has spread beyond this region. We may quell revolution in Kent and Essex today on the battlefield but it has gone beyond where we stand."

Ancel nodded. "I listened as the king read the dispatches aloud in his tent tonight," he confirmed. "Word came a few hours ago that the unrest in East Anglia has been curbed, which was good news, indeed. Did you know a mob attacked at the University of Cambridge and killed the royal officials present?"

Buckingham grunted. "Was it le Despenser who put an end to things?"

"Aye, he led the king's forces at Walsham in Norfolk County. All is quiet there now."

Buckingham looked grim as he said, "I fear this movement will reach as far north as York and all the way west to Somerset."

"If you are right, then it will be dealt with harshly," Ancel replied. "The king, though young in years, will not back down. He will mobilize whatever army is necessary to end the rebellion, no matter how far it stretches. I have found him to be mature beyond his years."

"What about Lancaster?"

Ancel grew thoughtful. Though Buckingham was a trusted nobleman and part of the king's inner circle, he still wanted to be discreet.

"The king has bided his time since he came to the throne at ten years of age. But I will say that with the bravery and determination he's shown these past two weeks, he is certainly coming into his own. Richard won't necessarily need his uncle to guide him much longer."

Buckingham nodded in agreement. "One thing these peasants have gotten right is that John of Gaunt is a corrupt, despicable man. Though royal blood runs through his veins, the king would be smart to rid himself of his uncle's presence and send Lancaster far away from court." He paused. "That is, if Lancaster survives. Many of his retainers and close friends have perished by the peasants' hands already. I am surprised the duke hasn't met a similar fate."

"He's a wily one, my lord. If anything, Lancaster will land on his feet, much like a cat tossed out a window, full of hellfire and using up another of its nine lives," Ancel observed.

The earl grunted and they returned to their stew, finishing in silence.

Ancel returned his empty bowl to a pile on the ground. "If you'll excuse me, my lord, I plan to stretch my legs and clear my head before donning my armor."

"Wait."

He stood still, wondering what Buckingham might want.

"You have been with young Richard from the beginning, have you not?"

"Aye. His grandfather, the old king, worried about what would happen to his grandson after his death. King Edward trusted my father, Geoffrey de Montfort, and he extended that trust to me. I have been close to the king since before he came to the throne. Though officially I am a member of the royal guard, my role goes far beyond those duties. I am the king's eyes and ears in places he cannot go and I will do anything to protect him from his enemies—be they on the battlefield or in hidden alcoves at the royal court."

Buckingham smiled. "I like loyalty in a man. The king does not plan to ride into battle this morning. Do you plan to remain by his side?"

"Nay, my lord. The rest of his royal guard will see to him. No enemy will come close to approaching the king when he is ringed by their protection. My talents will be best utilized on the field."

"Then may I invite you to my side when it is time to ride forth into battle?"

Pride swelled within Ancel. "I would be most honored, my lord."

"Collect your armor and meet me at my tent in an hour."

"Aye, my lord."

Ancel hurried back to where he had bedded down and roused a young squire named Will that he'd come to like.

The boy sleepily rubbed his eyes and brushed back his hair from his face. "You have need of me, my lord?"

"I require assistance with my armor, Will."

The squire didn't question him about why he would don his armor so early and Ancel liked that about the boy. He was always eager to please and asked thoughtful questions, storing away the nuggets of knowledge. Though Will helped several of the knights associated with the royal guard, Ancel decided he would ask the king if he could take Will under his protection so that the lad could serve Ancel exclusively. His gut told him the squire could be trusted and that he would make a good knight someday if given the proper instruction.

A quarter of an hour later, Ancel was ready to ride into battle. Only his horse needed to be readied.

"Will, please prepare Storm and bring him to me. I'll be at Buckingham's tent, which is next to the king's."

"Aye, my lord." Will frowned slightly and turned to leave.

"Anything wrong?" Ancel asked. He guessed what the boy might say.

The squire squirmed under his scrutiny. "It's just that . . . well, Storm is a handful. And that's on a good day, my lord. But I will do my best to see him prepared."

"I still have time before I plan to meet up with Buckingham. Would you like me to accompany you? I might be able to give you some ideas on how to handle Storm and other horses that tend to have minds of their own."

"Would you, my lord? I'd be ever so grateful," Will said, the relief obvious on his face.

"Come. We'll take on the task together."

MARGERY AWOKE, THIS time knowing exactly where she was. She unfurled the cloak from her body and sat up. Her belly remained full from last night's late meal but she knew it wouldn't remain that way for long. She pushed her hand into her pocket, fingering the ring and necklace that she'd placed there only yesterday afternoon. Her fingers then went to her neck and the silver chain there. She felt for the pendant and thought it wise to slip it inside her kirtle to keep it from view.

She leaned against the wall a moment. This was the first time she'd had to think about her mother's final words to her—that Lord Joseph Ormond wasn't her true father. Margery knew she had been born during the first year of her parents' marriage. No other children came after her arrival. She could remember a fragment of an argument between her parents regarding children, though she'd been too young to understand it at the time. Now she wondered if her father—no, her mother's husband—had suspected that his wife came to the marriage bed already with child.

And if Lord Joseph wasn't her father, then who might be? Why hadn't her mother married him instead?

The answer was obvious. Margery's parents had been betrothed from a young age. She supposed her mother had fallen in love with another man. Mayhap he, too, had been promised to someone else. What a tragic set of circumstances. Her mother had spent her life with one husband who gambled his fortune away and killed himself, only to wed a second one who was cruel in both word and deed.

But who could her true father be?

Then she understood that her father might not come from the nobility. Her mother could have coupled with a stable hand or a steward. Any man on her father's land. If so, then Margery's blood might be no better than what ran through the peasants that now attacked Highfield and beyond.

No, that couldn't be. If it were true that her father wanted her to have the silver pendant when she came of age, he must have been a man of some means. Silver was a valuable metal and the garnets in the pendant were both large and numerous. To give her mother a parting gift of such value, her true father had to be a man with money behind his name.

If only Margery had a few moments longer to spend with her mother. Marian Vivers had started to reveal her lover's identity and been cut off by the pressing circumstances.

Now, Margery would never know of her true origins.

She needed to quit wasting time fretting over things from the past that were beyond her control. What was important at the moment was to leave Highfield. The peasants had already murdered her mother and stepfather, along with others. If she fell into their hands, she would certainly meet the same fate they had.

She decided to return to the secret door in the solar and unbar it in case she needed another quick escape route into the passageway if she ran into the angry peasants again. She made her way through the dark passage to the solar door and slipped the bar free. Once she had done that, she returned to the door leading outside. Her fingers reached out and located the bar that locked the outside world away. Gingerly, Margery slid it aside and cracked open the door a sliver. Darkness greeted her, a stillness hanging heavily in the sweet air but she sensed dawn was not far off. She slipped from the secret hideaway which had saved her life, her feet landing on the ground. Sealing the door, she gathered the cloak Sarah had provided about her and made her way across the bailey, scanning the yard for any movement. She came across the discarded, lifeless body of her stepfather again and steeled herself. Passing it, she picked her way carefully in order to avoid the other dead bodies scattered about, the shapes of the soldiers who had remained at Highfield. These men had even taken over the harvest since so many local serfs had abandoned the fields in order to join in the rebellion. She guessed either they must have been caught unaware or been overpowered by the greater numbers of peasants who had swarmed the estate yesterday.

Margery couldn't do anything for the dead now, not even her beloved mother. Father Martyn would have to see to the Christian burials of all the dead at Highfield, though he was old and doddering. She wondered who might dig the graves for so many and decided she couldn't worry about it because it might drive her mad. Her focus needed to be on walking toward Billericay, the nearest town to Highfield. All Margery knew was that the city sat to the east of where Highfield stood. From there, she would need to learn where London lay.

As she headed toward the gates, Margery sent a prayer to the Virgin Mary, asking the Blessed Mother for her guidance and protection from any violence while on the road. Surely, she would come across a convent at some point on her journey toward London. The good sisters should be willing to take her in because of the events occurring throughout the countryside. She would remain behind the convent's walls till the insurrection died down. Hopefully, that would give her time to figure out where she could go.

Reaching the gates, she found them hurled wide open. Not a soul was in sight, either on the ground or up on the wall walk. Before she hurried through and set out on the road that ran between the fields of wheat, she decided to search the last body left at the entrance to Highfield. By his dress and the sword resting near his side, Margery knew the man had been a soldier. Already a rotten stench wafted up from him. She held her breath while she searched him and found what she was looking for. Holding up the baselard, she inspected it. The blade seemed sharp and would give her something to use to defend herself if needed. She'd been around kitchen knives for years, chopping onions and separating parts of chickens to roast. Surely, this small dagger wouldn't be any different to use.

But slicing up a dead bird was a far cry from stabbing a living man. If confronted, could she follow through and attack someone who threatened her safety? Margery hoped she wouldn't be tested in this way. She slipped the baselard into her boot. The cold steel against her bare leg made her aware of the dangerous path she was about to set out on.

Taking a deep breath, she pushed onward just as the sun began to rise in the east. By the time she reached the crossroads, Margery knew which way to turn and began walking in the direction of the sun toward Billericay.

Sarah came to mind as she trod along the deserted road and Margery prayed that her friend had survived the horrible events that had transpired yesterday. Sarah was a sweet girl two years younger than Margery. They'd become close friends over the years and performed many of the chores around the keep together. Cleaning always became a faster, more pleasant task with a partner and Sarah's sunny smile and high spirits brightened every day.

Walking alone on the road, Margery suddenly realized that she was free from Lord Umfrey Vivers. Though she hated how her stepfather's life came to a bloody end, he no longer controlled her in any way.

But what about Thurstan and Gervase?

Both her stepbrothers had been present at Highfield yesterday. She'd seen each while they broke their fasts. Did one or both of them escape the madness that had reigned at Highfield? She hadn't recognized them among the dead but, in truth, Margery deliberately hadn't looked at the faces as she'd passed by. Knowing how the serfs felt about Lord Umfrey and how they'd even accused her innocent mother of mistreatment, she knew if the mob had come across either Thurstan or Gervase, they would have killed the nobles on the spot. Both men were cut from the same cloth as their father—greedy, ruthless, and unforgiving.

As the sky grew lighter, Margery became concerned. Though she saw no one either behind or in front of her, tales of how dangerous travel could be filled her thoughts. Only last month, a traveling peddler had been found dead close to Highfield, all his wares missing, even down to his very clothing. She'd been horrified when Gervase recounted the news to her but he'd told her that what the thieves hadn't kept for themselves would have been sold at market, including the man's gypon and pants.

With that in mind, Margery decided to enter the woods that ran along the edge of the road. She would walk a parallel path to the road which would allow her to remain out of sight from others. It would make spotting any travelers easier for her, while they'd be less likely to see her from a distance. If she did spy anyone, she could push deeper into the forest until the stranger passed her by.

She continued for a long time. Her stomach began to gurgle loudly, insisting that it be fed. She also grew thirsty and wondered how far away Billericay still lay. Her feet already ached from so much walking and her body tired from being tense and alert to any unforeseen danger about her.

Pausing to catch her breath, Margery heard a sound and cocked her head to listen. She was certain it wasn't an animal in the forest. She glanced in both directions and saw no one in sight on the road. Shrugging, she began again and kept on for some minutes.

Then she heard something once more. She couldn't make out what the noise might be.

She frowned, uncertain if she should continue. But still, nothing was in sight and she needed to reach Billericay and beyond. Convincing herself she only imagined it, she pushed on. After hearing or seeing nothing for a while, she began to relax as she rounded a curve in the road. All at once, a buzzing surrounded her. She halted in her tracks and glanced in every direction. Proceeding cautiously, the air grew heavier as she sensed the presence of people.

Margery cut deeper into the woods and spotted movement ahead. Slipping from tree to tree, she finally came close enough to discover a huge group of men assembled.

God in Heaven . . . she'd stumbled into the very midst of the rebels.

Hundreds of men gathered, some on horseback, many on foot. A nervous energy surrounded them and she knew they were poised to attack. Her thoughts jumbled as she leaned her back against the tree, wondering what she should do.

Then a wail rose, growing in strength until she had to cover her ears from the noise. The very earth beneath her feet shook as the rebel army moved forward as one. She peered from her hiding place behind the tree trunk and watched them pour forth from the forest in a blur.

Though her body poised for flight, Margery knew she must remain in the forest. It was far too dangerous to leave now. Getting to Billericay would have to wait. But the tumultuous sounds of battle, while repelling her, attracted her all the same. She crept closer to the edge of the woods and watched in both horror and fascination as a mass of soldiers swept through the peasants. King Richard's men moved with precision. No wasted moves occurred on their part as the rebels began to flounder and scatter.

Suddenly, a ragged man came running toward her. He held his side, blood leaking between his fingers. A knight in armor on horseback chased him, wielding a long, heavy sword stained with blood. The man reached her and fell into her arms, almost causing her to lose her footing.

"Help me," he pleaded, as blood bubbled from his mouth.

Margery saw the horseman had almost reached them. In fear, she pushed the man back and dropped to her knees as the sword whizzed through the air. The rider rode past her into the trees as the rebel's head flew through the air and rolled when it hit the ground. Sickened by the sight, she looked over her shoulder and saw the knight turning his horse. Though she couldn't see his eyes through his helm, a chill passed through her.

This knight would now come for her.

A scream bursting from her lips, Margery lifted her skirts and ran for her life—straight onto the battlefield.

CHAPTER 5

ANCEL STUDIED THE opponent across the field. These remaining Essex rebels were the last men standing in the fight that had gone on the past couple of weeks in and around London. It surprised him how many sat atop horses. He wondered where those beasts had come from. Surely, they weren't all plow horses the serfs had used in farming.

He was ready to fight. Dawn had come and gone and the signal had not been given. Buckingham and Percy had sent scouts out, waiting for the right time to attack, but it had left the king's army restless and irritable as they anticipated their attack.

Finally, the battle cry rang out and Ancel unsheathed his sword, urging Storm forward toward the rabble of poorly-dressed and even more poorly-armed peasants. As the gap closed between the Crown's troops and the rebels, he noted a scattered few held weapons in their hands, which they must have claimed from previous skirmishes. Most, however, carried mere sticks or rocks, which they began to throw at their attackers as the king's forces drew near.

These would not repel the wave of Richard's men that thundered toward them.

He brandished his sword in his right hand and held the reins in his left as he reached the beginning line of serfs. His blade sliced through first one opponent, then another, as he toppled man after man from their horses.

After two passes, he'd downed over a dozen men. The grass already ran red with the blood spilled. Ancel pulled on Storm's reins and turned the horse in order to scan the area. Wild confusion spread throughout the ranks of the serfs still alive. Those on horseback dispersed without any organized retreat, riding in every direction, while those fighting on foot began to panic and run without thought. That would make it somewhat harder to end this engagement but one look at Buckingham waving on the king's army in encouragement let Ancel know that sooner, rather than later, this engagement would end the hard-fought resistance from the Essex and Kent men.

It seemed such a senseless waste that so many men had been killed—and for what? England already had lost many thousands to the wicked Black Death and now the death of hundreds—if not thousands—of rebels would create a manpower shortage even more severe. It would take years to recover from losing another generation of males before farming would thrive again. It wouldn't surprise him if soldiers were ordered into the fields in order to claim the harvest this year and in years to come.

A sadness washed over Ancel. These peasants never had a chance against a superior army of trained soldiers who fought for a living and yet the insurgents had decided to fight on despite their dwindling numbers and lack of weaponry. In a way, he admired their bravery for attempting to make a final stand yet their foolishness angered him at the same time. Women and children might starve now, thanks to their menfolk never coming home.

Ancel nudged Storm's flanks again in order to do one more sweep of damage to the rebels. As he galloped at full speed, attacking those in the path he rode, he spied a woman amidst the fighting and bloodshed. She stood frozen to the spot, terror evident on her face.

His heart went out to her as he wondered how she'd been caught up in the doomed rebellion. Mayhap a husband or sweetheart had urged her to come along but it shouldn't cost the woman her life simply because she followed the orders of a man. Ancel rode toward her and, at the same time, he saw a knight advancing in her direction, his sword swinging menacingly. The poor woman had her back to the fellow and would never know what struck and killed her.

Enough blood had been shed this day. Ancel pushed Storm and reached the peasant just as the soldier wielding his sword did. Ancel rode between the pair and bent low, snatching the woman around the waist and yanking her to safety as he rode off. While Storm continued to gallop, Ancel sat back up in the saddle and lifted the woman in front of him, an arm around her waist, gripping her tightly to him. She squirmed in protest but he held fast to her as he charged away from the chaos that surrounded them.

At first, he thought to ride close to where the king observed the action and then decided against it. This woman was present at the insurrection. The king, angered by the bold and disrespectful peasants causing such havoc, might instruct a member of his royal guard to cut her down, simply because she had the audacity to be left standing after so many noblemen in London and others had fallen.

Ancel refused to let that happen.

Instead, he rode to the edge of Norsey Wood and drew his horse to a halt. Dismounting, he brought the woman with him. He released her as their feet touched the ground. She stumbled and fell to her knees. Immediately, Ancel took her arm and helped her back to her feet.

She looked at him with brown eyes that contained flecks of warm gold as she struggled to breathe. Wisps of rich brown hair framed her heart-shaped face, having come loose from the single braid that fell to her waist. Her lush mouth trembled in fear.

She swallowed hard and got out, "Thank you, my lord." After several more anxious breaths, she added, "I am most grateful." Then she smiled and Ancel's heart skipped a beat.

"Who are you?" he demanded, for this ethereal beauty with milky white skin was no peasant, despite her unadorned, unlined cloak that held no coat of arms nor silken cords to fasten it. The wind had parted the garment, revealing a plain wool kirtle in light brown, much like a servant in a keep would possess and wear.

When she didn't answer him, he raised the visor on his helm and asked, "What were you doing in the midst of a battle?" His anger grew. "You could have been killed—and almost were—until I snatched you from the jaws of death."

Her face crumpled and her gaze dropped to the ground. "I know. I am sorry, my lord." Her eyes rose to meet his and she gave him a tired smile. "I seem to be in danger no matter where I turn. I do thank you for rescuing me, though."

"Start at the beginning, my lady, for though meanly dressed, you speak as one of the nobility."

"I am Lady Margery Ormond, my lord. I come from Highfield, which is west of Billericay. I've lived there with my mother and stepfather for many years. My father . . . died . . . and my mother wed Lord Umfrey Vivers when I was but five years of age. Sarah, one of our servants, gave me one of her kirtles, hoping I would blend in as a peasant."

Ancel almost laughed aloud at that thought. Anyone who got within ten paces of Lady Margery Ormond would know she was no serf. Her regal bearing alone would give her away in any situation. It rivaled the perfect posture of his mother, Merryn de Montfort.

"But how did you come to be here, my lady?" He waved an arm about. "Don't you know you are in the midst of an uprising? Peasants marched on London and took the Tower for a brief time. Fighting broke out in London and spread beyond the city to here, in Essex."

"Is that Wat Tyler you speak of?" she asked, curiosity lighting her face. "We heard rumors he led rebels from Essex and Kent to confront the king."

Ancel snorted. "He did that very thing, my lady—and lost his life as a result." He paused. "As do all of these Essex rebels at Billericay today."

They both looked back across the field and Ancel saw that the fighting was coming to an end. He guessed several hundred dead men from Essex covered the ground and would need to be buried before the day was done.

He turned back to the noblewoman and saw she swayed. Her face had turned ashen as she surveyed the area. Ancel reached out and caught her before she crumpled. Sweeping her into his arms, he moved away from the sights and sounds of the final minutes of battle and took her to the shade of a large oak. As he placed her against the trunk of the tree, he saw she had fainted.

Ancel couldn't blame her. Seeing this field awash in the blood of the dead, as well as hearing the cries of the injured, was enough to bring a seasoned knight to his knees, much less a sheltered woman of the nobility. He studied the stranger before him, her long, dark lashes swept against her pale cheeks. In her peasant garb, Lady Margery looked nothing like the women of the royal court in their elaborate clothing yet he thought her more elegant and graceful than any woman of his acquaintance.

He took her hand and waited for her to awaken, drinking in her fresh beauty. Something stirred within him, an unnamed feeling that he couldn't place.

Her lashes fluttered and her eyes opened. She glanced about, familiarizing herself with her surroundings.

"I apologize, my lord. I had not truly comprehended the scale of this attack. Seeing so many wounded and dead . . . it caused me to grow weak."

"I understand, my lady. You have my sympathy. No woman should have to view what you have seen this day." Ancel paused. "Are you still unsteady or do you think you can answer a few questions?"

She nodded. "I do not feel faint at the moment, my lord. I will do my best." She gripped his hand for support. A warm feeling flooded Ancel. It took him a moment to focus. He needed to learn more about her.

"Might I stand?" she asked unexpectedly. "I would feel more like myself if I could do so."

"Of course." He offered her his other hand and pulled her to her feet. Though reluctant to release her, he did.

She took several calming breaths and then nodded. "Go ahead. I will tell you what I can if it will help you understand what has happened in Essex."

"Why did you leave your home at Highfield? And how did you come to find yourself in the middle of this battle?"

"The serfs at Highfield . . . they . . ." Her voice trailed off. Tears welled in her eyes.

Ancel placed a hand on her shoulder. "Go on, Lady Margery," he encouraged softly. He needed to know what had happened to her.

She bit her lip to still it. "They murdered my invalid mother in her bed." Anger sparked in her eyes. "And they tortured and disemboweled my stepfather. Lord Umfrey's head now rests upon a spike at the gates of Highfield." She shuddered. "I know not where my two stepbrothers are—whether they were caught in the uprising and died or if they managed to escape as I did."

Her body began shaking uncontrollably as tears flowed down her cheeks. Ancel drew her into his arms as she wept, wanting to bring comfort. It amazed him that Lady Margery had escaped from her home with her life. And to think her mother had been viciously attacked while bedridden. He couldn't imagine seeing his own beloved mother dead, much less murdered at the hands of their farmers at Kinwick.

He let her sob till she quieted and lifted her head, staring off at the field again.

Tilting her chin till their eyes met, Ancel asked, "How did you survive such an attack within your home, my lady?" he asked gently.

An odd look crossed her face. "I hid. In a secret passageway. Only a handful knew of its existence. My mother could not walk. She urged me to leave when Sarah came to warn us of the coming trouble. I ran to the solar and concealed myself inside. I . . . I . . . heard them when they came for Lord Umfrey." Her voice broke. Fresh tears cascaded down her face.

"I remained hidden for a while but I regretted leaving my mother. I moved along the tunnel until I found a way to exit. But I was too late."

"You found your mother?"

"I heard her talking to the serfs who had stormed the keep."

His heart ached at the wistful smile that crossed her face.

"She stood up to them. Told them that neither she nor I had ever done anything wrong or mistreated any of them." Lady Margery paused. "They killed her anyway."

Her bitter tone let Ancel know she had heard her mother's death and had been helpless to prevent it.

"I remained secreted in the hidden passageway until I thought it safe to flee Highfield. I didn't know if the rebels had taken control of the estate and I couldn't chance them finding me there. I decided to make my way toward Billericay—even London—and hoped that I would pass a convent that might offer me shelter until this madness ended."

Ancel took her hands in his. "You are safe with me, Lady Margery. I will speak to the king and personally escort you back to your home. I am sure since your estate is nearby, he will want it secured. I will ask that I be allowed to remain in order to help restore order to Highfield."

A hopeful look crossed her face. "You would do me such a kindness? Oh, thank you, my lord. I have been so frightened. And I've worried about Sarah, my servant. Though I tried to convince her to come with me, she refused. She is my friend, my lord. I want to see that she is all right. I know she had nothing to do with the serfs who stormed Highfield and ransacked it, though I realize some of our tenants and servants may have also joined in."

"Then I hope we will find Sarah alive and well when we reach your home." He released her hands and suddenly felt bereft at the loss of contact between them. Instead, he offered her his hand. "Come, my lady, and we shall ride back to the king."

Lady Margery placed her hand in his and he led her back to Storm, who stood patiently waiting. Ancel placed the noblewoman atop his horse and climbed behind her. His arms went around her as he took up the reins. She leaned back into him, and it gave him a warm feeling to have her close.

Turning to look over her shoulder, she asked, "What is your name, my lord? You never shared it with me."

"I am Sir Ancel de Montfort, son of Lord Geoffrey and Lady Merryn de Montfort of Kinwick, and a member of the king's royal guard."

Her cheeks flushed a pretty shade of pink. "I am happy to make your acquaintance, Sir Ancel."

"I feel the same, Lady Margery."

With that, he spurred Storm on and they rode away from the field of blood and toward the king and his men. Ancel got as close as he could to the group surrounding Richard and jumped down, then lifted Lady Margery to the ground.

"Come with me, my lady." Ancel didn't think it safe to leave her next to the horse with so many men milling around. He offered her his arm and she slipped her hand through the crook.

He caught sight of Will and motioned the squire over. "Watch Storm," he ordered and saw the boy scramble over to the warhorse.

Ancel wove his way through the crowd, ignoring the odd looks tossed his way. He spotted the king and moved in the monarch's direction but found himself slowed by the noblewoman on his arm. He looked down at her and frowned.

She look terrified—even more so than when he'd snatched her from the battlefield.

"Do not worry, my lady."

"But 'tis the king!" she exclaimed. "And I'm sure I look a fright."

Ancel grinned. True, she had a smudge of dirt on one cheek and looked a little disheveled but her incandescent beauty was shining through.

"All will be well," he reassured her and tugged her the rest of the way.

"Your majesty," he called out.

Richard turned and his face lit up as Ancel bowed. "Sir Ancel! I am relieved to see you made it through the skirmish without a scratch." He glanced to Margery and smiled. "And who might this be?"

"Meet Lady Margery Ormond, sire."

She removed her hand from his arm and gave a deep curtsey. "You majesty," she murmured and then stepped back a few paces.

"No, come closer," the king admonished. "Leave it to Sir Ancel to find a pretty maiden in the midst of battle."

"May we speak in private, your highness?" Ancel asked.

Richard nodded and moved away from the ring of guardsmen and royal advisers that surrounded him. Ancel and Margery followed closely behind him.

Quickly, Ancel explained what had happened at Highfield and how Lady Margery had fled, disguised as a peasant, thanks to the quick thinking of a trusted servant.

"With her stepfather murdered by the local peasants and Highfield being as close as it is to London, I thought it best that we secure the estate. Lady Margery has two stepbrothers and we can look for them, as well. Hopefully, they survived the attack," Ancel said, though he doubted it. By the look on Richard's boyish face, Ancel believed the king agreed with him.

"Would it please your majesty if I took twenty men with me as I escort Lady Margery back to Highfield? I can see to bolstering the defenses and burying the dead. Since it's also harvest time, I can direct that, as well. I'm hopeful there will be serfs remaining who took no part in this insurrection and will help return Highfield to a working estate." He paused. "If it pleases you, sire, we could even use the place as a central location to station troops. From Highfield, they could ride out to various parts of Essex and Kent and shore up various manors and castles as needed."

The king pondered his request briefly. "Though I prefer you by my side, 'tis important that Essex, in particular, is stabilized. Using Highfield as a base is something I will take under advisement." He placed a hand on Ancel's shoulder. "You may have the score of men you asked for and another ten, as well, Sir Ancel. Return Lady Margery to her home and make sure the place is one friendly to the Crown. Find her stepbrothers if you can and restore them to their places of honor."

"And if they cannot be found or are dead?" Ancel asked.

"Then I must consider naming a new baron and award the land to him." The king paused. "Mayhap you would be interested, Sir Ancel."

The king's words shocked him. Ancel knew one day that Kinwick would come to him once his father passed. He hoped that day was long in the future. But to be able to have his own land and title at such a young age? The prospect was tempting.

"Lady Margery?" the king asked, eyeing her with interest.

"Your majesty?"

"Are you betrothed?"

She blushed profusely. "Nay, my lord. My stepfather said he had no interest in seeing me wed since I was not a blood relative. My mother had been ill for some time and Lord Umfrey thought it best that I remain at Highfield in order to run domestic affairs there."

The king frowned. "Hmm." Then he brightened. "If your step-brothers cannot be found, then mayhap I will let you remain at Highfield.

"As Sir Ancel's bride."

CHAPTER 6

ARGERY'S YEARS LIVING under the heavy hand of Lord Umfrey helped her remain silent at the king's bold statement. Other women might have sputtered. Or argued. Or swooned. Margery stood stoically and inclined her head to the young monarch. When she lifted it, her features stayed placid, helping her keep her thoughts to herself.

It surprised her to see how youthful England's king truly was, knowing she was older than the monarch by seven years. Yet Richard possessed a confidence Margery found sorely lacking in her own character. She had learned not to complain about anything. Lord Umfrey would never have tolerated it if she did. Moreover, she had learned to adapt to any situation around her. Fighting back was unacceptable. Disagreeing with any of the Vivers men would result in harsh punishment. If Lord Umfrey had taught Margery anything since she came to Highfield, it was to endure no matter what happened around you.

But a frisson of excitement rippled through her at the thought of wedding the handsome knight standing next to her. At least she thought he might be handsome. She'd only seen a small part of his face, thanks to the helm he wore. Vibrant hazel eyes had stared back at her, then reassured her of her safety once he'd lifted his visor. A kind smile had warmed her insides as he spoke to her, reassuring her in the midst of chaos. Glancing at the tall, broad frame encased in armor, she guessed he was over six feet in height. But he still remained somewhat of a mystery.

Would it possible to find herself wed to such a bold knight?

Margery had long ago given up on the idea of marriage so the idea of escaping Highfield through marriage had never occurred to her. Where once she'd had dreams of sharing her life with a husband and bearing his children, gradually they had been replaced by reality. Watching the erosion of the relationship between her mother and stepfather only reinforced that marriage wasn't something she would wish to be a part of, even if given the choice.

But now? Only time would tell.

As the king strode away from them, he called over his shoulder, "Choose the men you wish to take with you, Sir Ancel, and keep me informed of the situation."

Margery wondered at the relationship between the monarch and this courageous knight who had rescued her. She thought kings only listened to their advisers and royal councils, not a mere knight who was a member of his guard. Yet even through her inexperience, she could tell there was great trust between the two men.

"My lady?"

Margery turned, sensing her cheeks now burned in embarrassment. What if Sir Ancel had a sweetheart somewhere? What if he never intended to marry? The king had practically told the knight he would need to wed her if her stepbrothers had been killed in the rebellion. Of course, the king dangled ownership of Highfield and Lord Umfrey's title, as well. Though Sir Ancel had yet to see the estate and castle, he would naturally be tempted, as would any man, to possess his own land and the title that accompanied it.

"Aye, my lord?"

"I want you to stay here. I will send William Artus, a squire, to watch over you. It may be a few hours before we depart from Norsey Wood."

She glanced around. "But isn't the battle over?"

He nodded grimly. "Aye. But we will need to deal with gathering up the horses taken by the peasants and burying the dead."

"Oh." It made her think of all the bodies at Highfield. Guilt permeated through her that she had survived when others had perished.

"I will walk the field and choose the men to accompany us to Highfield, as well. How far is it from here?"

"I don't know, my lord. I had never left the grounds since I arrived there when I was five. I departed as the sun rose this morning and walked a good while but I cannot tell you the exact distance." She offered him an apologetic smile. "But I will be able to show you where the estate is located as we return."

The knight nodded curtly. "If you will excuse me."

Margery watched him leave, surprised to find herself wanting to trail after him. She looked around at all of the activity that went on around her. Even though she was surrounded by hundreds—no, thousands—of men, she felt very much alone all of a sudden.

Sir Ancel stopped and spoke to the same young man that he'd given his horse to. Pointing in her direction, she gave a friendly wave. The squire nodded and marched in her direction, leading the warhorse.

"Greetings, Lady Margery. I am William Artus but you may call me Will. Everyone does." He gave her a shy smile.

"Good day to you, Will."

"Sir Ancel said that you might be hungry."

She smiled at him. "I am famished," she confided. "I haven't eaten in some time."

"Then my first task is to find some food for you." He glanced around. "Would you be able to hold Storm's reins? Sir Ancel loves his horse more than most and charged me to watch over him. But it would be faster if I could leave Storm here and bring something back to you."

Though Margery had never been around horses and the thought of keeping the horse's reins should frighten her, she agreed.

"I'll be back soon, my lady. Speak to no one," he warned. "And keep your distance from Storm. He's most unfriendly to everyone but his master." Will handed her the reins and hurried off.

She held the reins loosely since the horse didn't seem to want to go anywhere. Men rushed by her. A few gave her a passing glance but most ignored her and focused on whatever task was at hand. After a few minutes, Margery decided to draw closer to the large horse in order to make friends with him. Though he was an imposing height, the animal didn't seem to be hostile as Will Artus had suggested.

Approaching him carefully, she said in a quiet tone, "Hello, Storm. I must thank you for your part in rescuing me from the danger I was in." Tentatively, she held out a hand and stroked the animal's nose, which felt like velvet. He seemed to like it, so she stretched to scratch him between the ears. The horse closed his eyes. If she believed a horse could smile, then Storm did so now. Margery began rubbing under his chin and down his neck. He quietly chuffed. She giggled, happy that he seemed so accepting of her.

"My lady!"

She turned and saw Will hurrying toward her, a crock in each hand and half a loaf of bread tucked under his arm.

"What are you doing?" the squire demanded.

Margery frowned. "Looking after Storm, as you asked."

"Drop the reins," the young man ordered.

Margery did as he asked and he shoved the crocks into her hands. The scent of stew wafted up, causing her stomach to gurgle noisily. Will reclaimed the reins from the ground and even nudged her back from the horse.

"Storm is not a friendly beast," Will scolded. "I warned you to stay back."

She looked at the warhorse. "Well, he does look fierce," she agreed. "I am sure all horses that go into battle do. But he's been gentle as a lamb with me. I believe he enjoyed the attention I gave him."

Will snorted. "No one would ever call Storm gentle. Only Sir Ancel can ride him and care for him. Storm merely tolerates me at best. I'm surprised he didn't bite off your fingers."

Margery laughed. "I think you are teasing me, Will Artus."

She gave him one of the bowls and lifted the other to her lips. Will tore some of the bread off and offered it to her. Soon, Margery had downed all of her stew and wiped the crock clean using the bread. Rarely had a meal tasted so good.

She wondered if it was freedom she tasted—and not only stew.

ANCEL SCOURED THE battlefield for the men he wanted to bring with him to Highfield. He wouldn't take any of the knights from the royal guard. In these uncertain times, King Richard needed to take special precautions. Ancel had promised the old king that he would look after the monarch's grandson. By not poaching any of the men who surrounded the king, men who would give their lives for him, Ancel would make good on that promise to King Edward.

Still, many others that he knew would be assets at Highfield.

He spoke to half a dozen trustworthy soldiers, then a dozen, then had up to twenty who would accompany him. It still wasn't enough.

Then he thought to speak with Buckingham.

Ancel found the commander closeted in his tent, Sir Thomas Percy at his side.

"Forgive me for the interruption, my lords," he said, "but I have need of a few good men—and you can help me in this quest."

Briefly, he explained Highfield's close proximity to London and how the king wanted it secured before he related his idea about making it a prime location to station troops that could be sent out through Essex.

"And Kent, if needed," Percy added, "though it seems as if the grumblings there have calmed. You say you need ten more men?"

"Aye, my lord. The king agreed to a total of thirty to get the castle grounds and its defenses back into shape."

"You may have ten of my men," Percy said.

"And I'll guarantee you ten of mine," Buckingham volunteered. "That way the place can be secured quickly and the crops seen to in a timely fashion. I will share with the king that using Highfield is a good idea to secure Essex. Any news of Lord Umfrey?"

"He was killed in the rebellion," Ancel said, not relating the torture the nobleman suffered.

"What of his sons? He had two. Or mayhap three," Percy said.

"Lord Umfrey's stepdaughter said there are two. Both are missing at the moment."

"And this noblewoman escaped the wrath of the peasants?" Percy asked. "By the Christ, she must be a most capable lady to have done so."

"Lady Margery looks like a fragile thing that might blow away if a strong wind arose," Ancel said. "But to show the fortitude and inner strength she did has certainly earned my good opinion of her."

"Come," Buckingham said. "I'll pull together my men and Percy can do the same so you can be on your way."

"Thank you again, my lords."

Within minutes, Ancel had a crew of two score surrounding him.

"Thank you for accepting this task," he told the group. "Highfield lies between Billericay and London. The king values its proximity and wants the estate back in noble hands. We'll need to repair any damage caused by the peasants who revolted there in order to secure the land and schedule a guard to patrol the wall walk, the estate, and the nearby roads. Besides keeping up your training and being ready to defend the property, some manual labor will be required."

"Such as what, Sir Ancel?" a soldier from the group asked.

"The dead will need to be buried. Some crops may need to be harvested until I can ascertain workers for the fields. You may be asked to ride out into Essex to curb any other signs of rebellion. If you agree, we need to leave soon."

A general murmur let him know the men were up to the charge. He saw their determined looks and knew though this force was small in number, it would be able to accomplish the tasks he set for them.

"Gather your horses and any other belongings and meet me at this spot within a quarter-hour."

The soldiers peeled away and Ancel went in search of Lady Margery. He spotted her and Will and headed in their direction.

The squire broke away and met him. "My lord, you must talk to the lady. She doesn't realize what she's doing is dangerous."

Ancel frowned. "What's wrong, Will?"

"She's . . . *petting* Storm," he sputtered. "She wouldn't listen to me."

Immediately, Ancel glanced over the squire's shoulder and saw Lady Margery's hand gliding along Storm's enormous side. Then she began to stroke the horse's neck down to his chest.

Storm held perfectly still.

His jaw dropped. No one could touch Storm except him without fear of losing a few fingers. While the horse had never given Ancel a moment of trouble, he possessed a nasty temper and snapped at anyone who came near. It was why Ancel usually cared for the horse instead of any of the squires attached to the royal household. Not that he minded. His cousins, Raynor and Elysande, had taught him much about horses and both Raynor and Geoffrey de Montfort had encouraged Ancel to always care for his own horse and not leave that task to another.

But to see the very petite Lady Margery engaged in a conversation with the warhorse as she moved her hands over him shocked Ancel.

He rushed over and heard her cooing to the horse.

"My lady?"

She looked up and gave him a brilliant smile. "I have made a new friend, Sir Ancel. I think I am in love with your sweet horse."

Her smile warmed him as a summer day might. Without realizing it, he returned her smile.

As she stroked the horse, she said, "I was never allowed in the stables at Highfield. In fact, I've never been on a horse in my life, except for when you rescued me from the battlefield. But if they all are as sweet and friendly as Storm, I believe I would like to learn how to ride." She glanced back at Ancel. "Mayhap you could teach me."

"Lady Margery, did Will not tell you that Storm has a temper? That he snaps at others? That you might lose a few fingers—if not your entire hand?"

She shrugged. "He said that very thing but I cannot imagine Storm behaving so rudely. I believe Will was being overly cautious." She looked at the horse and crooned, "You would never be ill-tempered with me now, would you, Storm?"

The horse nickered softly. Apparently, Storm had fallen in love with the fetching Lady Margery.

For a moment, Ancel thought he might have, as well.

CHAPTER 7

"HIGHFIELD WILL BE up on the left," Lady Margery said, turning toward him to make her voice heard over the thundering hooves of the horses.

They had ridden about three leagues from the outskirts of Billericay, which meant London lay less than twenty miles away. Ancel decided he would do what he could to encourage the king to place a large faction of troops at Highfield until peace had returned to Essex. It would prove an ideal location to send out an armed royal force in case unrest occurred in the area again.

A few minutes later, the forest ended. Ancel saw a long road surrounded by fields of wheat on each side and a large manor house in the distance. He led the group down the road and felt the noblewoman stiffen against him. Ancel knew she prepared herself for what they would find.

Open gates awaited them—as did the former baron's head placed in a prominent place, resting on a spike. Ancel couldn't blame Lady Margery for averting her eyes as they rode through without stopping. They'd already passed a few bodies on the edge of the fields and along the road and found others scattered about as they entered the outer bailey. He led the party past the training yard, seeing even more corpses, and then to the inner bailey, where he called for a halt.

He'd thought about what needed immediate attention on the ride here. They arrived mid-afternoon and he believed much could be accomplished since hours of summer's daylight remained.

"You five." Ancel indicated the soldiers to his immediate left. "Go into the forest to hunt for the next two hours and bring back as much game as you can carry. The peasants may have raided the buttery, so food will be a pressing need."

The soldiers turned their horses and galloped off.

He yanked the helm from his head and raised his voice so that it would carry across the bailey as he said, "The rest of you need to tend to your horses first. I'm not sure how large the stables are, so they may need to share with the horses already at Highfield. See that any horses or remaining livestock are also watered and fed."

Lady Margery spoke up. "No horses remain, my lord. I assume they were taken by the rebels. I'm not sure about the rest of the animals."

He nodded. "Then care for your horses and once you've done so, divide in half. One group needs to bring back the dead. Place them in an orderly fashion next to the training yard." He would need for Lady Margery to view the dead to see if she could identify either of her stepbrothers. "The others can begin to dig graves. Once the bodies have been retrieved, all can continue digging. I want the dead buried by the end of the day so that we can move forward to other tasks."

Ancel knew that he asked much of the men to accomplish so many tasks in such a short time but the group was large enough that he believed it could be done. The sooner the dead had been placed in their graves, the better. Already, the stench of death hovered over Highfield.

"They will need to check inside the keep, as well," Lady Margery said quietly.

"Of course." Ancel instructed the men to search inside the keep and retrieve those bodies first before continuing to the grounds and beyond.

He dismounted and handed Lady Margery down before tucking his helm under his arm.

"Stay here," he told her, not wanting her to overhear his next order.

Ancel summoned Sir Folcard and drew him aside. "Lady Margery's mother was murdered in her bed," he confided to the knight. "Find her now and wrap the body. Take her directly to the chapel. I don't want the lady to see her mother alongside the group of bodies going rotten in the sun."

"I'll see to it at once." Folcard motioned to another knight beside him. They handed their horses off to others and went inside the keep.

Ancel returned to Lady Margery, who stood close to Storm, stroking him and seemingly lost in thought.

"I know it is difficult for you to return and see your home this way."

She nodded.

"Have you a priest at Highfield?"

"Aye. Father Martyn, though he is quite advanced in age."

"We should seek him out." Ancel signaled Will to his side. "I'm trusting you to look after Storm for me, Will. Are you up to it?"

A stubborn look appeared in the squire's eyes. "Certainly, my lord. If Lady Margery can make friends with the wicked beast, then I can, too." He took Ancel's helm and then gathered the horse's reins and said, "Come along now, Storm."

Ancel suppressed a grin and offered Lady Margery his arm. He saw that she, too, hid a smile as she tucked her hand through the crook of his arm.

Wordlessly, she led him across the bailey and toward the small, stone chapel.

They entered the darkened space and Ancel blinked several times as his eyes adjusted from the strong summer sunlight to the dim glow inside the chapel. His eyes scanned the room and settled upon a white-haired man sitting on the steps leading up to the altar.

"'Tis Father Martyn," Lady Margery confirmed.

He led her to the old man. As they drew closer, Ancel heard the priest softly weeping.

"Father, 'tis I, Lady Margery," she said softly.

The bearded priest raised his eyes. "Saints be praised," he said, his voice breaking as he rose unsteadily to his feet. "I searched for you, my lady. When I could not find you, I prayed that you had escaped this nightmare."

"Father, this is Sir Ancel de Montfort. The king has sent him to fortify Highfield."

The wrinkled face broke out in a smile. "Greetings, my lord."

"And to you, Father Martyn." Ancel paused. "I would like you to say a mass for the dead of Highfield as soon as possible."

"Only one?"

"Aye. One for all of the dead. God will surely understand these are trying times. My men will soon gather those who are no longer with us and they will bury everyone who lost his life by day's end. If you would like, you may pray over each individual's grave."

Father Martyn reached for Ancel's hands. He bent and kissed the knuckles. "Thank you, my lord. I am old and weary. I had not the strength to attempt such a task."

"Your job is here, Father." Ancel looked to Margery. "I am having your mother brought to the chapel now. If you would like, I am sure Father Martyn could first say a separate mass for her soul and then one for the others."

Tears welled in her eyes. "I would like that."

Movement caught Ancel's eye and he turned to see Sir Folcard and the other knight bringing Lady Margery's mother to the front.

"Thank you," the noblewoman told them as they laid the wrapped body at the top of the steps.

"I am sorry for your loss, my lady," Sir Folcard said. "I must apologize, though. We could not find clean linen to cover your mother. I am guessing the peasants stole any spare bedclothes."

The two knights bowed and exited the chapel. Father Martyn took a few minutes to prepare before beginning the funeral mass. Ancel eyed the bedclothes that encircled the body. He didn't know how the baroness had been killed but he could see the large bloodstains on the sheets surrounding her body. Anger flared within him at the senseless death of a helpless woman at the hands of a crazed mob.

He led Lady Margery to a seat and sat next to her. As the mass began, he took her hand in his, hoping to offer comfort. She gave him a grateful smile.

The mass ended. Father Martyn offered words of solace to Lady Margery and promised he would now begin a separate mass for the men on the estate who'd lost their lives. Lady Margery thanked him and Ancel led her outside.

"Are you up to accompanying me to the training yard?" he asked.

"You need me to view the bodies," she said. "To search for Thurstan and Gervase among them before the men bury them." A pained expression crossed her face.

"Aye. Can you do this?"

She nodded. Ancel realized their hands were still joined. He released the fingers wrapped around hers and offered her his arm once more. Lady Margery took it and they crossed the bailey, moving toward the training yard.

Having all the dead gathered in one place would be convenient for burial but the area reeked. The hot June sun baked into the bodies as flies swarmed over them. Ancel found himself breathing from his mouth to avoid as much of the rancid smell as he could. As they drew near, the sight of the long row of bodies saddened him. He couldn't imagine what Lady Margery might be feeling as he led her to the beginning of the line.

They walked slowly so she could study each body they passed. Some wore the clothing of serfs and he assumed these might have been those unwilling to join in the rebellion or ones who had even fought back. Others seemed dressed more as soldiers would be. He asked her about it and she explained that several of their tenants had deserted to join the rebellion, causing Lord Umfrey to send most of his soldiers into the fields for the harvest. Ancel supposed the soldiers had been unarmed and attacked there without warning, which explained the numerous bodies littering the road leading to Highfield.

Then she stopped. "This is Gervase."

Ancel recognized her stepbrother was dressed differently from most of those they'd passed. The cloth he wore was of a finer material and dyed a rich color, though bloodstains had ruined the well-fitting cotehardie.

"You're certain?"

Her cheeks appeared drained of all color. "I am. I know his face, even through the bruises and cuts. The color of his hair. 'Tis Gervase. He's the younger of my stepbrothers."

Ancel signaled a soldier over and told him, "This is Gervase Vivers, Lady Margery's stepbrother. He will need to be buried within the family plot. See that it is done."

"Aye, my lord."

They continued walking the rest of the line. Reaching the end, Ancel asked two soldiers who'd placed the last body before them how many more dead remained.

"This is the last of them, my lord. We're off to join those digging the graves."

He glanced at Lady Margery. "So you have another family member still missing." He found it interesting that she wrinkled her nose at his remark and wondered about how close she had been with the Vivers who resided at Highfield.

"Sir Thurstan, my older stepbrother, is not among the dead," she said flatly. "If anyone could escape trouble, it would be Thurstan."

"Then we will wait and see if he returns. If he does, then he will be the new baron."

"If he doesn't, Highfield will be better off," she snapped.

Curiosity led him to ask, "Why do you say that, my lady?"

Her eyes narrowed. "Thurstan Vivers is even worse than Lord Umfrey. He is lazy. Spiteful. Greedy. A lecher who cares more about his conquests than he ever would the people of Highfield. Though he has attained his knighthood, Thurstan holds to none of the tenets in the code of chivalry."

Ancel saw anger heated her cheeks and her small hands balled into fists.

"He has gotten almost a dozen of our serfs and servants with child while another five women in the nearest village have also given birth to his babes. I will state in no uncertain terms, my lord, that most of these women were taken against their will and several were virgins. Yet, Thurstan takes no responsibility for his actions, accusing those who came to Lord Umfrey to complain as being liars. He also refuses to go to mass, saying he cannot waste precious hours of sleep worshipping something he doesn't believe in. And Thurstan is all smiles when he is with his father, but the moment Lord Umfrey leaves a room, Thurstan is the first to belittle his father. He makes jokes with Highfield's soldiers at his father's expense. I hope you can see that the people of Highfield would be better off with no baron than with Thurstan Vivers as their liege lord."

Ancel's skin prickled at her words, his gut tightening at the abominations perpetrated by this so-called knight. It worried him that Vivers might have also hurt this brave noblewoman. Carefully, he asked, "Did he ever harm you, my lady?"

Her mouth set in a firm line. She remained silent for a few moments and then said, "Nay. He made me . . . uncomfortable, though." Her eyes met his. "Thurstan had recently returned from fostering and earning his knighthood and was to remain at Highfield. From the moment he arrived, he began making . . . lewd remarks to me. To intimidate me. Only yesterday, he cornered me . . ."

Her voice trailed off as tears welled in her eyes. Ancel saw the noblewoman's reluctance to share what might have occurred between them most recently. He also knew what he would do to Thurstan Vivers if the man surfaced—and then it would be certain that no one would ever find this knight again. Ancel would see to bringing justice to the bastard. Not only for his abuse of others, but for terrorizing this brave woman.

She composed herself and said, "I knew not to speak back to Thurstan but I'd begun to fear what might come to pass."

"You didn't go to your stepfather?"

Lady Margery shoulders sagged. "Lord Umfrey would have done nothing. In his eyes, his sons were perfect because they resembled him in every way, from their looks to their manners. I was little more than chattel to him, someone to cook and clean and make sure his household ran to perfection. If Thurstan chose to force himself upon me, there would have been no consequences."

She paused. Ancel caught the fear in her eyes, then saw anger replace it. "I hope the serfs did find him, my lord. I hope they did to Thurstan what they did to his father."

CHAPTER 8

MARGERY IMMEDIATELY REGRETTED the words she had uttered aloud to Sir Ancel. She knew better than to give voice to any opinion, especially to a man.

Hoping to appease him, she said, "Forgive me, my lord. I am distraught. I did not mean to wish harm to come to my stepbrother. I misspoke."

The knight frowned in displeasure. "Never show remorse for speaking the truth, my lady," he gently chided.

"I know better than to speak my mind. I apologize. It's been a stressful time for me. I forgot my place." She cast her eyes downward, too upset to say anything more to him.

He placed his hands on her shoulders and squeezed gently till she reluctantly looked up.

"I come from a strong mother who makes wise decisions and never feels the need to hide her convictions. She raised my twin sister, Alys, and my younger sisters, Nan and Jessimond, to do likewise. I value the opinion of a woman as much as one from a man." His hazel eyes grew warm. "Especially one that I admire as much as I do you."

She didn't know what to say to such outlandish talk. Why would he say he admired her? It was evident Sir Ancel was different from every man she'd ever met.

"Never hide anything from me, Margery," he added softly.

She swallowed. "I won't, my lord."

"Good." He dropped his hands to his sides. "I hope your stepbrother makes himself scarce. For if he does return, I will thrash him within an inch of his life for his untoward behavior to you." He paused. "I meant what I said before. You have nothing to fear. You are safe with me. I won't allow anything to happen to you."

Margery's heart began to beat quickly. He had called her by her Christian name. He would protect her from anything—even Thurstan Vivers.

"Thank you," she said, her throat thick with unshed tears.

"Are you ready to go into the keep?"

"Aye."

Sir Ancel took her hand and placed it upon his arm and escorted her from the training yard. Each step away from the corpses brought her relief but her heart continued to pound violently. Margery was afraid he would hear it and think her still afraid.

But she wasn't. Whatever she felt inside was some new feeling, something she'd never experienced before.

And it had everything to do with the bold knight by her side.

They entered the keep and went first to the great hall, which lay in darkness. Only embers smoldered in the fireplace.

"Getting a fire going should be my first task," he told her.

Fortunately, wood remained and Sir Ancel patiently fed the embers. In time, the blaze grew larger and they could see the room better. All the trestle tables still remained pushed against the walls but Margery saw that all the tapestries had been stripped from those very walls. They went to the kitchen and she found the remnant of a small candle. Lighting it, they explored and found the cooking pots and knives still in place but many of the cups and bowls were missing. The buttery had been cleared out. It looked odd to see it standing empty. All of her spices were also gone.

Sir Ancel led her upstairs to the solar, which had been ransacked. The bedclothes had been stripped. The rugs and candlesticks were missing. Chairs lay broken. Only the sturdy oak table and benches had withstood the onslaught from the mob.

"We should check the other bedchambers," she said, leading him back to the great hall and to the other side of the manor house.

Going up the stairs, she avoided the room she shared with her mother and entered the one Thurstan and Gervase used when they were in residence. It looked much as the solar had. Anything of value had been taken.

"Where is your room?" Sir Ancel asked.

"Across the hall. I shared it with my mother."

"Do you think you can see it, or would you rather wait?"

"I can. With you here. I don't think I could go inside alone."

He took her hand, his fingers warm as they held firmly to hers.

Margery led him across the hall and opened the door. She took a deep breath and stepped inside. Holding the candle high, she glanced around the room. It looked much as the solar did. The chest containing the few clothes she and her mother owned had been split apart. Nothing remained. It made her especially thankful that her mother insisted that she take the few pieces of jewelry with her. She realized the casket the jewels had been in was missing and wondered if the woman who'd belittled her mother had been the one to take it. Margery would never forget the sound of the woman's grating voice and hoped, one day, she would be able to confront this serf and claim justice for her mother.

She looked at Sir Ancel, a deep scowl on his face. "It looks as if you have only the clothes on your back, my lady. And stained ones, at that."

Margery glanced down to the kirtle Sarah had given her. The dried blood from the dying man who had clutched her covered the front. It would never come clean.

"My own clothes are underneath this," she told him. "So I do have something to wear."

"We should have had you remove this hours ago," he said. "May I?"

She set the candle on the floor and allowed him to untie the borrowed cloak, which he tossed onto the mattress before he pulled the bloody kirtle from her. An odd quickening inside caused her breathing to become erratic.

He wadded up the kirtle. "You'll need to burn this." He looked down at her questioningly. "These are your clothes?"

Margery glanced down at her attire. "Aye, my lord."

The knight shook his head. "These aren't the clothes of a lady."

She shrugged. "Lord Umfrey was tight with his coin. I made my clothes from the material that I could afford."

He took her chin in his hand. A rush of warmth raced through her. "Then the first thing we do tomorrow is find something more suited for your position. I'll send someone back to Billericay."

"That's not necessary, my lord, when so much needs to be done here. I can scrub floors in what I'm wearing now. In fact, I'll keep this kirtle in order to work in it." She reached out to claim it but he dropped it to the floor.

His hand slid away from her chin till it cupped her cheek. "You won't be scrubbing floors, my lady. We'll find servants to do that for you. Is there a village nearby? Mayhap you could accompany me as I hire servants to repair the inside of the keep."

Margery gazed at him wide-eyed, butterflies exploding in her stomach at his touch. "But I have always scrubbed the floors, my lord. Tended the garden. Cooked all the meals."

"You cooked all of the meals," he said, his voice low and neutral in tone. But she heard something within it.

"Aye, though Sarah always helped with the cooking. 'Twas what was expected of me."

"Highfield doesn't have a cook?"

"Nay, my lord."

His callused thumb tenderly stroked her cheek. "Then we will also hire a cook, as well as servants. And I'll need to see if any of the serfs still remain on the estate. I would appreciate you accompanying me. You will know their names. They might be more willing to talk to me if you are present."

"All right." She barely got the words out. All she could think about was his touch.

His hand fell away.

"But this will all cost money, my lord. Quite a bit, I'm afraid. I haven't a clue where Lord Umfrey kept his. Unless..." Her voice trailed off as she remembered the large chest she'd discovered inside the hidden passage. It had only been a few feet inside and would have been convenient for the nobleman to access it from the solar.

"What is it?" he asked.

"I think I may know where Lord Umfrey kept his coin. Do you remember I told you I hid in a secret passageway?"

"Aye. You said you entered it from the solar."

Her excitement grew. "I found a chest inside. It was locked but I'm almost certain that it contained Lord Umfrey's monies. I can show you."

ANCEL FOLLOWED LADY Margery back down the stairs and across the great hall again. They went up a different staircase and entered the solar once more.

It upset him how she'd been made to dress and how Lord Umfrey and his sons had treated her. Instead of being a valued family member, Vivers had used her for manual labor, no better than a slave. And it sounded as if his elder son had thought to use Margery in an even more vile way.

He hadn't realized he touched her until he became aware of her warm skin beneath his fingers. Ancel had longed to stroke the porcelain skin. Run his fingers through her rich brown locks. Even place his lips on hers.

No woman had ever affected him this way.

Was this how it started?

Ancel had a shining example of how love and marriage worked. His parents seemed more deeply in love with each passing year. He'd watched his cousins, Elysande and Avelyn, fall in love with good men. Growing up, he'd admired Cousin Raynor almost as much as his own father and Raynor had one of the strongest marriages Ancel had ever seen.

Even his own beloved twin, Alys, had wed a few years ago and now had children of her own. Even before they could speak when they were young, Ancel knew Alys' heart. When she fell in love with Kit, Ancel sensed in his bones how utterly happy Alys was with Kit. The connection they had assured him how much love she felt for her husband.

Could he be as lucky as others in his family and find that kind of deep love and friendship with a woman?

With Margery?

When the king suggested that Ancel might marry Margery, he'd brushed off Richard's spontaneous remarks. But now? The idea appealed to him.

For now, he would protect these new, odd feelings and continue to learn more about her as he accomplished what needed to be done at Highfield.

Margery went to a spot and knelt. "There was a tapestry covering it before but it's gone now." She touched the stone wall and began pushing against it. Suddenly, the stone moved back and she nudged it further.

"You have to crouch to enter," she warned him and frowned. "You are so large, I'm not sure you'll even fit, my lord."

Raising the candle in front of her, she bent and ducked inside. Ancel followed her, understanding why she'd said what she had. The passageway was narrow and would restrict movement.

"Here it is," she said.

He looked and saw the locked chest she'd described.

"I hadn't seen it before. I had nothing to light my path. Later, when I had a candle, I was on the other side and never returned this way. I only came back to this door after the candle had burned out to unbar the door in case I needed to use it again."

Ancel couldn't imagine her feeling her way along somewhere she'd never been before, frightened and alone in the dark as blood-thirsty rebels murdered everyone Margery knew.

"I'm sure you are right and this is where Lord Umfrey hid his wealth. We can return later with a hammer and break the lock. I'd also like to explore this hidden passageway. Without my armor."

He backed out of the passage and stepped into the solar. Margery followed, the candle almost at its end.

"We should return downstairs," he told her. "I want to see how the men are doing with the burial plots and if the hunters have returned with game for us to eat."

They went back to the great hall. Margery excused herself to right the kitchen.

"Have the soldiers bring whatever they caught to me so I can begin to prepare something for the men to dine upon. In the meantime, I'll straighten this mess and see if I can locate more candles. If not, I will have to make some tomorrow."

"After we go to the village and find servants to help you," he reminded her, enjoying seeing the blush stain her cheeks as she remembered their trip to the village. "I'll send the game to you as soon as it arrives."

Ancel went outside and, after removing his armor, pitched in to help finish digging the graves for the dead, only stopping to send the soldiers who brought back game to the great hall.

One told him, "My name is Bartram, my lord. I am a fighting man but I know my way around meat. I would be happy to help Lady Margery. I can skin a few of the deer and the rabbits and help cut the meat up and get it on to roast or boil."

"That would be much appreciated, Bartram."

By the time the last body had been placed in the ground, Ancel was covered in dirt and sweat. He went with the others to wash at the troughs, scrubbing away as much grime as he could. It had grown late, the day passing from light to dusk and finally dark by the time the men adjourned to the great hall. The smell of roasting meat caused his mouth to water.

Bartram came to him. "The rabbit stew is ready, Sir Ancel. The deer will take longer. I can sit with it and turn the spit. We can partake of the venison in the morning."

"It will be good to have food in our bellies for we will have a long day ahead of us," Ancel told the soldier.

He watched as Margery doled out stew to the men. Many had brought their own bowls, so they didn't run short. She apologized for not having her spices in order to season it properly but Ancel noted she'd added onions to the broth. He thought it tasted heavenly.

The men bedded down in the great hall once they'd had their fill. Ancel found Margery. She looked tired.

"Would you like me to escort you to the solar?" he asked.

"Why?" A puzzled look crossed her face.

"I thought it would be uncomfortable for you to sleep in the bed-chamber you shared with your mother."

"Oh. That is very thoughtful of you, Sir Ancel. It would distress me to be in my old room, though it will seem quite odd sleeping in the solar."

"I also didn't think it appropriate for you to bed down among the men."

She nodded. "Then I suppose I should go upstairs."

He escorted her up the staircase and stopped at the door.

Margery looked up. "I cannot thank you enough, Sir Ancel. You have my enduring gratitude." She placed her palms against his chest and leaned on her tiptoes to kiss his cheek. Her warm lips against his skin stirred something deep within him.

Cupping her face, he said, "Call me Ancel." Then he bent and pressed his mouth softly against hers for a brief moment.

"Goodnight, Margery."

CHAPTER 9

MARGERY AWOKE, UNSURE of her surroundings and then remembered the events of yesterday. Her fingertips went to her lips and she relived the moment when Sir Ancel's lips had brushed against hers.

She had never been kissed. Never come close to being kissed. It had ended before she'd even known it began.

But something more than a kiss had occurred between them. Of that Margery was certain.

She rose and pushed aside the jumbled thoughts that began flooding her mind. She had no time to think about the kiss now. She only wished she could have focused on it last night but once she'd scrunched up her cloak and placed her head against it, she'd fallen swiftly into a dreamless sleep. The past two days had been the most trying and eventful of her life and there was plenty of hard work ahead in order to restore a semblance of order to Highfield. Margery didn't have the luxury of lying abed and thinking sweet thoughts of a handsome knight and his kiss.

It frustrated her that even the chamber pot had been stolen from the solar. She made her way to the garderobe, holding her breath while in the tight space. Hurrying away, she went downstairs and slipped through the snoring bodies in the great hall until she reached the kitchen. Surprisingly, Bartram had beaten her there. The soldier sat by a lone candle.

"Good morning, my lady," he greeted in a soft voice. "You're up and about early."

"I usually am. I was used to baking bread before mass began each morning," she shared.

One eyebrow shot up. "You were, were you? Hmm."

He made no judgment aloud but Margery knew her words surprised the soldier.

"All the milled flour is gone," she explained, "so I thought I would see what else was available to feed the soldiers."

"The venison I've prepared will be enough for the men out there," Bartram said. "I spoke with Sir Ancel. He told me that the two of you would go to the nearby village today and try to replenish the stores."

"We need so many things," she said ruefully. "The rebels ransacked the keep and took most anything not nailed down."

"I found barrels of ale," he said, "but no wine."

She shrugged. "We can do without that. But I want to purchase as many chickens as I can, for their eggs and to eat the birds, as well. Sheep, too. And then we need flour for bread and tallow for making candles. And most certainly spices. I cannot cook without them. Nothing would be edible without spices."

He chuckled. "Your list seems to grow longer and longer, my lady."

"Good morning."

Margery turned in the direction of the familiar voice. "Good morning, my lord." Catching sight of Ancel had her heart pumping madly. His dark, thick hair was rumpled from sleep. She longed to run her fingers through it and tame it. Though the light was dim, she could see the bristles from his unshaven face and found them quite attractive.

"Does Father Martyn say mass each morning?" he asked.

"Aye."

"Then I will be sure the soldiers are roused. After breaking our fast, I want to explore the castle's defenses and set the men to repairing things. Once I've done that, I would like to escort you to the village. Is it far?"

"Kirkby lies a league or so west of Highfield but I've never been to it before."

"I see." His mouth set in a hard line.

Margery hated seeing him upset on her behalf, especially since her mistreatment lay in the past. "But I look forward to going there, my lord. I know we have many supplies to purchase."

"What we can't find there, we can send to Billericay if need be. Or even London," he added.

The rest of the morning passed quickly for Margery. The soldiers rose and attended mass, which seemed shorter than usual to her. The morning meal was a success, thanks to Bartram's handling of the spit. Though the meat could have used some salt, nevertheless it was tender and soon gone. Ancel put Bartram in charge of the hunting party that had gone out yesterday and told them to bring back as much meat as they could again. He also encouraged Bartram to continue with preparing the food until a cook could be found.

Good to his word, Ancel reappeared after a few hours, an ax in hand.

"The men are hard at work under Sir Folcard's supervision. Right now, I want to return to the chest and see what Lord Umfrey kept inside it."

He escorted her to the solar and Margery once again touched the wall until she felt it spring back. This time, Ancel went inside and dragged the heavy chest from the passageway. Using the ax, he slammed it against the lock until it broke. Removing it, he lifted the lid.

As Margery expected, Sir Umfrey's gold had been hidden inside, along with many pieces of jewelry. It saddened her that her stepfather had never thought to gift her mother with a single bauble in all their years of marriage. A fresh wave of grief washed over her, knowing she would never see or speak to her beloved mother again.

"With this, we can easily replace whatever you feel is needed at Highfield and can hire enough workers to tend to the fields." He removed several coins and slipped them into a pouch that he'd withdrawn from under his gypon. "As well as hire servants to clean and a cook."

Margery shook her head. "I can do the cooking, especially with Bartram's help, my lord. But it would be nice to have a few servants to help with the rest."

Ancel's hand went to her face and brushed back a stray wisp of hair. "You are a lady, Margery. A noblewoman. Though Lord Umfrey never treated you as such, you are nonetheless deserving. You may help manage the chores but you will never have to do intense labor again—and that includes cooking. 'Tis the hardest work of all. Besides, Bartram is a soldier. Not a cook. He's more valuable to me on the wall walk than in the kitchen."

She forced herself to breathe as his hand lingered. "Whatever you think is best, my lord."

His hand slid to her neck as his thumb brushed slowly against her bottom lip. "Ancel. Remember? At least when we are alone."

"Ancel." The word came out a whisper. She longed for his lips to touch hers once again but, without warning, his hand fell to his side.

He closed the chest and pushed it back into its hiding place. "When we return, mayhap even after the evening meal tonight, I want you to show me the whole of this secret passage. Where it goes. Where it ends."

"All right," she agreed reluctantly, not favoring being in the small space again.

Ancel led her to the stables and the stall where Storm resided. She watched as he saddled the horse and walked alongside the beast as he led Storm outside.

"I will teach you to ride soon, Margery. But for now, you can ride with me." He placed her on Storm's back and climbed behind her. His arms encircled her and she leaned back, a feeling of contentment filling her.

June was near its end and the weather was glorious, sunny with a slight breeze. The ride to Kirkby didn't take long, thanks to the giant strides of the warhorse they rode. Ancel lifted her from Storm and asked her about everything she needed. Margery ran through her list, naming all the goods and livestock she thought would be required to get Highfield up and running so they could feed the soldiers.

"What about parchment and ink?" Ancel asked. "I must keep the king informed of the progress at Highfield and I would also like to write to my parents at Kinwick and let them know I am safe despite the recent uprisings."

Margery thought it considerate of him to write to his parents. The notion of Thurstan or Gervase writing to Lord Umfrey was laughable. It only showed her how different Ancel de Montfort was from most men.

"Our steward had some but I haven't checked to see if any remains. I doubt any of the serfs took it." The steward's body had been one of many she had passed yesterday. He'd been a quiet, efficient man. It was hard to think he'd lost his life merely because he worked tirelessly for the nobility.

Ancel must have caught the expression on her face and figured out no one at Highfield held that position because he said, "A steward will also be someone we must hire to help run the estate." He took her hand and placed it atop his arm. "Come, my lady."

Margery was interested in everything they saw at Kirkby. She couldn't recollect ever having been in a village or town in the past. Very few memories remained from her early childhood before she and her mother had come to live at Highfield.

They passed a blacksmith's shop and she paused.

"We will need a blacksmith," she told Ancel.

"Did yours join the rebellion? Or mayhap was he one of the bodies buried yesterday?"

Margery shivered. "He was one of the men who came to Mother's bedchamber. I recognized his voice. If he dares show himself at Highfield, I will hang him myself." Anger coursed through her at the memory.

Ancel squeezed her hand. "Then let's speak to this smithy and see if he might be available."

He led her inside the open shed. Margery felt the intense heat from the blazing fire and saw a stout man with a heavy, black beard remove something from the flames before he pounded away at it.

"Good day," Ancel called out loudly as he looked around. Margery could tell Ancel assessed the work on display.

The smithy turned. "The same to you, my lord. I am Matthew Cheyne. And who might you be?"

"I am Sir Ancel de Montfort, sent by the king to secure Highfield from the rebels. We are in need of a blacksmith. I don't know how occupied the villagers keep you but you would be busy and well paid if you decide to come live and work at Highfield, Matthew."

The man stroked his beard thoughtfully. "My two daughters are married and gone but I have a wife and my son, who is six and ten. John works with me and his skill already surpasses mine. Could I bring them with me?"

"Agreed." Ancel offered the smithy his hand. "Might your wife be interested in working inside the keep? We could use some extra hands."

An eager smile sprang up on Matthew's face. "That would be most welcomed, my lord, though Eua is gone for a few weeks visiting our daughter in Billericay. My wife will assist with the birth of our first grandchild and stay on for a bit but John and I could start as soon as you'd like."

Ancel turned to Margery. "Is there a cottage that comes with the position?"

"Nay, but there is living space behind where Matthew and John will work."

"Then John and I will finish up our obligations here and come to the castle tomorrow morning," Matthew promised. "Thank you again, my lord, my lady. I look forward to being at Highfield."

They went to the few places of business and purchased what they could but Margery realized it would take a trip to Billericay to fulfill all their needs, especially finding enough livestock. At least they'd been able to buy plenty of tallow, so she could start making candles and soap immediately. Ancel arranged for one of the villagers to load the goods on a cart and bring everything to Highfield, along with several chickens and a few sheep.

As they returned to Storm in order to leave Kirkby, Margery heard her name. Joy filled her heart as she spied Sarah running toward them. She met her friend and hugged her tightly.

"I'm so glad to see you, Sarah. I was worried about what happened to you after I left."

Sarah beamed at her. "Oh, my lady, I felt the same way. 'Tis so good to know you are alive. But what are you doing in Kirkby?"

Ancel had come to stand next to them. Margery introduced the knight and explained how they'd come for goods to replenish the keep.

"We also need servants," Ancel said. "Would you be willing to return to work at Highfield, Sarah?"

"Of course, my lord," Sarah said with enthusiasm. "Lady Margery and I work well together."

"Lady Margery won't be doing as much of the heavy work as before," Ancel cautioned. "In fact, we are in need of several more servants to help with the cleaning and a cook, as well. Might you know anyone we could hire?"

Sarah looked at Margery. "*More* servants? Truly?"

"Aye. Sir Ancel believes Highfield needs more than we've had in the past."

Sarah nodded in understanding. "Then I would ask my mother and sister to come along. Mother would be perfect as the manor's cook, while Agatha could work with me. She just lost her husband and didn't know what she would do, especially with all the recent troubles. This is a godsend. When would you need us, my lady?"

"Come today if you can." Margery laughed. "There is plenty to be done."

"Then you will see us by sundown," Sarah said. She looked to Ancel. "And thank you, my lord. I promise we three will work hard."

"I don't doubt that, Sarah. And pass along the word that Highfield also needs farmers for the harvest, ones who can remain as tenants. Good day to you."

Ancel helped Margery onto Storm and they returned to the estate.

"I'm sorry we weren't as successful as I'd hoped," he told her. "Kirkby didn't have much to offer."

"Still, we have a new blacksmith and cook. I would not have expected hiring both so soon."

"And servants to help you," he reminded her. "I will go to Billericay soon and see about the rest, including finding a new steward to help manage the estate. We also need to go out and see what tenants remain and seek others to replenish the labor force. The harvest won't wait much longer."

They parted ways. Margery went to check the blacksmith's quarters and did her best to ready it for the Cheynes' arrival tomorrow. The cart arrived with the supplies they'd bought and two of the soldiers unloaded it for her as she directed them where to place everything. Sarah and her relatives came after that and Margery showed Maud the kitchen, promising to spend more time with the older woman tomorrow as they baked bread together with the new flour. By then, the soldiers appeared for their evening meal. Bartram and his crew provided amply and there were even leftovers for the next day's meals.

After the meal ended, Ancel drew her aside.

"Will you return with me to the solar?" he asked. "I would like to explore the passageway now since I have much to do tomorrow."

The thought of entering and walking deeply into the narrow space again caused panic to flare inside Margery. Still, Ancel would be with her. No one would be chasing her, ready to kill her if she were discovered.

"If you like," she replied neutrally, trying not to show her fear.

"Bartram found an oil lamp. I'll retrieve it to light our way," he told her. He did so and accompanied her to the solar.

"Let me try to figure out how to open it this time," Ancel said.

Margery stepped back and allowed the knight to poke and prod until the stone sprang open. He urged it forward and picked up the lantern.

Though her mouth was suddenly dry, Margery gave him a small smile as he ducked inside the narrow passage. Steeling herself, she followed him.

CHAPTER 10

A NCEL CROUCHED LOW, thinking his back would be stiff tomorrow from bending over so much. The path hidden in the walls of the keep proved narrow and confining. His broad shoulders came close to rubbing against the walls in the tight space. Even holding the lantern out to see what lay ahead, the way was murky—and eerie.

"You traveled through this in the dark when you made your escape?" he asked Margery.

"Aye."

Her voice seemed small and quiet. He couldn't imagine the terror she'd experienced. Fleeing an angry mob wanting to murder you was nerve-racking enough. But to do it in the dark in an unknown place? And as a woman? Once again, he admired Margery's bravery and quick thinking as she sequestered herself inside this hidden pathway.

They reached a point where the corridor widened and Ancel saw it forked in two directions. He asked, "Which path should we take?"

"I went to the left the first time I reached this point," she replied. "It will lead to the opposite side of the keep and come out at . . . my former bedchamber."

Ancel realized that was when she had been forced to listen to her mother's death. He shouldn't ask her to relive such a painful time.

"Mayhap this wasn't a good idea to have you accompany me," he said. "I know it brings back unpleasant memories."

"We can go on," she said, a catch in her voice.

"Give me your hand," he instructed.

She held it out and his engulfed her tiny one. He'd hoped to bring her strength and reassurance yet, for him, a feeling of peace descended. Holding Margery Ormond's hand had come to be his favorite thing in life.

Except for that brief kiss.

He pushed that thought aside and focused on the business at hand. Leading her to the left, it took some minutes before they came to a dead end.

"Are we there?"

"Aye." Margery moved forward and slid a bolt that secured the opening before pushing the half-door. She exited the hidden tunnel and he followed, still keeping her hand in his.

"A tapestry used to hang here," she indicated. "That's one reason I never suspected the entrance being here, though you've seen how difficult it is to open even if you know it exists."

"How did you know about the one in the solar?"

She explained how her stepbrothers had allowed her into the solar to show her the hidden way but refused to let her play with them or use it since she wasn't a true Vivers. Ancel knew that was only part of the story. Boys could be cruel to girls and he knew no friendliness existed between Margery and her stepbrothers. He could only imagine their brutal taunts.

"I truly had forgotten about it until the pressing danger somehow forced me to remember."

"You know it saved your life."

"Aye," she said softly. "If only I could have gotten Mother inside."

His thumb rubbed across her knuckles. "She is with God now and no longer suffering."

Margery's eyes dropped to the floor and she nodded. Ancel gave her a moment and then said, "Come. Show me the rest," and they reentered the passageway.

He led the way again, holding fast to her hand, somehow needing to do so as much as he hoped she needed him, as well. They arrived back at the fork and followed the new path until it ended. Ancel pushed open the secreted door and they stepped out into the cool night air, looking around to see exactly where he was. Though he doubted he would ever need to make use of the hidden passageway, he'd wanted to learn everything about it. Being prepared had served him well in the past.

"If you like, we can return to the keep from the outside," he suggested, knowing she might dread taking the darkened pathway again. "I hold you in high regard, Margery. I can't imagine navigating something unknown such as this narrow passage as you did, much less in total darkness. Though you feared for your life, you pressed on and even tried to rescue your mother. Even the bravest of knights would have seen this as a formidable challenge."

She nibbled on her bottom lip and desire shot through him. His hand tightened on hers.

"I didn't feel very brave. Most of the time I was paralyzed with fear," she admitted.

"But you continued on," he pointed out. "That's courage, Margery. Being afraid and not letting it stop you from what you have to do." He paused. "When I ride into battle? I feel terrified. But I press on because I must."

"You know fear?" she asked, disbelief on her face.

"I think most men who ride into battle are terrified. Very few men enjoy war. But as a knight of the realm, I fight for king and country and will do it every time I'm asked to defend England."

"I hope I am never that scared again, Ancel," she confessed. "I don't ever want to be so afraid. I want a quiet, simple life."

He studied her a moment. "Have you thought on the king's words, Margery?" he asked softly. "On staying here, at Highfield, as my wife?"

Her mouth trembled. "I've wanted to. But I haven't. Part of me wishes for it desperately. A husband. Children. Making Highfield into a home that's full of happiness—and love." A single tear cascaded down her cheek. "But a part of me is terrified that Thurstan will ride back through the gates and I will, once again, be a prisoner with no choice."

Ancel set the lantern down and cupped her face. "Even if your stepbrother returns, you don't have to stay here."

Her sad eyes gazed at him. "But where would I go?"

"Wherever I go," he said simply.

With that, he pressed his lips against hers, feeling their softness. Her hands clutched his gypon, bunching it as she kneaded him.

He broke the kiss and saw disappointment in her eyes.

"Come." Ancel retrieved the lantern and quickly brought her back inside the hidden tunnel. He slid the bolt against the door and sat, tugging her down and placing her in his lap, one arm going about her waist. Soldiers patrolled not only the wall walk but the grounds of the castle. He didn't want anyone coming across them. What he needed was privacy.

Margery felt warm against him. Her hands rested on his shoulders. His hand cupped the nape of her neck.

"I have thought of nothing else but kissing you," he revealed, then covered her mouth with his.

Ancel began slowly, not wanting to frighten her, knowing she was inexperienced. He kissed her lips. Her temples. Her brow. Her eyelids. Slowly, he ventured back to her mouth and let the tip of his tongue outline her lips before it ran along the seam. She opened to him and his tongue entered her mouth, leisurely exploring it, enjoying her taste, her scent, the feel of her in his arms.

Tentatively, her tongue touched his. He sighed his pleasure and Margery grew bolder. Soon, she matched him as their tongues warred with one another, mating. His ran along the roof of her mouth and she shuddered, a moan escaping from her.

Then darkness surrounded them, the oil in the lamp exhausted. Her fingers tightened on his shoulders.

"I'm here," he told her. "I won't leave you. I'll never leave you."

Ancel's mouth found hers again and plundered its sweetness. His fingers caressed her throat, brushing against a slender chain. They moved lower, touching the swell of her breasts as he kissed her hungrily. Margery pushed closer to him, her fingers now locked behind his neck. He palmed a breast and squeezed it gently. It swelled, filling his hand. He found her nipple and dragged a fingernail across it slowly, over and over, feeling it pebble in need against the cloth of her cotehardie.

Margery wriggled against him, causing his manhood to rise. Ancel knew he had to put a stop to things. He brought his hand back to the nape of her neck and stroked it as he pulled his mouth from hers.

"Oh my."

He heard the wonder in her voice.

Ancel kissed her softly and said, "We will spend a lifetime exploring one another, my love, but we must wait to be wed before we go further into love play."

Her head fell against his chest. "You truly want to marry me?"

"I do."

Her fingers playfully tickled his neck. "Is it me you want, or is it Highfield you desire?"

"Highfield would be a nice reward but you are the one that I wish to warm my bed and bear my children. An estate cannot do that."

"But if Thurstan does come back?"

"Then I will offer for you. I will tell him the king thought of it first."

"Thurstan is obstinate and might say no, drunk on the power of being the new baron. What if he refuses?"

"No one refuses Ancel de Montfort," he teased and kissed her again.

This time, she broke their kiss. "Actually, Thurstan is not my closest relative. He would have no say over who I wed. Only my father would."

Her words puzzled him. "But didn't your mother wed Lord Umfrey after your father's death?"

Margery snuggled against him. "Mother married Lord Umfrey after Lord Joseph Ormond's death."

It dawned on him what she meant. "So she was with child before she wed her first husband?" Ancel asked.

"Aye. I knew nothing of this until moments before I fled. Mother gave me an amethyst ring and a pearl necklace that she had kept hidden from Lord Joseph. He was a gambler and lost everything. He killed himself and left Mother and me in disgrace."

Ancel stroked her back. "Did she tell you your father's name?"

"Nay," He heard the disappointment in her voice. "Only that my real father wanted me to have a silver pendant inlaid with garnets when I came of age. I slipped the necklace on and pocketed the other jewels. Mother told me she wished she had time to tell me more but Sarah insisted I leave then." Margery paused. "If I had stayed, I would have learned the truth—but I would have lost my life."

"So you have no clue how, other than this necklace, to identify your father?"

"Nay."

"For your sake, I hope Thurstan doesn't return. If he does, I will make sure the king insists that we wed. But I promise you, sweetheart, I will do whatever I can to help you discover the identity of your father and reunite the two of you."

"You would do that for me?"

He chuckled. "I think I would do anything for you, my lady."

Margery kissed him with enthusiasm. It was all the invitation Ancel needed. They kissed for what seemed like hours, till his lips were sore and he knew hers must be, as well.

"Enough of this. We need to make our way back," he told her.

"I am the expert of navigating this place in the dark. I shall lead you this time," she boldly proclaimed.

Ancel took pride in her determination as she brought him back to their original starting point. They emerged into the solar.

Before he sealed the doorway, Margery said, "I'd like to place my ring and necklace inside the passage for safekeeping. They came from my mother and she received them from her father, the Earl of Waudum, before her first marriage." She removed a piece of cloth from her pocket and handed to him. "They are wrapped inside this handkerchief."

"Would you like me to place them inside the chest?"

A look of distaste crossed her face. "Nay. That belonged to Lord Umfrey. I don't want them to mix with anything of his."

Ancel took the wrapped jewels and placed them several paces past the wooden chest.

Emerging from the half-door, he replaced the stone in the wall and stood, happy to be able to stretch to his full height.

Noticing the delicate silver chain against her throat, he asked, "May I see the pendant from your father?"

Margery pulled the necklace from where it fell in the valley between her breasts and lifted it for him to inspect.

Ancel studied the intricate design, a generous amount of garnets scattered throughout.

"I think I have seen this pattern somewhere before," he shared. "I can't recall where at the moment."

Excitement filled her features. "Mayhap if you do, it will lead us to my real father."

CHAPTER II

ANCEL SPENT THE next morning with the soldiers in the training yard, putting them through various exercises in order to evaluate their skills. It was an exceptional group of men—disciplined, talented, and dependable.

Will motioned him over. Ancel had assigned the squire to keep near Margery, so it concerned him that the young man had left her side and was outside, far from the manor house. He handed the sword he'd used to demonstrate a move to a soldier and hurried over.

"My lord, Lady Margery said to tell you there's a group of serfs that have gathered in the great hall."

Ancel took off running toward the keep before Will finished his sentence.

"Wait, my lord!" cried Will, chasing after him. "They're a peaceful group."

He stopped in his tracks, forcing himself to take a deep breath. The thought of Margery surrounded by an angry mob had frightened him beyond measure. It revealed just how deeply his new feelings ran for the petite beauty.

Will caught up to him, breathing hard. "They heard you put the call out. For workers. For the harvest." The squire swallowed and gulped more air. "Lady Margery wanted you to speak to them. That's all. Everything is fine otherwise, my lord."

"Thank you, Will. I'll see them now. You can return to the training yard for a while."

The young man broke out into a huge grin and hurried away,

eager to join in with the other two squires helping the knights.

Ancel had chosen Will to stay close to Margery today since he trusted the squire. Though she had Sarah and Agatha with her to begin righting the keep, he felt more comfortable knowing that Will shadowed her. Will had grumpily agreed to the task, though Ancel had overheard the lad complaining to a fellow squire about having to play wet nurse to the women inside the keep.

He found Margery awaiting him at the door leading into the keep's entrance. His heart skipped a beat at the sight of her.

"Will said you had need of me." He gazed into her brown eyes, the amber rimming them catching the light of the summer sun.

She gave him a warm smile. "They've been turning up all morning. Some are tenants from Highfield. Others are from places nearby. I thought it best if you addressed them as a group and decided who should stay or go."

"Do you recognize any from the attack on Highfield? Any of your own people who turned traitor?"

Margery shook her head. "It's possible a few participated. But now that the king's army ended the rebellion at Billericay, I believe all they want is to be able to work the land in peace in order to feed their families."

"Let's go speak to them." Ancel opened the door for her and they entered the great hall.

Glancing around, he guessed probably sixty or seventy people gathered in the large room. A third were mature men and another third were young men, while the rest were women and young children. It was likely that some of the women had lost husbands in the uprising and the younger men their fathers.

He escorted Margery to the dais and seated her while he climbed upon it and remained standing to survey the crowd.

"I am Sir Ancel de Montfort, a member of the royal guard and here at the king's command. I have King Richard's full authority and have been charged to secure Highfield and protect the inhabitants both here and in Essex from any lingering problems caused by the recent uprising."

Pausing, he let his words sink in. Ancel wanted them to understand exactly who he was and why he was here.

"The rebellion is over and done. Highfield's crops need harvesting. New livestock will be purchased and need tending. If you have come to work hard on the land and provide for your families, then I am happy to have you here."

A general murmur and nodding of heads pleased him.

"I want to speak to everyone present. Lady Margery will introduce me to you if you are known to her and that way I will know if you are a previous tenant or choose to be a new one. The lady will also help in assigning plots of land and cottages for you and your families to live in. Those who are selected to remain at Highfield will be expected to attend mass each morning in the chapel and break their fast in the great hall afterward.

"For now, pull the trestle tables from the walls and be seated. We will come around and talk with you."

Ancel reached out a hand and helped Margery rise. They descended from the platform as the peasants began rearranging the trestle tables and benches and seating themselves.

"Over there," Margery said. "Do you see the tall man with the reddish beard?"

Ancel nodded. "What about him?"

"He's Giles Downer. He lost his wife in childbirth last month. 'Twas their first. I know he's an excellent worker and knowledgeable about farming and animals. He would be someone you could place in charge because he has the respect of the others."

"I smell bread has been baked. Have Maud put some of it out with tankards of ale for the group. I'll talk to this Giles Downer first."

Downer impressed Ancel with his demeanor and knowledge, so Ancel placed the man in charge of the rest of the workers. Downer seemed to know most everyone in the room, even the people Margery didn't know. The three of them circulated among the tables and spoke to everyone present. After two hours, they had their labor force and the workers had cottages assigned to them. Immediately, Downer divided those present into various teams and sent everyone out into the fields.

"No need to wait till tomorrow, my lord, when you can put idle hands to work today. 'Tis only noon. We've all afternoon in which to work, then the people can settle in to where they will live once the light fades."

It impressed Ancel that Giles already had a firm hand on the situation. Ancel told him, "You will receive double that of the other tenants, Giles. If you put anyone into a leadership position and you feel they are owed more, let me know. Or our steward. I plan to hire one in the next day or so."

"Aye, my lord." Downer paused. "These are good people, despite what happened here. I don't think you have a need to worry."

"I have confidence in you," Ancel said, "but there will be a strong military presence at Highfield in the foreseeable future."

The soldiers streamed in for the noon meal as Downer left. Between the meat Bartram's group provided and the bread Maud and Margery had baked that morning, the men seemed satisfied. Now that the harvest would be taken care of and the defenses had been brought back to a desired level, Ancel decided he could make a quick trip to Billericay for what they hadn't been able to purchase at Kirkby.

He turned to Margery, whom he shared a trencher with. The corner of her mouth had a small spot of grease from the meat. Ancel refrained from reaching out and wiping it away with his thumb.

Or licking it with his tongue.

No woman had ever stirred such deep physical need within him. Margery might be small in size but one look from her could fell him.

"I'm leaving for Billericay," he told her. "Although I would like to take you with me, I want to ride hard and fast and finish the business at hand. I know you want to continue making the candles with Sarah and Agatha since we've been in short supply."

Ancel saw she tamped down her disappointment. "You remember everything from my list, my lord? The things we still lack?"

"I do. Bedclothes, spices, materials for clothes. Needles and threads. More chickens and sheep. Wine. Parchment and ink. Farm implements. A steward."

She laughed and his heart melted at the sound of hearing her happiness. "Well, the wine isn't necessary but it would be much appreciated. You have an excellent memory, my lord."

"I'll make a return trip to Billericay when I have more time to see about horses. Or mayhap even go into London for them. Would you like to accompany me there?"

Her eyes lit up. "To London? Of course! Who wouldn't want to see London?"

This time, Ancel laughed. "You thought Kirkby was large and you haven't even seen Billericay yet. London will probably overwhelm you."

"I don't care," she proclaimed. "I would love to see it. With you." She smiled shyly.

"Then plan on it. I will even take you to see the king again."

A frown creased her brow. "I have nothing to wear to meet the king."

"But you already have met him," he reminded her.

"And I looked like a fright. Nay, I would not embarrass you, my lord. I can wait for you somewhere if you need to speak with him."

Ancel planned on bringing back material worthy to clothe Margery. She had been neglected far too long. If Billericay didn't have what he sought, he would send Will to London to find something to suit her.

He lowered his voice. "You always look lovely," he said. "I wish I could not just tell you that but show you. Mayhap when I return tonight we can find some time to be alone."

A blush tinged her cheeks. "I would like that, Ancel," she said quietly.

Standing, he offered her his hand and helped her rise. "Then I'm off. Stick with candle making and nothing more physical than that."

Margery snorted. "I'm not some delicate creature, you know. I wager that I have as much stamina as you do, my lord."

A thought of her naked in his arms, their bodies slick with sweat from an entire night of love play heated his loins. He would show her what stamina was—and enjoy every moment of it.

ANCEL PUSHED STORM along the road to Billericay. The warhorse enjoyed being unleashed and they arrived quickly. Ancel found a place to stable the horse for a few hours and then made the rounds of the town, purchasing items needed inside the keep first, from candlestick holders to bedclothes to linen bath sheets. He'd made an extra trip to Lord Umfrey's oak chest and had ample coin for the goods. He bought extra flour, as well, knowing how quickly bread seemed to be gobbled up by hungry soldiers. Rounds of cheese came next and then spices. He stocked up on some vegetables since peasants had overrun Margery's garden. She would salvage what she could and replant what she needed. Ancel arranged for carts to deliver the merchandise since those from Highfield had been stolen. He already had Matthew Cheyne and his son working on wheels. Cheyne had known of a carpenter in Billericay that might be willing to relocate to Highfield. Ancel sought the man out and hired him on the spot. Soon, Highfield would have carts again and the new carpenter could help in building new furniture to replace what had been looted or ruined.

Buying rugs baffled him and the selection seemed small. He decided this was something Margery could help him with when they journeyed to London. He also decided to put off choosing stores of wine for now. He did purchase a few casks to tide Highfield over. London would certainly have a better selection.

It was odd how he didn't miss the city at all, nor did he miss his duties in the royal guard. At heart, Ancel knew he enjoyed country life more than that at the Palace of Westminster. Since coming to Highfield, he did many of the things his own father performed at Kinwick. Ancel wondered once more if Thurstan Vivers would show up. If he didn't, Ancel hoped the king would make good on his word and award Highfield to him. Ancel would love to bring the estate back to a point where it thrived.

With Margery by his side.

Discovering a place to buy chickens, he bought every single bird with the promise of more to be delivered to Highfield by the end of the week. Margery would be pleased to have hens and their eggs. The merchant also guaranteed to have fifty sheep brought to the estate.

Bells began to chime from a nearby church. Ancel counted five and knew he wouldn't be able to conduct all of his business in the time left. Hiring a steward was too important to be rushed so he decided to wait on finding one for now. Instead, he made a final stop to look at material for new clothing for Margery.

Ancel looked at the different fabrics and colors, trying to picture what Alys wore since she was close in age to Margery.

"May I help you, my lord?"

He turned and saw a thin woman of two score. "I could definitely use your help." Ancel explained that he needed cloth for a noblewoman who had lost everything she owned.

The woman sighed. "Stupid, bloody rebellion. At least your lady did not lose her life as others did. Come, I can recommend what she needs to replace. And what about combs? Soaps?"

"I am at your disposal, madam."

Ancel wound up buying several bolts of material for Margery. It appalled him how she'd been forced to dress by Umfrey Vivers. He wanted her clothing to reflect her position. He limited what he bought because he knew the variety would be greater in London. In fact, he'd already decided when he sent Will with a missive to the king that he'd give the squire coin to select some fine materials to bring back to Highfield.

"Is the lady handy with a needle?"

"I suppose so. She's mentioned making her own clothes." He thought a moment. "Do you know of an available seamstress that might be willing to come to Highfield for a time?"

"My daughter is ten and seven, my lord. She is as fine a seamstress as can be found in Essex. Let me fetch her."

Soon, Ancel had been introduced to Christine Morley, the woman's daughter.

"I'd be happy to come to Highfield, my lord. At a large estate, there's always sewing to be done. If the baroness is pleased with my work, I would consider staying."

"The baroness recently passed," he told the girl. "You would work for Lady Margery, her daughter." He didn't want to reveal that Margery might be the next baroness. Though not superstitious, Ancel wanted to wait to hear from the king before he said anything about whether he would be the new baron or not.

"Do you know a carpenter named Harry Bacon?" Ancel asked.

"Aye," Christine said. "He made a table and chairs for us three or four years ago."

"He is to be Highfield's new carpenter and will travel there in the morning with his tools. I'm sure there would be room in his cart for you and your things. Would you like me to arrange that?"

Christine readily agreed. Ancel doubled back and firmed up with Harry to bring the seamstress and bolts of material with him when he left for Highfield the next day.

Satisfied with all he'd accomplished, Ancel walked back through the town to retrieve Storm. He would return to Billericay in a day or two to find a steward. As he crossed an alley, he heard a whimper. Always on the alert to danger, Ancel pulled his sword and proceeded cautiously. The whine came again near a pile of garbage.

Then he caught sight of a floppy ear as a puppy poked its head out and looked up at Ancel with a pitiful expression. The dog wriggled around but didn't come forward when he called to it. Ancel leaned down and found the animal's hind legs were trapped under a barrel. He lifted it and the puppy crawled away.

Toward Ancel.

He plopped on Ancel's boot, exhausted, his eyes closed as he rested his head.

"Poor thing. You must have been struggling a long time to get out from under that barrel."

He lifted the black and white pup to his chest and saw it was a water spaniel. They were trained to flush game for falcons or for hounds and oftentimes were adept at swimming and could retrieve water fowl. Most importantly, they were known for their good nature.

Impulsively, he said, "You are coming home with me, my fine fellow. I have just the lady that will be pleased to have you as her companion."

Ancel couldn't wait to see Margery's face.

CHAPTER 12

MARGERY TRIED NOT to show her concern when Ancel didn't return by the evening meal. She sat on the dais alone, missing his company, though dozens of lively conversations filled the great hall. She looked out, happy to see so many people present—soldiers and serfs alike—all looking tired but full of life as the day came to an end.

Mealtimes under Lord Umfrey had been somber affairs. Very little conversation flowed throughout the room. Umfrey himself spoke occasionally to Thurstan or Gervase, usually to grumble about something. The nobleman never addressed her and Margery had liked it that way. When he did take note of her, it was because he wanted something done in addition to the many duties she had to fulfill each day.

They still needed to hire more servants. Margery had Sarah and Agatha help her and Maud prepare tonight's meal and the two sisters were the only servers. Margery was thankful Ancel had insisted on installing a cook. By watching Maud, Margery could tell how talented the woman was and knew she would be an asset to Highfield. Still, it would be nice to have a few more hands to clean and help cook and serve the meals. She wondered if Ancel had employed any servants while in Billericay.

Thoughts of the roaming bands of highwaymen on England's roads caused her to worry about his safety since he had traveled alone to the town. Yet of all the men she had known, Ancel was the most capable. If trouble presented itself, she doubted anything would happen to prevent him from returning to Highfield.

To her . . .

Margery longed for his kiss again. For his touch. In a short time, Ancel de Montfort had come to mean her entire world. She never knew she could be so happy, especially at Highfield. What had once been her prison, with Lord Umfrey as her jailer, now became a place of happiness. She knew the estate would thrive under Ancel's hand— as would she.

From their brief time together inside the secret tunnel, Margery knew a world of mystery awaited her. Ancel's touch had made her body tingle and throb and long for more. She prayed a selfish prayer to the Virgin Mary, one that had Thurstan Vivers dead and never returning to Highfield. Her stepbrother had been vile and uncouth and terribly lazy. She hoped she never saw him again and that the king made good on his promise and awarded Highfield—and her—to Ancel.

Even if Thurstan came home, Margery believed that Ancel would sweep her away as he'd promised. Whether to the royal court in London, where, hopefully, she could find someplace to serve, or to his parents' estate, it didn't matter. Highfield would not be safe for her under Thurstan's hand.

It did make her curious about her real father, not Lord Joseph Ormond, a man she barely remembered and had no respect for. How had her parents met? How did they come together? Margery wondered if she would ever know the true tale but it had felt right to share what little she knew about it with Ancel. She longed to share everything with the dashing knight. The thought of sharing her body with him had her shivering in anticipation.

Sarah and Agatha cleared the tables as the meal ended. The tenants, some old and some new, left in groups to settle in to their abodes, while the soldiers sat about telling stories or tossing dice. Margery decided to retire to the solar and hoped Ancel might visit her there upon his return.

It made her uncomfortable sleeping in the same bed where Lord

Umfrey had slept. She'd awakened from a nightmare last night, the sounds of her stepfather's screams ringing in her ears. As she looked around knowing he'd been taken to his death from this very room, a chill penetrated her body. She went to the bed now, stripped of bedclothes by the angry peasants, and picked up the torn, bloodied cloak that she'd worn at the battlefield. Wrapping it around her, she left the bedchamber and went to sit at the table in the solar, thankful that it still remained.

A knock sounded and she rose to answer it. A giddy feeling ran through her and she hoped Ancel had arrived and come to visit.

Margery opened the door and was greeted by his sunny smile. She would never grow tired of it, no matter how many times he shared it with her. Then her eyes fell to his chest and what he had gathered in his arms.

"A . . . puppy?"

Ancel laughed and swept inside the room. Margery closed the door and faced him as he held the small dog up for her inspection.

"What do you think?"

She closed the distance between them and petted the animal's head. It looked painfully thin. But the dog's liquid brown eyes called out to her, tugging on her heartstrings. Then it licked her hand and gave a small woof.

"See, he likes you," Ancel proclaimed, his eyes merry. "Here. Take him."

Margery gathered the puppy in her arms and brought him against her. He rested his head against where her heart beat. She was convinced the dog smiled up at her.

Looking back at Ancel, she said, "I don't recall a puppy being on the list, my lord."

His eyes lit in mischief. "You are teasing me, Margery Ormond. And no, he wasn't one of my purchases so he didn't cost a single coin."

As she stroked the dog, Ancel explained where he'd found the animal and how he'd freed it.

"I thought he would make a good companion for you. He's a water spaniel, so if you don't want him, I suppose one of the men would know how to train him so he could be used for hunting once he's matured."

She gazed down at the warm bundle of fur and her heart melted. "Nay, my lord. I want him all to myself." She cocked her head and asked the dog, "What shall we call you, my little one?"

"'Tis a boy," Ancel confirmed. "I checked." He thought a moment. "More of him is black than white but all four paws are white. How about Whitefoot?"

Margery playfully tugged on one of the puppy's hind paws. "What do you think, Whitefoot? Do you like that name?"

The dog wiggled in her arms so she put him down. "I think that's a perfect name for him. But I'm sure he's hungry. And his fur and paws are filthy," she added, looking down at her now-muddy cotehardie.

"I've taken care of that," Ancel said. "Sarah is heating water for a bath and Maud said she would bring up something for him to eat."

Margery laughed. "Already you are quite spoiled, Whitefoot," she declared. "A bath and then dining in the solar? Next thing we know, you will think you are royalty and demand to sleep in a bed."

Another knock sounded and Ancel admitted Sarah and Agatha, both carrying pails in each hand. Their mother followed a few paces behind the women.

"He's a right cute one," Sarah said as she set her pails down.

Margery saw one of them was empty. Sarah poured water halfway up into the empty one and then removed a bar of soap tucked under her arm.

"Put him in, my lady, and I'll give him a good scrubbing," she said.

"No, Sarah. You've all had a long day. Sir Ancel can help me wash Whitefoot."

"Whitefoot? Is that his name?" Agatha asked. "Oh, he looked up. Hello, Whitefoot." She giggled as the puppy began running in circles, chasing his tail.

"Here's some food for Master Whitefoot," said Maud. "He's got a bit of roasted chicken to nibble on. Poor little mite. We'll need to fatten him up."

"Thank you all," Ancel said. "We can manage the rest."

The three women left and Margery fed Whitefoot his dinner by hand. Between bites, he licked her fingers. She hoped, at first, that he did so in affection but she realized it was because they'd become coated in grease from the meat.

They bathed the dog, no small feat since he twisted and squirmed from start to finish. After rinsing him, Whitefoot had shaken the excess water off and run around till he tired himself out. Margery and Ancel watched his antics, highly entertained. The dog finally curled up next to Ancel's boot, resting his head on top of it.

"Thank you for my gift," she told him. "Whitefoot is better than anything that was on my list. But how did your trip to Billericay go?"

He told her of all the goods and livestock that he'd purchased and when everything would arrive. She couldn't believe he'd been able to find so much and arrange for its delivery in such a short length of time.

"I also hired a carpenter who will arrive in the morning," Ancel shared. "With all of the furniture that was broken or stolen, he'll be busy for some time crafting new items. His name is Harry Bacon and he will bring a seamstress, Christine Morley, with him."

Margery frowned. "But we don't need a seamstress, Ancel. I am perfectly capable of—"

"I know you are," he said as he took her hand and entwined his fingers through hers. "But Christine is coming all the same. She can make a new wardrobe for you and clothing for any of the servants, aprons or whatnot, and she can even help you with weaving new tapestries. I know how those help keep out the cold. Winter will be here before we know it. It's not too soon to begin thinking of that."

Everything seemed to be right in her world. Margery had a hard time believing how things had turned upside down and inside out in such a short time. Ancel thought of everything, even bringing her Whitefoot. Feelings she'd never known stirred inside, though Margery refused to put a name to them.

"I will need to head back to Billericay to seek a steward. I didn't have enough time to speak to anyone who might fill the job. It's one of the most important ones on an estate . . ." His voice trailed off. "No, I won't be going to Billericay," he said firmly. "I had said I would send a missive to my parents. I think I know of someone at Kinwick who might be willing to fill the position."

"This is a man you trust?"

"Aye, much more than meeting with strangers in Billericay." Ancel brought their joined hands up and brushed a kiss against her knuckles before releasing her hand. "I will write to Mother and Father now and inquire about Clifton Walters."

Margery rose. "Then I will bid you goodnight."

Ancel took a step toward her. A soft growl floated up from the ground. He leaned down and lifted a sleepy Whitefoot from his boot and then placed his hands on her shoulders.

"Goodnight, sweetheart." He brushed his lips against hers. "Sweet dreams—to you and your sleeping pup."

ANCEL LEFT THE solar and retreated to what he determined had been used as the steward's office at Highfield. He had investigated the room before his trip to Billericay and found parchment and ink there, though he had bought more while in town since the supply was perilously close to running out. He hadn't spared the time to examine any of the estate's records. At this point, he preferred training with the men and ensuring that Highfield was well protected from any attack. He would allow the new steward to wade through the murky waters of numbers in the ledgers, which he often didn't have the patience for, unlike his younger sister, Nan. If allowed, Nan might drown herself in numbers. He chuckled at that thought.

Drawing out quill and ink, he readied them and placed a fresh sheet of parchment on the desk. He would be brief, which his father would appreciate and his mother would bemoan, but Ancel wasn't ready to tip his hand as to what the king might or might not do regarding Highfield. Dipping the quill into the ink, he composed the missive.

Greetings, Mother and Father —

I am sure news of the peasants' uprising has reached you. It started in London and spread beyond to Kent and Essex. Know that it has been crushed and that I am safe and well, though not with the royal guard at present. After the king's army fought the rebels at Norsey Wood outside Billericay, some ten leagues east of London, I was charged with securing a place called Highfield, an estate only six leagues east of London. The estate's proximity to London and its being in the heart of Essex (where the rebels originated), made it a chief concern of the king.

For now, I am in charge of the place, since its baron was murdered in the rebellion, as was his younger son. The elder, who would inherit the title and land, has yet to be found. I have a small force of troops that the king let me handpick. Buckingham and Sir Thomas Percy, the co-commanders at the battle fought at Norsey Wood, each lent me ten of their finest men, as well. The estate is secure and being fortified against future attacks. I have had to recruit new tenants to deal with the wheat harvest. Things are running smoothly and a great part of that is due to the assistance I have received from Lady Margery Ormond, the previous baron's stepdaughter. She is a gracious noblewoman and has the manor house well in hand, which allows me to focus on safeguarding the estate.

One reason I am writing to you is to inquire about Clifton Walters. I know he was training under Diggory, our own steward. Would Walters be available to come to Highfield and serve as its steward? I trust Diggory, who knows more about Kinwick than anyone except Father and I remembered he thinks highly of Walters. With Walters having trained under Diggory, I know he would be prepared for any situation. The king would also be grateful to see Highfield running smoothly and thriving once more.

I cannot say how long I might remain at Highfield. I am the king's man and will do his bidding. I hope, if and when I return to London, that I can visit with you there if not at Kinwick itself. I miss you both.

Your loving son,
Ancel

He let the ink dry on the parchment as he read through the message twice. He said what he'd needed to without revealing anything regarding his feelings for Margery or his hopes for gaining possession of Highfield.

Satisfied, Ancel rolled the parchment and found sealing wax. He would give this to Will Artus in the morning and have the squire ride to Kinwick.

CHAPTER 13

A NCEL EXITED THE chapel after mass and stopped Will. He removed the rolled parchment from his gypon and handed it to the squire.

"This is for my parents, Lord Geoffrey and Lady Merryn de Mont-fort. They reside at Kinwick Castle." Ancel gave Will instructions on the best route in which to reach his home and a few coins for the road. "You may break your fast first but I want you to ride out when you're done."

"Do I wait for a response, my lord?"

"Aye. In fact, I am hoping that a man name Clifton Walters will accompany you back to Highfield to serve as its steward. It should take you three days to reach Kinwick. You may stay the night once you've arrived and then return."

Will tucked the missive inside his gypon. "Thank you, Sir Ancel, for trusting me with this mission."

Ancel watched Will hurry off and catch up to the two other squires. He smiled, knowing how his mother would fuss over the boy and feed him until Will would think he might burst. A wave of homesickness washed over Ancel. Though he enjoyed being part of the king's guard and had liked his brief time at Highfield even more, Kinwick would always be home. He hoped one day he would be as good a parent to his children as his parents had been to him.

With Margery by his side.

The more he thought of her as his wife, the more Ancel grew to like the idea. Most men would not bother to look past her tremendous beauty but he admired her spirit and intelligence. Margery would make an excellent mother—and he would enjoy making their children with her.

Tamping down the lust that rushed through him at that thought, he started toward the manor house. Before he reached it, he saw that a rider approached. Ancel recognized the soldier as Terryn Althilos, a fellow knight in the king's guard.

He acknowledged the man, who swung from his horse. "Greetings, Sir Terryn. What brings you to Highfield?"

"The king's orders, Sir Ancel. He wants you to accompany me back to London at once."

Ancel kept a neutral expression on his face. "Did he say why?"

"Nay," Terryn replied. "I bring no missive, just his majesty's command that you return quickly."

"Is this permanent, or will I be able to finish my assignment at Highfield?"

"I couldn't say, Ancel. The king is guarded in both actions and words these days," Terryn confided.

"Then let me fetch my armor while you water your horse."

Terryn laughed. "I'd say I would go to the stables to do that and have someone saddle your horse but I'll wager Storm's nasty temper still gives everyone fits and you'll need to ready your horse yourself."

Ancel smiled. "My horse does have a mind of his own. He tolerates Will Artus at times, though, and, interestingly enough, Storm has grown quite fond of Lady Margery, who lives here at Highfield."

"Storm is fond of . . . a lady?" Terryn snorted in surprise. "What is this world coming to?"

"Ah, if you saw the lady in question, you might understand Storm's resistance crumbling."

Terryn looked interested. "You know, Ancel, we could make time to break our fast before we leave for London. I would like to catch a glimpse of Lady Margery and judge for myself why Storm has gone soft."

Ancel signaled a soldier over. "Take Sir Terryn's horse and see that it's watered and fed. Not too much, for we'll be on the road to London soon."

He led his fellow guardsman into the great hall and over to the dais where Margery was seated, sipping ale.

"My lady? I would like to introduce Sir Terryn Althilos to you. He is a member of King Richard's royal guard. And this is Lady Margery Ormond of Highfield."

Terryn bounded onto the dais and captured Margery's hand. "'Tis an honor to meet you, my lady." He bent over her hand and brushed his lips against her knuckles.

A flash of jealousy rippled through Ancel.

"I am happy to meet you, my lord. Would you care to join us and break your fast?"

Terryn smiled. "I would like that very much, my lady." He seated himself next to Margery and gave Ancel a sly smile as Agatha poured ale for them.

Immediately, Ancel came to Margery's other side and told her, "I am to accompany Sir Terryn back to London for an audience with the king."

The look of distress on her face caused him to reach out a hand to touch her face. He quickly dropped it back to his lap before anyone knew what he attempted, least of all Terryn, who was draining his cup of ale and hadn't noticed Ancel's indiscretion.

"Will you be gone long, my lord?" she asked neutrally.

"I don't know," he said honestly. "I may be gone a day. I may not return at all."

"I see." She turned back to her trencher.

Ancel noticed Margery didn't eat anything. Instead, she tore her bread into pieces and then tore those pieces into smaller ones. He quickly finished his meal and rose.

"I need to claim my belongings from upstairs, my lady, and speak to Sir Folcard. I will place him in charge of Highfield's defenses for now."

"Will you send a message if you are not returning?" she asked.

"Aye."

Ancel left the great hall, his gut twisting. Surely, this couldn't be the way things ended. He'd only been at Highfield a handful of days and still had so much he wished to accomplish. He would have to convince the king to let him return if Richard wanted him to remain at court.

He reached the bedchamber he'd been using, the one her stepbrothers slept in when they were at Highfield. With no squire to help him, it would take longer to don his armor.

"I can help you," a familiar voice said.

Ancel turned and saw Margery standing in the doorway. He rushed to her and yanked her inside the room, slamming the door. His mouth sought hers as he crushed her to him. Need for her filled him as he kissed her deeply.

He broke the kiss and gazed at her longingly. More than anything, Ancel wanted to make this woman his in every imaginable way.

"I'm sure the king is merely being cautious," he said. "The need to keep Highfield and the road to London safe is too pressing for me to be gone from here long."

"But what if he wants you to return to London for good?" she asked. "I could tell he places great faith in you, Ancel. He may prefer to send another knight to Highfield in order to keep you by his side so you can advise him."

He took her hands in his. "If he does, then I will send for you. It may take a while, for you are a valuable asset to Highfield, indispensable for getting it up and running properly again. But I promise you, my love, we won't be parted for long. You are as much a part of me as my sword arm. I would be nothing without you."

Taking a deep breath, Ancel voiced what was in his heart. "I love you, Margery. Now. Always." He brought her hands to his heart. "Feel it, my love. Every beat calls out your name. Every breath I take, I think of you. Whether we are meant to be together here at Highfield or in London or even at Kinwick, we will be. This is my solemn vow to you."

He kissed her again, the kiss possessive, claiming her, branding her as his.

"I love you so much, Ancel. So very, very much," Margery told him. "And I swear I will be faithful to you and wait for you, for as long as it takes."

Wordlessly, she stepped away from him and began helping him put on his armor. When he wore every piece except for his helm, she placed two fingers against her lips then raised them to his. Pressing her fingertips against his mouth, she gave him a smile and turned away.

Ancel watched the sway of her hips as she left the room and swallowed.

It was time to go to London and see what the king wanted from him.

ANCEL AND TERRYN reached London without any problems. The road was clear of trouble. They saw many serfs working in fields as they passed, leading Ancel to believe that the rebellion in the east had truly run its course. As they arrived in the city, he saw many buildings had either burned to the ground or collapsed and stood as rubble. It would take the city time to rebuild. He hoped peace would prevail while that occurred.

They made no stops until they arrived at the royal palace and stabled their horses. Ancel took the time to rub Storm down and see that he got a good measure of oats. The warhorse seemed happy back in his familiar stall.

"You are to go directly to the king," Terryn said. "Even if he is with another, you have been granted access to enter." The knight gave him a wry smile. "If the king wishes you to remain at court, I give you permission to whisper in his ear to have me return and see to Highfield—and the lovely Lady Margery. I'll admit that I was quite taken by her beauty and grace."

Ancel refrained from slamming his fist into Terryn's handsome face and calmly said, "I will let you know." He planned to recommend no other man to the king. If Ancel had his way, he would be back at Highfield by nightfall.

Winding his way through a myriad of halls, he chuckled to think how they had confused him to no end when he'd first come to reside at the palace five years ago. The time had gone by quickly because he enjoyed serving his king but all Ancel wanted now was to be fruitful at Highfield, with Margery by his side, preferably as his wife.

Arriving at the king's rooms, he nodded at various noblemen waiting for an appointment with the monarch and made his way past the knights standing guard. Without knocking, he slipped into the first of the king's rooms. A soldier motioned for him to continue. After passing through five more rooms, Ancel spied the king sitting at a table with Michael de la Pole and Sir Christopher Heron. The son of an upstart merchant who traded in wool, de la Pole had risen swiftly at court and definitely had the monarch's ear, while Heron was a nobleman friendly with de la Pole. Ancel paused in the doorway, not wanting to interrupt their conversation.

"So you think these are the best choices for me? For England?" asked the king. He glanced over and grinned when he saw Ancel. "Welcome back to court, Sir Ancel. Please, come and join us. I'd like you to hear this."

Ancel came forward, nodding to acknowledge the others. Looking at the king, it seemed as if Richard had matured since the last time they'd seen one another. Ancel supposed the difficult decisions the monarch had made during and after the peasants' rebellion would age anyone.

"We are discussing brides for the king," de la Pole said.

Ancel's brows shot up. "I didn't know your majesty was inclined to wed at this point."

Richard shrugged. "Most kings marry young. I am already ten and four and this war with France keeps dragging on. We must find a way to make a strong political and military alliance, as well as fill our coffers with a large dowry. After all, what father would not want his daughter to wed the king of England?"

Ancel could see the king's point. He suspected a large part of the peasants' uprising had to do with the taxation situation in England, brought upon by the quickly emptying royal coffers, thanks to the lingering war with the French. Ancel's own father had fought against the bastards at both Crecy and Poitiers over a score of years ago and still the war between the two countries crawled on, draining both countries' treasuries. The Duke of Lancaster had tried to replenish the royal treasury through a new taxation program but its unpopularity had been the breaking point, causing the peasants to rise up and protest against the policies established by the king's uncle.

"Who are you considering as your wife, sire?" Ancel asked Richard.

De la Pole answered instead. "We have two suitable women, Sir Ancel. I have already sent Lord Myles Peveril to Milan to negotiate with Bernabo Visconti. His oldest daughter, Caterina, would bring a huge dowry with her, as well as pose some interesting trade proposals. I plan to leave London tomorrow and join Lord Myles in the negotiation."

"And the other choice?" Ancel asked.

De la Pole cleared his throat. "I have already traded several letters with King Charles of Bohemia. Sir Christopher leaves for Prague tonight and he will open up the discussions for me. I will join Sir Christopher after I speak with Visconti in Milan. Anne of Bohemia is the king's eldest daughter. She is the one we are considering for England's queen, even more than the Visconti woman."

Ancel could understand why. As head of the Holy Roman Empire, Charles was the most powerful monarch in Europe, ruling half of the continent's population and territory. A marriage between Richard and Anne would be of great diplomatic significance. It was also well known that Charles had no love of the French. Having the Holy Roman Empire as England's political and military ally would send a strong message to the French king.

If Ancel had to guess, Anne would be the choice over the Italian noblewoman, no matter what size dowry she could bring to the

Crown's treasury.

"I think you've said your piece, de la Pole," Richard declared. "You and Sir Christopher need to be on your way. Keep me informed of your progress."

"We will, sire," de la Pole said smoothly. "I have confidence you will have the bride best suited for you and England. Lord Myles will report directly to you once he leaves Milan. Sir Christopher and I will return as soon as negotiations have been completed in Prague."

The two men left and Ancel asked, "So Anne of Bohemia is the true choice and Caterina Visconti is merely a negotiating ploy, I assume?"

Richard shrugged. "Something like that. I don't care which of them I wed and bed. But 'tis good to see you, Ancel. I have missed our talks, my friend. And I have much to share with you. Have a seat. In fact, pour us some wine first."

Ancel did as asked and returned two golden goblets to the table.

"I want to hear about Highfield but first I must tell you what I've decided upon with my advisers and new royal council's input."

"I am eager to hear what you have to say, sire."

"First, the battle at Billericay did end the insurrection in the east. Order has been reestablished. Because of that, I am rescinding the previous grant to rebels. The royal charter I signed a few weeks ago was done so under duress. It has now been revoked. However, I did truly listen to what the peasants had to say and have made changes in my royal council. I will grant pardons to almost all of the rebels, with a few of their leaders being the exception."

The king drew in a deep breath and expelled it. "Most importantly, there will be no more poll tax to try and fund the French war. Uncle was wrong about that in ways too numerous to count."

"What?" His words shocked Ancel. "Do you mean to seek peace with France?"

Richard nodded. "It's time, don't you think?"

Ancel chose his words carefully. "I think the people as a whole will be pleased."

"I also plan to raise rural wages. I want noblemen throughout the kingdom to follow suit. We are sorely lacking in laborers, Ancel, both from the losses due to the Black Death and now the large number of serfs killed in this uprising. We are going to have to pay the poor a living wage in order to keep them in line, both now and in the future."

"I think these are wise decisions, your majesty. It may take the noble class more time to be accepting of your ideas, though."

The monarch slammed his hand upon the table. "They *will* be accepting, for I am their king! I am determined that the threat to my royal authority will never occur again. I will *not* be challenged by anyone, be they noble or poor."

"And what of your uncle, John of Gaunt? You've implied that Lancaster's policies led to much of the recent troubles."

Richard's eyes narrowed. "Uncle is fortunate that he was away from London when the peasants revolted. True, they burned his palace to the ground but at least he is alive—unlike many of those he surrounded himself with. I have ordered him to stay away from court for the time being until things quiet down. He is only uncle to the king—not the king himself. I fully assert my rights, Ancel. No one is in charge of this nation but the king, and I am he."

Ancel hoped the young monarch knew what he was doing.

"I do plan to send a force throughout England to quell any thought of uprising that might linger. Four thousand armed troops will be sent across the land." Richard paused.

"I would like you to be one of the leaders of this army, Ancel. What do you say?"

CHAPTER 14

WHAT DID HE SAY?

W Ancel wanted to refuse. But what knight could deny the wishes of his king? Ancel took his knightly oath seriously. His purpose in life was to serve both king and country, putting aside any personal desires. But maybe the monarch would agree to a compromise.

"Sending out an army of that size would send the desired message, sire. 'Tis a wise idea and would thwart any smoldering ideas of rebellion." He paused. "But what of Highfield? At your request, I have been working on the castle and its defenses, as well as patrolling the road near it that leads to London. With the estate's proximity to the city, I believe it should be a priority. In fact, I was going to suggest to you that you send another two dozen troops there for now until you are assured that the situation to the east is in hand."

Ancel saw the king was torn but he pressed on. "Mayhap I could spend some time with this army and then attend to things at Highfield afterward."

At this point, he'd already pushed Richard enough regarding the issue. Ancel must accept whatever order came from the monarch's lips.

"Hmm. It seems as if I need you in both places." Richard pressed his lips together, lost in thought. Finally, he said, "I like your suggestion. Spend the rest of the summer with my army, Ancel, then you may return to Highfield in the fall to follow through and make sure the estate is well guarded and provides protection to the area, as well as see that it is prepared for winter. If everything is to your liking, then you may return to court and my royal guard by year's end."

"What if Thurstan Vivers never returns to Highfield? What if he was killed in the peasants' rebellion, as I suspect?" pressed Ancel.

The king looked blank a moment and then nodded. "Ah, I remember the situation now. So there's still been no sign of the man who should be the new baron?"

"None at all, your majesty. Though we found the bodies of his father and younger brother, Thurstan Vivers was not among the dead." Ancel patiently waited, hoping he wouldn't have to prod the king to remember what had been dangled as a prize for Ancel.

Richard came to a decision. "Then I will make good on my promise and give you the land and the title. You deserve a reward for your service to me. My grandfather chose well when he asked you to watch over me these past five years."

"And the lady?"

The king smiled. "Oh, she was a rare beauty, that one." He studied Ancel a moment. "So you are interested in wedding her?"

"Aye," he said firmly, not expanding on his answer. Let the king think what he would. "When will the army march forth?"

"They leave at dawn tomorrow."

"Then with your permission, sire, I would like to return to Highfield immediately. I want to place Sir Folcard in charge and discuss with him what should be done this summer before I return in the autumn. And, hopefully, share with him that you will send more men."

"I grant you this request and swear to provide the soldiers you seek. Be back ready to ride in the morning."

Ancel excused himself and left the king's rooms. He passed many courtiers but chose not to linger. In the limited time he had, he only wanted to get back to Margery. Retrieving Storm, he decided she needed a surprise other than Whitefoot. He was glad now that he'd brought the pup back to her, for the dog would help keep her company until he could return to Highfield—hopefully, for good. And if Thurstan Vivers appeared in the meantime?

Ancel still would claim Margery as his bride.

Cantering through the streets of London, he came to a shop where he had purchased luxurious fabrics of silk and satin as gifts for his mother and Alys. His little sister, Nan, favored dressing as a boy despite her beauty, so any feminine gift to her would have gone to waste. His remaining sister, Jessimond, had only turned five recently and didn't need beautiful clothes—yet. Already, Ancel could see that the youngest de Montfort girl would turn many a man's head in the future.

Entering the merchant's shop, Ancel browsed until he found the bolts of cloth he desired. The owner measured and cut silk, velvet, and taffeta in colors of scarlet, green, and a deep russet. He hoped Margery would be pleased with his selections. Now that Highfield had a seamstress, Christine Morley would make certain that Margery was clothed appropriately for her station. Ancel never wanted her to feel out of place and he planned to take her with him when he next saw the king.

He gathered his purchases and made a hasty retreat to Highfield. Ancel would squeeze as much time as he could with Margery before he returned to London and the king's army.

MARGERY STOPPED AND scooped up Whitefoot, burying her nose in his fur. The puppy had slept with her last night and followed her everywhere she had ventured today. The lone exception had been mass this morning. She hadn't wanted to bring him into the chapel and face Father Martyn's wrath, though she doubted his old eyes could have seen the dog from a distance.

Knowing Ancel had planned for Will Artus to leave to deliver a missive to Ancel's parents at Kinwick, Margery had pulled aside another squire and bid him to take Whitefoot back to the kitchen and watch over the dog till she returned to break her fast.

"But I will miss mass," the boy protested weakly while he eyed the dog longingly.

She hid her smile at his show of reluctance. "You have my permission. Keep the puppy occupied and out of trouble."

"Aye, my lady." He'd grinned and lifted Whitefoot from her arms.

Once Ancel left for London with Sir Terryn, Margery reclaimed the dog and he fast became her shadow, moving from room to room as she went throughout the keep. The carts with all of the goods that Ancel had purchased arrived and she spent the morning directing where everything should be placed. The keep looked more settled now with bedclothes on the mattresses and pillows placed atop the beds, as well as kitchen goods replaced and new candlesticks for all of the bedchambers.

"My lady?" Sarah said. "You're needed in the bailey. The carpenter and seamstress have arrived."

Margery had forgotten they were coming. She hurried from the keep and saw a burly man with a thick, blond beard standing beside a small, trim woman with dark hair.

"Greetings," she called as she approached them. "Welcome to Highfield. I am Lady Margery Ormond."

"Harry Bacon, my lady, and 'tis Christine Morley who accompanies me. She is your new seamstress, while I am the castle's new carpenter."

"We are pleased to have both of you at Highfield. Harry, would you help carry in Christine's things? Then I'll show you the shed where you'll share workspace with our smithy, Matthew Cheyne, and where you'll be living."

Margery had decided to move the Cheyne family to a small cottage located close to the gates, while allowing Harry Bacon to live next to the smithy's shed. Matthew and John had been happy to relocate yesterday and the smithy told Margery that his wife, Eua, would be happy with their new home since the cottage was larger than where they had been staying. Matthew expressed his hopes that Eua would return soon from helping their daughter and grandchild.

It took two trips to get the seamstress and her baskets settled.

"I'm eager to start sewing for you, my lady. First, I'll need to measure you, though." Christine frowned. "It won't be soon enough. Pardon my saying so but you sorely need something new to wear."

"I will return soon, Christine. Why don't you go to the kitchen and have Maud, our cook, give you something to eat? I'll get Harry out to where he will work and live and then join you."

"Aye, my lady." Christine left and Margery walked with Harry to where Highfield's carpenter would craft what was needed for the estate. She introduced him to Matthew and John, who were working on new wheels for the estate's use.

"This is a fine space, my lady," Harry told her, "both to work and live in. I am grateful to come to Highfield."

"I hope you will enjoy being a part of Highfield, Harry. Go ahead and bring all your tools inside and set them up as you please. Then come to the great hall and eat something since the noon meal has already passed. We can walk through the keep together so I can show you what furniture I'd like you to start working on first."

Margery left Harry's company, Whitefoot trailing after her. She sought out Christine and allowed the seamstress to measure her.

"Sir Ancel bought some nice cloth for you, my lady. Come, have a look."

She fingered the soft wool Christine had brought with her and especially liked the gray and blue bolts of material that Ancel had purchased.

"Let's talk about how you'd like me to make these up," Christine said, "though I do have a few ideas now that I've seen you."

Margery shook her head. "Nay, I will leave that task to you. I am clueless as to what should be made and how to do so. I have never had much in the way of clothing and know nothing about fashion."

Christine nodded sagely. "Then leave things to me, Lady Margery. By the end of the week, you will be happy to dress each morning in what I sew for you."

Margery thanked Christine and returned to the great hall, where her new carpenter awaited her. They toured the inside of the keep, while she pointed out to him where certain pieces had stood before they'd been damaged or taken and what she wanted replaced. The carpenter also had several ideas for furniture he could create for other spots, pointing them out.

"I like all of your ideas, Harry," she told him. "Highfield's carpenter has also made furniture for others on the estate in the past. We have several new tenants and I'm sure they will need your services soon."

"Sir Ancel promised me I would be busy, my lady. 'Tis the way I like it. And I will tell you now that I am looking for a wife. I want sons that I can teach carpentry skills to so that they may follow in my footsteps."

Immediately, Margery thought of Sarah and what a good wife and mother her friend would make. Harry seemed like a good man, else Ancel would never have hired him. As if the servant read her mind, Sarah appeared in the corridor and joined them.

"My lady, Sir Ancel has returned from London. He is waiting for you in the solar."

Her heart slammed against her ribs in anticipation of seeing him. "Thank you, Sarah. Please make sure Harry can find his way out of the keep. You might also want to accompany him back to his quarters and see if there's anything you can think of that he needs."

Her friend's eyes lit up as she glanced at the carpenter. "Of course, my lady." Sarah gave Harry a friendly smile. "Come along, Harry. We'll get you fixed up in no time."

As the couple walked down the hallway, the carpenter looked over his shoulder and gave Margery a shy smile.

Margery lifted Whitefoot from the floor since she knew the small puppy would not be able to keep up with her as she hurried to the solar. Pushing open the door, she spied Ancel arranging bundles on the table. She shut the door and placed the dog down and rushed into his arms.

The knight enfolded her, his mouth seeking hers in a long, hot kiss that went on for minutes. Breathless, she sucked in a deep breath after he broke the kiss. But something wasn't right. Ancel searched her face as if memorizing her features. A bad feeling stirred in her gut. Before Margery could ask him if anything was wrong, he released her and indicated the wares on the table.

"I've brought you fine cloth from London," he declared. "I hope you will think I made some wise choices in what I selected for you."

"You didn't have to do that, Ancel. You had already brought back plenty of fabric from Billericay and provided Christine Morley to sew for me."

He shook his head. "The selection at Billericay was limited. London had a much wider variety to choose from." He shook out the first bundle.

Margery's eyes widened in delight as she saw the material. She fingered a green silk, watching it ripple like water running in a brook. Then her hands brushed against a russet velvet. She lifted it to her cheek and sighed.

"I've never had anything as fine as this. Thank you, Ancel. You spoil me."

"Just like Whitefoot," he added. "I plan on indulging you both." Then he grew serious.

"Something is wrong," she said, setting the fabric aside. "I knew it by the way you looked at me a moment ago."

He frowned. "Not wrong. Just not as I would have wished it to be." He drew in a deep breath and took his time expelling it. Margery patiently waited.

"The king wants me to ride out with his army," he explained. "It means I will be gone from Highfield the rest of the summer."

Margery's teeth sank into her lower lip. Tears sprang to her eyes. She blinked quickly, not wanting them to fall.

Ancel took her hands. "I would prefer remaining here with you but I must follow the king's command, my love. He has given me permission to return to Highfield in the autumn."

"What . . . what of ceding Highfield and the title to you?" she asked. "Did you speak of that possibility with him?"

"If your stepbrother hasn't returned by the time I reach Highfield again, then the king will fulfill his promise."

Margery leaned on her tiptoes and kissed him. "That's good news, indeed."

"It is. Though the king may desire for us to be at court with him. We may have to spend part of our year in London and the rest at Highfield."

She squeezed his hands. "I really don't care where we go—as long as we are together."

Ancel smiled. "You already sound like a de Montfort." He sat on the bench next to the table and pulled her onto his lap. "Let me tell you about the many couples in my family and how the men and women live their lives in love."

Margery entwined her arms around his neck. "I think I will enjoy hearing this."

CHAPTER 15

THOUGH ANCEL WOULD rather have spent all the hours he had left at Highfield with Margery, he needed to prepare for his absence. After sharing something of his family and the love matches that various couples had made, he sent for Sir Folcard to join them in the solar and then arranged with Maud to take the evening meal with Margery.

Alone.

Folcard arrived. "You have need of me, my lord?"

"Aye, Sir Folcard. Have a seat." Ancel indicated for the knight to sit on the opposite side of the table from him and Margery since it was the only place available. He looked forward to their new carpenter creating additional chairs for the solar.

"I am leaving Highfield and will travel with the king's army for the next couple of months. Though order has been restored in eastern England, the king wants to suppress any thoughts of rebellion in other areas. He's sending a force of four thousand soldiers to travel the land in a show of strength. I am to accompany them for the remainder of the summer, so I'm leaving you in charge of the defenses at Highfield."

Folcard inclined his head. "Thank you for your confidence in me, Sir Ancel."

"You will keep to the training schedule that we have established and continue assigning men to patrol the road both to the east and west of Highfield. I would like you to meet regularly with Lady Margery and give her reports so she is aware of the military status surrounding her home. A new steward should be arriving soon and he can handle business for the estate. If you have need of any funds, see him."

"What of the tenants, my lord, and the responsibilities regarding the land?"

"Giles Downer has proven most capable. I will discuss with him what tasks to complete in my absence." Ancel thought a moment. "I asked the king for another two dozen men to supplement those already at Highfield. They should arrive shortly."

"Very good, my lord. Additional troops will come in handy."

Margery asked, "Are our barracks large enough for that many more men?"

"I hadn't thought of that," Ancel admitted. "I will speak to Harry Bacon about extending the current building. John Cheyne can help Harry with this project. Sir Folcard, the soldiers under you might need to help our carpenter with expanding the barracks. I'd rather that happen while the weather is warm so that we won't have to worry about when cool winds arrive."

"That won't be a problem," Folcard assured him. "We can balance building and training."

"If you don't have any questions, then please send Giles and Harry to the solar so that I may meet with them."

Folcard excused himself.

Soon, the farmer and carpenter arrived and Ancel explained how he would be gone from Highfield for the rest of the summer. Ancel spoke with Harry first, explaining how the barracks would need to accommodate more men.

"So drop whatever you are doing. Sir Folcard and his men will assist you when they can, as will the new additions arriving at Highfield."

"We'll begin at once, Sir Ancel," Harry said. "It will be completed before you know it." He left the solar with a spring in his step.

"Giles, I'd like you to remain in charge of all the tenants while I'm gone and direct their activities. You'll need to finish the hay harvest as quickly as possible so that the fields can be ploughed and fertilized.

And if, for any reason, I'm delayed past summer's end?" Ancel knew he must plan for that possibility, not knowing what the king's troops would find out on the road.

"We'll start the wheat harvest next month, my lord and seed the ploughed fields," Giles said. "And come September, if you're not back, I can have the tying and winnowing take place."

"A new steward should arrive in the next few days. I want you to meet with him and Lady Margery every week. If you have any concerns, express them to her and Clifton Walters. I've bought some sheep that will also need shearing soon," Ancel said.

"Everything will take place as you've asked," Giles said. "You can count on me, my lord. I won't let you down."

"Very good. Thank you, Giles," Ancel told the farmer. "You've done an excellent job so far."

"And I plan to keep doing it, my lord." Giles flashed a grin. "Be safe, my lord. I hope to see you soon."

The farmer left as Sarah arrived with a large tray of food.

"What's this?" asked Margery.

"I thought we'd sup alone tonight," he told her. "Come, Sarah. You can leave everything here."

She placed the tray on the table and unloaded it. "Anything else, my lord?"

He shook his head. "Thank you. And thank your mother, Sarah. Maud has already proven herself to be an excellent cook. I will miss her cooking while I am away."

The servant smiled. "I shall tell her you said so, my lord. Mother will enjoy the compliment." She closed the door behind her and they were finally alone.

Ancel poured wine for them. He'd purchased a few casks during his trip to Billericay and asked for Margery to make wine available in the solar. They sat and enjoyed a meal of tender heron and stewed plums, with a small round of sharp cheese. Margery fed Whitefoot a few bites of the bird. The puppy finally curled up near the hearth. Ancel treasured each moment with Margery, knowing how he would miss her during the long days and nights ahead.

He told her that he'd accessed the secret panel earlier and removed several gold coins for her to use while he was away.

"If you need more, feel free to take it. It's money that belongs to Highfield and should be used to better it."

Once they finished their meal, she asked, "When do you leave?"

He saw how she put on a brave face. "I can stay a few hours longer." Rising, he offered her his hand and picked up the candleholder before leading her into the solar's large bedchamber. Glancing around, he saw the improvements in the room that had occurred.

Placing the candle down, he said, "We are not formally betrothed but you are my intended. If you don't mind, I would like to be able to stretch out on the bed and hold you in my arms."

She gave him a shy smile. "That would be nice."

Ancel lifted her long braid and untied the ribbon at its end. Slowly, he unplaited the braid until he freed her locks and ran his fingers through the silky waves. Then he drew back the new bed curtain and had her climb onto the bed. He lay down next to her and pulled her close, inhaling the scent of honeysuckle on her smooth skin. He buried his face in her luxurious, thick hair as his hand rubbed up and down her spine.

"I want to leave you with a parting gift," he said softly.

"But you've already given me so much," Margery protested. "I have Whitefoot, who is already my shadow in all that I do. I will soon have clothes made up from the beautiful materials that you bought in Billericay and London. What more could I want?"

His hand glided down to cup her buttock. He gave it a gentle squeeze. "I want to pleasure you, my love. I promise not to spill your virgin's blood but I would leave you with a memory of what is to come between us once we wed."

She touched his cheek. "I am yours, Ancel. You know that."

He kissed her deeply, hoping to show how much he cared for her. Though he had kissed many a pretty girl over the years, each kiss with Margery stirred new feelings within him. As his mouth plundered the sweetness of hers, he reached for the hem of her clothing. Finding it, his hand slipped under the layers and brushed up her calf.

"Mmm."

Ancel's fingers danced up her leg in feathery strokes as Margery continued to murmur. Then he reached the apex where her womanly core hid. His fingers grazed against the velvet slit.

"Oh," she said.

"It's all right. I won't hurt you," he said.

"But . . . but . . ."

"This is but one thing that happens between a man and a woman." Her body tensed. "Relax, sweetheart."

"I will try to, Ancel," she said meekly.

But Ancel didn't want meek. He wanted to pleasure Margery until she cried aloud. Slowly, he pushed a finger inside her. She jolted against him. Stroking her leisurely, it pleased him to hear little noises coming from the back of her throat. He kissed her again, his tongue beginning to mimic the motion of his finger. He pushed another one inside her and heard her gasp as he rubbed against her tender nub.

"You like that."

"Uh, aye," she said weakly.

"You'll like this even more."

Ancel let his fingers speak for him, speeding up, slowing down, enjoying the satisfied sounds that came from her. Her breathing grew shallow and rapid, as small moans escaped from her lips. She began to whimper as her juices flowed. Her nails dug into his shoulders as she began pressing herself against his hand. He increased the speed again till she writhed in a frenzy.

Suddenly, she stiffened against him and began calling out his name. Ancel quickly covered her mouth with his, the kiss silencing her as she bucked wildly against his searching hand. Then she shuddered and grew still. Her hands dropped from his shoulders and fell beside her. He slipped his fingers from her and enjoyed seeing the sated look on her face.

"That's only the beginning of love play," Ancel told her.

Margery swallowed. "I thought I might die, the pleasure was so intense." She paused. "There's more to it?"

"Aye."

A slow smile touched her lips. "That must mean I can do for you what you did for me. Make you feel as I did." Her eyes lit up. "Make you call *my* name."

"Another time, love."

She sat up. "Nay, Ancel. Now," she said firmly.

Margery's eyes gleamed as she lowered her lips to his. She nibbled at them, teasing them apart, until her tongue touched his and sparks ignited between them. Then she slung a leg over and straddled him, her tongue continuing to war with his. Immediately, his manhood sprang to life.

She broke the kiss and let her lips traveled along his jaw and then she nipped at his throat playfully. His hands slid up her thighs and clasped her waist. Without warning, she grasped the hem of his gypon and yanked, pulling him forward, which allowed her to bring it over his head. Margery let the gypon fall next to her and then brought her lips back to his throat. They glided across it and then began a march down his bare chest. Ancel groaned.

Raising her head, her gaze met his. "Do you like that?"

He grinned. "You know I do."

"I do, too," she admitted and returned her mouth to his belly. Margery licked her way across it, the muscles leaping to life, and then she slowly blazed a path back to his mouth.

Ancel's body was on fire. He grasped her waist again as she kissed him, holding her in place in order to keep himself in check.

And then her hands tugged on his pants, pulling them down until she freed his cock. Her hand grazed against it, causing him to squeeze her waist. Her fingers locked around it as she continued to plunder his mouth. Slowly, she began moving her hand back and forth. He groaned deeply.

"Does this feel good?" she murmured against his lips.

He nodded.

"And this?" Her hand increased in speed.

He moaned.

"Now?" she teased, pulling and pushing and squeezing until all rational thought left Ancel. All he knew was the touch of her hand pleasuring him as her kiss captivated him.

The pressure built within him as her loving fingers and tongue worked their magic. He released his hold on her, his hands searching the bed and finding his gypon. Ancel slipped it between them as he climaxed and hoarsely cried out, her hand still warm against his heated shafted as he spilled his seed in the bunched gypon.

Slowly, Margery's shining face came back into view, flushed with excitement, her lips swollen from their many kisses.

"Did I please you?" she asked eagerly.

Ancel tossed the gypon to the ground. "More than you could know."

She sighed contentedly and bent to brush her lips against his. He kissed her softly and pulled her down against him, her head resting against his beating heart. Rolling to his side, he cradled her tenderly. Almost immediately, he heard the even breaths of sleep coming from her.

Ancel listened to her breathing, enjoying her warmth against him. He looked forward to a lifetime with this woman, the only woman for him. He would have what his parents shared. What he'd witnessed with Alys and Kit. Love for Margery filled his heart. Their separation would only make it grow stronger, for Ancel couldn't imagine feeling this way about anyone other than Margery.

He dozed for a bit and then awoke, knowing he must now leave her. His lips brushed against her hair as he slipped from her embrace and the bed. Ancel refused to awaken her. He didn't wish for a tearful goodbye. Looking at her angelic face as she dreamt the night away was how he wanted to remember her in the coming days and weeks until he returned.

Opening the bedchamber door, Whitefoot appeared in the doorway, his tail wagging merrily. He picked up the puppy and took him to the bed. Placing the dog on the mattress, Whitefoot quickly curled up against his mistress and closed his eyes.

"Take care of her," Ancel whispered to the dog before he left the bedchamber.

He'd left his armor in the bedchamber her stepbrothers had shared and went there now to don it. It took him longer than usual and he wished that Will Artus was present to help him. The squire should return soon, hopefully with a new steward in hand. Ancel had done everything to keep Highfield running during the absence of one but now it was time to depart.

Returning to the stables, he prepared Storm for their ride back to London. He rode through the gates and turned west at a gallop, seeing no one until he drew near the city. Dawn would break soon. As he approached its gates, a group of soldiers poured through them, headed his way. Ancel recognized Sir Terryn Althilos at the front. Ancel signaled his fellow guardsman and rode toward him.

"Is this part of the king's army?" he asked.

"Nay," Terryn told him. "We are two dozen men sent by the king to Highfield while you are gone." The knight paused. "I am to assume command until your return." Terryn smiled broadly. "I look forward to being in charge of the soldiers—and getting to know Lady Margery, of course."

Ancel refrained from ripping his friend's heart out.

Just barely.

CHAPTER 16

Four months later . . .

MARGERY AWOKE IN the darkened chamber. The curtains pulled around the bed kept out some of the cold of the mid-November day. She closed her eyes again, sensing it was still too early to dress.

And closing her eyes, she could relive the brief time she had lain next to Ancel in this very bed.

Every day, her heart ached at their separation. The two months he should have been gone had dragged into more than double that. She remained busy during the day but the nights saw loneliness creep inside. With each day Ancel was gone, it caused her another day of worry. Was he safe? Would he return? Did he still love her as much as she loved him?

Life had run smoothly at Highfield during his absence. The morning after his departure, she awakened to learn that the king's extra soldiers had already been received. The royal guardsman who had first summoned Ancel to the king's presence had accompanied the group. King Richard had placed Sir Terryn Althilos in control at Highfield. Though the knight leaned on Sir Folcard for some things, he obviously enjoyed being in a position of power.

Moreover, he had flirted outrageously with Margery those first few days. She hadn't known that's what the knight was doing until Sarah clued her in. Margery only knew his suggestive looks and play on words made her uncomfortable. Once Sarah set her straight, she had requested a private meeting with Sir Terryn—and informed him to act like the knight he was pledged to be.

"Do your duty to your king and Highfield," she requested. *"And know that King Richard has offered Highfield's land and title to Sir Ancel if my stepbrother does not return. That also includes my becoming Sir Ancel's bride."*

Sir Terryn had grown serious about his assignment after she informed him of that—and been nothing but a gentleman ever since. He had alternated the soldiers in the training yard so that some went through exercises while others helped build the extension to the barracks and others guarded the estate and patrolled the roads beyond.

Margery enjoyed her meetings with Clifton Walters, the new steward who had trained at Kinwick. Will Artus had returned with Clifton and a missive for Sir Ancel from his parents. Informing the two men where Ancel now was, Clifton urged her to read it and act accordingly since she was Lady of Highfield now. When Margery admitted to the steward that she could not read because her stepfather expressly forbade her learning how to do so, Clifton had waved aside that notion and said he would teach her himself.

She proved to be a good student and, with Clifton's help, Margery had been able to read the four missives Ancel had sent to her during his absence, thanks to the hours she had labored over her letters. They had all been brief and she assumed Ancel had little time to pen missives to her. But one had come to Highfield for each month he was gone.

He'd apologized profusely when he told her he couldn't break away as soon as he wanted. The king's army had traveled as far north as York and then to the west country, suppressing small pockets of rebellion along the way. Ancel's last message to her said that many of the rebel leaders had been rounded up. Over fifteen hundred had been executed or killed in battles that had been fought. That let her know how serious the situation was and why the king had insisted that Ancel remain with his army.

Finally, Margery pushed herself from the bed and dressed quickly, enjoying how she now had clothes that made her feel feminine, thanks to Ancel's thoughtfulness regarding her wardrobe. Today was an important one—the marriage of Sarah to Harry Bacon—and she wanted everything to be perfect for her friend.

Mass had been delayed this morning since everyone would attend the nuptial mass later in the day. She went first to the kitchens, where Maud already labored over food for her daughter's wedding feast. Sarah, Agatha, and two other servants Margery had hired from Kirkby were hard at work as Maud barked orders to them. She joined in and helped ready the small morning meal, getting it out to the tables of hungry soldiers and serfs who'd gathered.

Sir Terryn approached her. "Is the wedding still at noon, my lady?"

"Aye. I hope the men not on duty will be allowed to attend the nuptial mass, my lord."

"They will," he assured her. "I'll also let them come to the feast and fill their bellies before they trade off and allow their fellow soldiers to do the same."

Margery signaled Giles over. The man had proven to be a valuable leader in getting both the hay and wheat harvests in on time. When Ancel failed to return, Giles had taken on the responsibility of seeing that the sowing and milling occurred and started the serfs weaving during all of October. Now that they were halfway through November, he supervised the men in butchering, salting, and smoking the meats that would see Highfield through till the springtime.

"Remember, Giles, that today is the wedding," she reminded him. "The workers only need to work until shortly before noon."

"Aye, my lady. I'll see that everyone gathers outside the chapel in time for the wedding."

"Thank you."

She returned to the kitchen and ordered Sarah to follow her, motioning to Agatha before she left. Agatha nodded in understanding, privy to what they'd discussed last night.

"Follow me." Margery led Sarah to the solar, where the bathtub awaited her in the center of the room.

"'Tis your wedding day, my friend. You're to have a hot bath."

"Truly?" Sarah's smile warmed the entire room. "You have already been so generous, my lady, giving me material and having Christine make me something to wear for the ceremony today."

Margery placed a hand on Sarah's arm. "You have been my true friend for many years, Sarah. If not for your warning when the rebellion began, I wouldn't even be alive. You saved me from the death that came for my mother and the others." Hope fluttered in her heart. Thurstan had yet to return to Highfield. Surely, if he still lived, he would have turned up by now to claim his rights.

Agatha and the others appeared with buckets of hot and cold water then. Margery had them pour a mixture of both into the bathtub as she streamed scented oil into the water. The sweet smell of honeysuckle wafted up.

"Oh, I will smell as you do, my lady!" Sarah said with enthusiasm.

"Harry will be so pleased," Agatha said. She hugged her sister. "I am so happy for you."

"Everyone should go now, else Maud will coming looking for you. I'll tend to Sarah."

Margery helped wash her friend's hair and then allowed Sarah to scrub herself while she laid out the cotehardie that the servant would wed in.

"Is there a bath sheet, my lady?" Sarah asked.

She laughed. "Here it is. Let me help dry you."

Margery dried and then dressed Sarah, stepping back to admire her. "You look lovely."

"I feel like a queen," Sarah said.

"Harry will certainly approve."

Sarah blushed at the mention of her groom. "Oh, Harry is always complimenting me, my lady."

"You seem happy when you speak of him," Margery noted.

"I am. Harry is kindhearted and hard-working. He will make a good husband and father." Sarah giggled. "He's told me he wants at least half a dozen sons—and a few daughters thrown in along the way."

"Let's hope you're with child by the morning," Margery declared.

Using her own comb, she ran it through Sarah's hair until no tangles remained. "Shall I braid it for you?" she asked.

"Aye."

Margery created two elaborate braids and wound them around Sarah's head. She then took a circlet that she'd been working on for the last few days and placed it atop her friend's head. Margery had wound various autumn leaves throughout it and the bright oranges and reds stood out against the girl's yellow hair.

"I think it's time, Sarah."

Margery led Sarah from the room and down the stairs. The great hall stood empty but the enticing smells of the food to come made Margery's stomach gurgle in anticipation. They made the quick journey across the bailey to the chapel where everyone from Highfield stood, minus the group of soldiers on duty, waiting for the bride so that the ceremony could commence.

As she listened to the vows spoken between Sarah and Harry, Margery again prayed that she and Ancel would be able to do the same once England calmed down.

Father Martyn finished with the ceremony. Before he invited everyone inside to celebrate the nuptial mass, an odd tingling prickled her neck. Her heart began racing.

Ancel had returned.

Margery looked over her shoulder and then turned in circles as the people of Highfield brushed past her to enter the chapel. Disappointment filled her when her search proved fruitless. Turning to follow everyone ahead of her, she found her hand grasped. Warmth flooded her as she glanced up.

Ancel smiled down at her.

"It seems like forever since I have seen your sweet face," he said, bending to brush his lips against hers.

Margery's knees buckled. He grabbed her elbow to support her. "Come inside. We'll talk after the mass ends." He grinned. "I see Harry Bacon made quick work of wooing Sarah."

She found her voice. "They are most happy, my lord. Harry is ready to get Sarah with child tonight."

Ancel chuckled, then his eyes grew heated. "Harry is not the only one who desires a child from the woman he weds."

Margery remembered what his fingers had done to her and shivered.

He slipped her hand through the crook of his arm. "Come, my love."

They entered the chapel. Margery did not remember a single word Father Martyn uttered. All she was aware of was Ancel's shoulder touching hers. His thigh pressed against her own. She glanced down and wished she could wrap her hand around his. Oh, how she had missed this man!

The nuptial mass ended. Sarah and Harry left the chapel first. They spied Ancel and waved as they passed by him. Others noticed the knight had returned and, as they streamed from the building, many came and greeted him. He promised Sir Terryn and Giles Downer that he would meet with each of them for a progress report after the feasting ended.

Spying Clifton Walters, he threw his arms around the steward. "I am pleased that you came, Clifton."

"Thank you for the opportunity, Sir Ancel. I have enjoyed the short time I've been at Highfield."

"We'll meet later today—or mayhap tomorrow—in order to catch up about the affairs of this estate. I also want to hear all of the news from Kinwick."

Clifton chuckled. "The only thing you need to know right away is that Lady Merryn misses you dreadfully. Her last words to me were to convince you to come for a visit once you had the opportunity. 'I'm counting on you, Clifton,' she told me. 'I expect to see my boy at Kinwick sooner rather than later'."

"That sounds like Mother." Ancel looked at Margery. "You will love Mother."

"Everyone adores Lady Merryn," Clifton confirmed. "And Lord

Geoffrey, as well." He eyed them speculatively. "I will see you later, my lord."

Finally, they stood alone and began strolling leisurely back to the keep.

"You look lovely," he told her. "I hope you have enjoyed your new attire."

"I have. It is so different and beautiful from what I have worn in the past."

"I'm glad you are happy, Margery. I know I am, now that I have returned. You were in my thoughts day and night."

It thrilled her to hear his words.

"I must ask, though, about Thurstan," Ancel said. "Has there been any news of him?"

"None," Margery confirmed, not bothering to hide her smile.

"Good. I gather you haven't mentioned to anyone what the king has promised, based upon Clifton eyeing us up and down after I mentioned you meeting Mother."

"Only Sir Terryn," she confirmed.

Ancel frowned. "Why him?"

She shrugged, wanting to downplay the knight's former attentions to her. She didn't want to be the cause of trouble between Ancel and his friend. "I thought it appropriate that he know," she said primly.

He laughed. "Terryn is famous for chasing anyone in a skirt." He stroked her cheek. "I'll admit, I was jealous when I found out he would be coming to Highfield in my place."

"You'll never have a reason to be jealous, Ancel. I love you. Only you. No other man could ever turn my head. Not even the king of England," she proclaimed.

They entered the manor house and Ancel told her, "I stopped in London to see the king on my way to Highfield. I needed to give him a report regarding my observations of what had gone on in the field. He is recalling his armed forces. I believe we will stay at peace."

"What of the king wanting you to come back to London?"

"He told me to take a week's respite and see that Highfield was in good order. Then I am to return to the royal court—with you accompanying me."

Her grip tightened on his arm. "He wants to see me?"

"Aye. I'm sure it's only to confirm that your stepbrother is gone. Mayhap, he'll draw up the papers to transfer Highfield to me during that time."

"And then we can wed after that?" she asked, exhilaration filling her.

"I want to wait," Ancel confided. "I don't want us to marry in London. If it's all right with you, I'd prefer the ceremony take place at Kinwick. I have many relatives who would wish to come and meet you. Kinwick is quite large and could accommodate many more guests than Highfield. Unless, of course, you'd rather marry here. After all, it's been your home for many years."

"Nay. Let's journey to Kinwick. I am eager to meet your family and see where you grew up."

He smiled. "I want you to. Someday, you will be its countess."

They joined Sarah and Harry on the dais in the great hall. Margery had invited the couple to sit with her as the guests of honor. Ancel congratulated them on their marriage and wished them well. Conversation flowed freely, as did wine. Margery had insisted that Clifton go to Billericay in order to purchase several casks for today's festivities. After many courses of delicious food, the dancing began. Margery found herself swept up in it but no matter where she was, her eyes always returned to find Ancel.

Hours later, the happy couple left to celebrate their marriage in private. Slowly, things ground to a halt inside the great hall as everyone pitched in to right everything.

Ancel pulled her aside. "I'm going to meet now with those I left in charge. I'm curious as to what's been happening at Highfield. But after that?" His eyes twinkled in mischief. "I will visit you in the solar." He lifted her hand and grazed warm lips against her knuckles.

Margery hurried upstairs. With every step, her heart cried out, "Ancel is home."

CHAPTER 17

ANCEL AND MARGERY rode out with five other knights, bound for London. He had sent Will Artus ahead of them in a cart with Margery's trunk. They would meet the squire outside the palace.

For now, Ancel enjoyed having the woman he loved in his arms as they made their way to the city. He hadn't had time to teach her to ride before he left to join the king's army but since his return she had sat upon a horse and walked it around a pen twice in the past week. She seemed to enjoy the experience and Ancel knew he would make a rider of her. Whitefoot had sat patiently outside the fence each time, eager to regain her attention. She had asked if they could take the dog along with them to London but he didn't think it a wise idea. Sarah had offered to look after Whitefoot, so the dog went to stay with her and Harry.

As they neared London's gates, Margery gasped.

"I cannot believe how large it is."

"Wait till we are inside. You will experience sights and sounds like nothing before," he guaranteed.

Their party rode through the gates. Ancel enjoyed Margery's delight at everything they saw. She couldn't believe how many vendors there were or the number of people who swelled in the streets.

He motioned for the other riders to stop and dismounted. Handing Margery down, he said, "We need to let you taste a London pie. There's nothing quite like the mix of sweet and savory in them."

Ancel brought her to a stall and looked over the selection, choosing two pies. "We'll share so you can sample some of each."

She took a bite of the first one he'd purchased and sighed. "What's in this? 'Tis heavenly."

He sampled it. "Ground pork, flavored with honey and black pepper."

"I could eat this every day," she declared. Then she traded with him and bit into the second pie. "Oh, I like this even better than the first one. Here, try some of it, Ancel."

He let her feed him. "Mmm. That is good. This one is fish pie with cinnamon, sugar, and ginger."

"I taste more than those spices." Margery took another bite. "Definitely cloves. And pepper, but not quite like regular pepper."

Ancel ate more, rolling it around his mouth. "Oh, 'tis white pepper."

Her eyes lit up. "We must buy spices while we are in London and bring them back to Maud. In fact, we should take her both of these pies and see if she can come close to copying the dish."

He laughed. "Eat up, for now. I don't know when we'll return. When we do, remind me to stop and we'll bring pies for Maud."

They finished and returned to Storm. Half an hour later, they'd wound through the busy streets and reached the royal palace. Will awaited them in the cart.

"Stay here, Will. I will send for you and let you know where to take Lady Margery's trunk." He thanked the other soldiers for their escort and dismissed them, instructing them to return to Highfield.

Ancel led Margery inside the palace, through countless hallways teeming with courtiers. She said very little as they passed through corridors and rooms.

At one point, she halted their progress.

"Is something wrong?" he asked.

"No," she said breathlessly. "I simply want to take in all the grandeur."

He supposed, at one time, the trappings of the palace had impressed him. After so many years residing here, he simply looked at it as a very large place where hundreds of people lived. Ancel let her study everything around her before leading her forward.

They arrived in a large hall where dozens of men awaited an appointment with the king. He found Robert de Vere, Earl of Oxford, standing in a group. The man was a few years older than Richard and fast becoming one of the king's trusted confidants. Oxford saw him and came to greet him.

"Sir Ancel, how are you?" He glanced appreciatively at Margery, wearing a cotehardie of green silk. "And my lady, I would enjoy making your acquaintance."

"This is the Earl of Oxford," he told her. "May I present Lady Margery Ormond?"

The nobleman took her hand and kissed her fingers. "The pleasure is all mine, my lady. I don't believe I have seen you at court."

"Nay, my lord. I have never been to London."

Oxford looked back at Ancel. "You are escorting Lady Margery, Sir Ancel?"

"I am. The king wishes to see us."

"He is quite busy today." Oxford shrugged. "It's all about the upcoming royal marriage."

"Has a bride been chosen?" Ancel asked.

Oxford nodded. "Not only chosen but she arrived late last night."

"Is it Anne of Bohemia?"

The nobleman assessed Ancel for a moment. "I see you are quite well informed, even having been away from court," he said coolly. "My lady." He bowed curtly and walked away.

Margery sniffed. "I thought he was nice at first but that was certainly rude to walk away so abruptly," she pointed out.

"Oxford is close to the king. He doesn't like it when others appear to be, as well. It seems the king will be tied up for now with his bride arriving. Come. We will get you settled and then I will seek out someone who will let the king know we have arrived in London and are eager to gain an audience with him."

IT PROVED ANOTHER three days before they met with the king. Normally, Ancel would have let his impatience rule the day and forced his way past the royal guardsmen but each delay only gave him more time with Margery. He used that to his advantage. They were always surrounded by people at Highfield. Of course, London's streets burst with crowds—but none of them cared about the two of them.

They walked leisurely along the Thames, getting to know one another. He took her to St. Paul's Cathedral and delighted in how she reacted to the magnificent church. They visited merchants and bought a few odds and ends, including spices for Maud to use in cooking. But most importantly, they cherished their time together. Ancel's decision to make Margery his wife was reinforced in a hundred ways. He enjoyed her honesty and sense of humor and admired her intelligence and curiosity.

Finally, the summons came to visit the king in his private rooms. Ancel explained that this was a rare treat because most audiences with the king occurred in other halls within the palace. They arrived and were granted admittance, where a guardsman led them to an inner room.

As they entered, three men were on their way out and stopped to greet them.

"Ah, Sir Ancel. You have returned from the long march," Michael de la Pole said. "And where did you find this lovely creature?"

Margery blushed. "I am Lady Margery Ormond from Highfield, my lord."

De la Pole nodded. "I have heard of the estate, my lady." He took her hand and pressed a kiss upon it. "Michael de la Pole. Adviser to King Richard. And this is Sir Christopher Heron and Lord Myles Peveril, Earl of Mauntell. Both men have been of great assistance in finding a new queen for England."

Heron and Peveril bowed to Margery and also kissed her hand.

"'Tis nice to meet each one of you," she said politely.

"We must be off," de la Pole said. In a quiet voice he added, "You will find the king in a very good mood, de Montfort. Good day."

The three men left and Ancel walked Margery toward the king. Her fingers tightened on his arm.

"Greetings, sire," he said and bowed as Margery curtseyed to the monarch.

"Sir Ancel. And Lady Margery. It took you long enough to get here," he said in exasperation.

"But, we were not granted an audience before today, sire. We have waited three days to see you," Margery said innocently.

The king's brows shot up. "Is that so?"

"No need to get into that now, your highness," Ancel said smoothly. He didn't want to talk politics and how various courtiers jostled for time with the king—and prevented others from doing the same.

"Nevertheless, you are here. Come, have a seat. Would you care for anything to drink, my lady?"

"Nay, sire." She loosened the strings of her cloak and pushed it from her shoulders.

The king turned to Ancel. "Tell me of Highfield first."

Ancel elaborated on the state of the property and the extent to which the soldiers stationed there guarded not only the castle and its lands but the road to London. Richard nodded several times, looking pleased at the information. Then he shared with Ancel news of the army's return to London. They spoke for nearly an hour about the campaign that had lasted through the summer and well into autumn.

At last, the king ended that part of the conversation and included Margery once again.

"My lady, I must ask if your brother has returned to Highfield while Sir Ancel has been off fighting with my army."

"'Tis my stepbrother, your majesty, and nay, Sir Thurstan Vivers has never returned. His body was not discovered among those slaughtered by the peasants who attacked Highfield, though we did find my stepfather, Lord Umfrey, and his younger son, Gervase."

The king nodded, satisfaction evident upon his face. He turned to Ancel. "Then I will have the papers drawn up that will award Highfield, all its lands, and Lord Umfrey's title to you." He paused, his eyes lighting up. "And you may wed Lady Margery as part of the agreement, though that will have to wait for a few weeks. Tomorrow is Saint Andrew's Day, so we will be in the season of Advent. No marriages—not even my own—may occur during that time."

"We heard that you will soon wed Anne of Bohemia, sire. May I offer you congratulations?"

"Thank you, Ancel. The lady and I will wed soon after the new year."

Ancel hadn't realized that he and Margery would not be allowed to wed during Advent. It disappointed him but he had an idea on how they could pass the time.

A knock at the door sounded and a servant stepped inside.

"Lady Anne is here as you requested, your majesty."

"Have her come in," ordered Richard.

Moments later, a young noblewoman entered and crossed to where they sat. She dipped into a low curtsey and then rose gracefully. Ancel thought her to be close in age to the king. She was plain but had kind eyes and a sweet smile as she greeted them.

"My lord. My lady."

He returned her smile. "I am Sir Ancel de Montfort and this is Lady Margery Ormond. Welcome to England, Lady Anne. I hope you will enjoy your new home and country."

"The king has been most generous to me. I have a wonderful set of rooms and look forward to our marriage."

"Lady Margery will also wed Sir Ancel," the king informed his betrothed. "I am awarding Sir Ancel the title of baron and a new estate for his faithful service to me." He looked back to Ancel. "You may remain at Highfield until spring. That will have given you enough time to see the estate settled and running. Hire the soldiers you need to keep it well protected but I want you back at court, Ancel. No later than the beginning of May.

"You know I treasure your advice. And whether you serve in my royal guard or as one of my advisers, I need you in London. I have sent away many members of the royal council and other advisers after the uprising, hoping to appease the people. I am looking for new men to stand by me and make England great."

"I will be honored to serve in any way you ask, your majesty. But what of Lady Margery? May I bring her to court when I return?"

"If you wish." The king studied her a moment. "Mayhap you would like to serve my queen as one of her ladies-in-waiting, my lady."

Margery said, "If Lady Anne wishes it, then I will be happy to come to court."

Ancel saw Lady Anne give Margery a shy smile as she said, "I would enjoy having you with me, Lady Margery. I am eager to make friends in my new country. Mayhap you could also help me practice my English."

"Then it's settled," proclaimed the king. "The next time we all see one another, we shall be old, married people."

Everyone laughed at the king's joke and Ancel saw that their meeting had come to an end. He slipped Margery's cloak around her shoulders and they left the royal chambers.

"I was so nervous in his presence," she confided.

"No one would have guessed that, my love." Ancel drew her hand to his lips and tenderly kissed her fingers.

"Is it time to return to Highfield?" she asked.

"Aye. Pack your things and I'll have Will return home with your trunk."

Ancel escorted her to the room she had been staying in and left to find the squire.

"'Tis time we returned to Highfield, young Will. Bring the cart around and I'll help you carry Lady Margery's trunk to it."

Will did as asked and left for Highfield. Ancel led Margery to the stables and readied Storm for their return trip.

As he lifted her into the saddle, he said, "We have one more stop to make."

Ancel directed Storm to a busy street in the heart of London and led Margery inside a small shop.

A gray-haired man of two score greeted them. "How may I help you today, my lord?"

"We are in need of a wedding ring," Ancel said.

The jeweler's eyes lit up. "Come with me."

He led them to a counter and pulled out a tray of rings. "See if any of these appeal to you."

Ancel glanced at the selection and then at Margery. "Is there one you like in particular?"

Tears brimmed in her eyes. "I hadn't thought about a ring." She gazed from one piece to the next. "They're all so lovely."

The jeweler spoke up. "Why don't you try a few on, my lady? Sometimes they look different when resting upon your hand."

He lifted one from those displayed and slipped it onto her finger. She thought a moment. "Let's try another."

The craftsman gave her several before she asked to try one on a second time. It was a slender silver band.

"This is the one," she said. Turning to Ancel, she asked, "Do you like it?"

"I do. This ring looks as if it belongs on your finger." Ancel glanced to the jeweler. "Wrap it up, please."

The merchant did so and Ancel paid him. Then a thought occurred to him.

"Would you mind looking at a pendant? We are trying to find out its origin."

"Certainly, my lord."

Ancel removed the necklace from Margery and handed it over. The man studied it carefully, turning it over.

"It has a mark here," he indicated, showing them something small etched on the back. "This would be the man who crafted it. If you could find him, you might learn more about when the piece was created and even who bought or commissioned it."

He returned it to Ancel, who replaced it around Margery's neck.

"It's a fine piece of craftsmanship," the jeweler said. "A very unusual design. Good luck to you in discovering where it came from."

Ancel secured Margery's wedding ring in his pouch and they left the shop.

As they mounted Storm, he asked, "Where did your mother come from?"

"All I know is that she lived west of York. Her father was the Earl of Waudum."

"Before we return to court in the spring, I think we should take a trip to that part of England. Mayhap we can track down the jeweler who created the pendant for your mother and discover your true father's identity."

"Could we?" Margery asked, hope filling her eyes.

"I think it would be just the trip for the new Baron and Baroness of Highfield to take."

CHAPTER 18

MARGERY PRICKED HER finger again and put aside her sewing. She sucked on her finger, trying to draw the blood out. Today was the day Ancel's parents would arrive at Highfield and she couldn't seem to concentrate on any task.

On their way back from London, Ancel had shared with her his idea to invite his parents to visit Highfield. Margery knew he took pride in the castle and the estate and the improvements that had been made throughout. Now that the land and title would soon be his, he was eager to show it to his family, as well as have them meet the woman who would become his wife and Kinwick's future countess. He'd written to his parents the day they returned from London and asked for the de Montforts to come for a visit. The plan was for Lord Geoffrey and Lady Merryn to remain a week and then Ancel and Margery would return to Kinwick with the couple. They would spend the Christmas season at the de Montfort estate and then wed after Advent ended.

She looked forward to meeting Ancel's parents. He spoke so fondly of them. Margery only wished that her mother was still alive to see her only child wed.

A knock sounded on the solar door and Agatha popped her head inside.

"My lady, Sir Ancel says that his parents have been sighted. He requests that you join him downstairs in order to greet them."

Margery stood. "Thank you, Agatha. Please bring refreshments to the solar at once. They will be parched after their journey."

"Aye, my lady."

The servant left and Margery smoothed her skirts. She took her sewing and placed it inside a chest in the bedchamber. Glancing around, the room looked tidy and ready for their guests. Ancel's parents would be staying in the solar. She thought it only right for them to have a place of honor during their visit to Highfield.

And when she and Ancel returned from Kinwick, it would become their bedchamber. The room where her new husband would teach her all about the mysteries of love. The place where they would make many babes and she would give birth to them. Margery hugged herself, joy bursting from her.

She made her way outside and saw Ancel standing, tall and proud. Joining him, she slipped her hand through the crook of his arm.

His hand covered hers, while his glance spoke of his love for her. A calm descended upon her. She felt confident to meet his parents now.

Riders rounded the corner, the first bearing the de Montfort banner, followed by over a dozen horses. Immediately, Margery spied Ancel's parents in the center of the escort party. Lady Merryn's rich, chestnut hair shone like fire in the sunlight, while Lord Geoffrey looked like an older version of his son. Seeing him made it easy to know what her future husband would look like in the years to come. Both waved to her and Ancel with smiles on their faces.

Ancel rushed to his mother and helped her from her horse. He kissed both her cheeks soundly and then embraced his father.

"Come and meet Margery," she heard him say as he brought them to where she stood.

Lady Merryn broke away from her son and reached Margery first. She was struck by how beautiful Ancel's mother was, though she knew the noblewoman to be over two score in age.

"Lady Margery." Merryn de Montfort held her hands out. Margery took them and they kissed one another's cheeks. "I have looked forward to meeting you ever since we received Ancel's missive. We are so very happy to be invited to see Highfield."

"I am delighted that you and Lord Geoffrey could come for a visit, my lady."

"Please, call us Merryn and Geoffrey." Her eyes sparkled. "There is no need to stand on ceremony since you are to be our new daughter-in-law."

Margery beamed with pride. "Aye. Ancel and I will wed at Kinwick if you will give us permission to do so."

"Of course, you may marry at Kinwick," Geoffrey said. "'Twill be yours one day." He kissed Margery's hand and then wrapped her in a tight hug. Releasing her, his warm smile seemed familiar.

"You are very much like your son," she told him. "Or rather, Ancel reminds me of you."

Ancel came and slipped his arm around her waist. "Mother said I came out of the womb looking like Father. And Alys resembles Mother quite a bit."

"I can't wait to meet Alys and all of your other siblings," Margery said. "And your cousins. I don't think I can begin to remember all of their names."

"We can't wait to tour Highfield," Merryn said, "but I am eager to get you back to Kinwick so we can plan your wedding. You'll be surprised how many relatives Ancel has. They'll all want to be in attendance when you speak your vows."

"Please, come inside the keep," Margery said. "I know you've had a long journey."

"Three days in the saddle isn't so bad," Geoffrey proclaimed. "I like getting out and about."

As they mounted the stairs, Ancel asked, "Did you ride through London?"

"No, your mother doesn't like it much. We went around the city and picked up the road east of there."

"You don't enjoy London?" Margery asked. "I visited it for the first time last week and found it fascinating."

"She has nothing against the city itself," Geoffrey confided. "Merryn is always afraid that if we go to London, I'll be stuck at the royal palace."

Merryn slipped her arm through Margery's. "The king—the old one—always wanted Geoffrey to reside in London and sit on his royal council. I preferred a quieter life at Kinwick."

"And that means I prefer a quieter life. If I know what's good for me," her husband teased as he winked at Margery.

Merryn shot her husband a look. "Geoffrey, we should do our best to make a good impression upon Margery. That means behaving appropriately."

His eyes twinkled. "I will do my best, my love." He brought his wife's hand to his lips and gave it a kiss in apology.

"Don't worry, Lord Geoffrey," Margery reassured him. "I've decided already that I like you both—mischief and all."

The nobleman laughed heartily. "Oh, I like your bride-to-be, Ancel. You have chosen well, my son."

"I have," Ancel confirmed, the twinkle in his eyes matching that of his father's.

They entered the keep and took their guests to the great hall. Merryn also wanted to see the kitchen, so Margery showed it to her and introduced her to Maud. They returned to the men and adjourned upstairs to the solar.

"This is cozy," Merryn said. "And I could use some wine and cheese. I didn't realize I was famished. Thank you for your thoughtfulness, Margery."

The two couples ate and talked for a few hours. Margery heard stories about Ancel and Alys while they were growing up and many of them had her in tears because she laughed so hard.

"Alys has twins of her own now, as well as a younger boy," Merryn said. "They get into as much mischief as she and her brother did."

"What of your other children?" Margery asked.

"We have two more sons," Geoffrey said. "Both foster with the Earl of Winterbourne, whose estate lies an hour north of Kinwick. Hal is ten and seven and Edward is ten and five. They both idolize Ancel and want to be knights as he is. Hal is determined to become a royal guardsman, while Edward wants to do everything Hal does."

"Our middle daughter, Nan, is ten and two," Merryn said. "She is better with her bow and arrow than any of our boys—including Ancel—while Jessimond, our youngest, is only five. You will meet all of them soon, plus more cousins than you can swat a stick at—and their children."

"I am an only child, so I look forward to marrying into such a large family," Margery shared.

"What of your parents?" asked Geoffrey. "Are they still alive?"

Margery took a deep breath and explained how her widowed mother married Lord Umfrey many years ago and how they had both been killed in the peasants' rebellion in June.

Merryn took her hand. "I am sorry to hear of this, Margery. We didn't know." She squeezed Margery's hand in comfort. "I hope that you will come to look upon Geoffrey and me as parents."

"I would like that, my lady," Margery said quietly. She chose not to speak of Lord Joseph Ormond and how he wasn't her true father. Mayhap, if she and Ancel learned any news of her birth father, they could share that knowledge with Ancel's parents.

Ancel took her hand. "Though the king has determined that High-field will come to me, marrying Margery is what I treasure most." He grew serious. "I have watched for all these years and seen how the two of you have loved one another. I always wanted, one day, to have what you have between you. I never thought I'd find it. I wasn't even looking for it."

He turned and gazed lovingly at Margery. "But once I met this woman, I understood what love is. She is the only one for me." He turned back to his parents. "I wanted you to know that. We are a love match, as the two of you were. We feel blessed to have found each other."

Merryn smiled at them through tear-filled eyes as she patted Margery's hand. Geoffrey beamed as a proud father.

In that moment, Margery knew she'd found a new family.

MARGERY DRESSED IN the velvet that Ancel had brought back from London. He'd told her the deep russet color made her eyes and skin glow, so she was more than happy to wear it tonight while they celebrated the last night of Geoffrey and Merryn's time at Highfield. The week had passed quickly as they'd shown the de Montforts the estate and the surrounding area and introduced them to many of their tenants and workers.

She opened the door to the hallway and found Ancel waiting for her. He looked handsome in a hunter green cotehardie.

"I thought I would escort you downstairs," he said. "After this."

His lips touched hers for a moment. She longed for more from him but knew they needed to head to the great hall.

"Have you packed what you will need for our trip to Kinwick?" he asked as he led her to the stairs.

"Almost. I'm waiting for one last thing—what Christine has been working on for me to wear at our wedding. I tried it on yesterday afternoon and she had a few finishing touches to make. Everything else is already in my trunk but I'll be ready for our journey after we break our fast tomorrow morning."

"Mother is pleased that you've planned a special meal for them tonight."

"I can't say enough good things about your mother. And your father. They are wonderful people and have been so gracious and friendly to me."

"They adore you, as well. Mother already claims you as another daughter. I think she believes it was her idea that we should marry."

They entered the great hall and saw that most everyone had already been seated. Ancel led her to the dais and they greeted his parents.

Suddenly, Sarah appeared before her. Her friend seemed distraught.

"My lady, I must speak with you." She glanced over her shoulder.

"Can it wait until after we've dined?" Margery asked.

Sarah frowned. "I suppose so. But it's important that we talk tonight." She hurried away, her head down. Margery hoped everything was all right between Sarah and Harry.

As servants brought out the haddock and venison, Margery caught sight of someone new serving the meal to the soldiers and turned to Ancel.

"Do you know that woman? I'm not familiar with her."

Before he could reply, Agnes set a trencher in front of them.

"That's Eua, my lady. She's Matthew Cheyne's wife. Eua just returned from Billericay, where she's been staying with her daughter. The girl had her first babe and from what Eua says, it was a most difficult birth. She stayed on until her daughter got back on her feet."

"I remember now," Ancel said. "When I hired Matthew as our new smithy, he told me his wife was away. I said we could certainly use her help inside the manor house once she returned."

"I see. If I don't speak with her tonight, I'll be sure to do so before we leave tomorrow."

More courses came out and it pleased Margery how well everything tasted. She could tell Merryn and Geoffrey enjoyed their food by how much they ate. As the meal drew to an end, she told Ancel she wanted to say a few words to those gathered.

Rising to her feet with her pewter cup in hand, Margery opened her mouth to speak—until she heard that grating voice from months ago.

"More wine, my lady?"

A wave of nausea ran through her as blackness rushed up and clouded her vision. She wavered, her hand tightening on the cup. No, she refused to faint.

Not when justice must be meted out.

"I asked if you wanted more wine, Lady Margery."

Margery lowered her gaze to Eua, the new servant who stood in front of the dais offering her wine. Slamming down her cup on the table, Margery shouted, "You murdered my mother!"

She watched as the woman tensed and panic filled her faded, blue eyes. The servant looked around wildly as silence blanketed the great hall and then her head dropped.

"Stop," Margery ordered calmly. "Look at me, Eua Cheyne."

The smithy's wife reluctantly raised her eyes. In them, Margery saw the panic subsiding, only to be replaced by anger.

And resentment.

"I heard you as you berated my mother," she accused the woman standing before her. "*My mother*—who was bedridden and helpless. A kind, gentle soul who had done nothing to deserve a death sentence from someone she had never even seen."

Margery took a deep breath and gripped the table for support. "I saw what you did to her. I found her. Her throat cut. The bedclothes drenched in her blood. I will never forget that last sight of her—and you are to blame."

"She deserved it!" Eua spat on the ground and then waved a hand about as she faced those gathered in the great hall. "All nobility deserved what happened to them." She spun around to face those on the dais again. "I only wish we could have found you that day. I would have enjoyed slitting that pretty throat of yours and watching the life drain from you as I did your sainted mother."

Margery knocked her cup from the table. "My mother was considerate and brave. I will never forget what she looked like when you had finished with her. She deserves justice—and I will claim it for her."

Suddenly, Matthew Cheyne appeared behind his wife. The smithy looked as if he'd aged a dozen years since Margery had seen him yesterday.

"Eua, what have you done?" he whispered.

She glared at her husband. "I marched for the poor that day, Matthew."

"But we had nothing to do with Lord Umfrey and his family. Why would you—"

His wife laughed harshly. "You are so weak, Matthew. A puppet of the rich. You bow to them and make their weapons and shoe their horses, all while they trample on good people such as you. Your son. *Me.*" She shook a finger at him. "I would do what I did a hundred times more if I had but the chance."

Matthew shook his head. "You are not the woman I wed. You are a vile, wicked stranger."

Sir Terryn had risen to his feet and latched on to Eua's arm.

"Let go of me, you swine. You are as bad as the rest of them." She struggled to release herself from his grasp. When she couldn't, she went still.

Turning to Margery, the unrepentant woman said, "You want justice for your beloved mother? So be it."

With that, she reached with her free arm and snatched the blade resting at Sir Terryn's waist, swiping it across her throat. A thin red line appeared on her neck and then gushed freely as Eua fell to the floor.

Margery screamed and then the world went black.

CHAPTER 19

MARGERY FELT STRONG arms lifting her. She tried to open her eyes but found it took too much effort. A familiar masculine scent invaded her nostrils and she knew Ancel carried her. It caused her to relax and she gave in to the darkness again.

The next thing she knew, hushed voices spoke around her. This time, she fought to keep her eyes open and found she was lying in the bedchamber she had shared with her mother.

A scream formed on her lips, the image of Eua Cheyne cutting her throat, her blood spurting everywhere. Margery threw her hand over her mouth to keep it from escaping.

A heavy weight sank next to her. Ancel captured her wrist in his large hand, rubbing his thumb against the tender underside. The motion calmed her. She glanced up and saw Merryn standing on the other side of the bed. The noblewoman sat beside her and took her other hand as she stroked Margery's hair.

"Do you need anything?" she asked softly.

Margery shook her head. Tears welled in her eyes. She noticed Sarah standing at the foot of the bed, a sympathetic look on her face.

"You wanted to warn me," she said to her friend. "About Eua."

"Aye. I saw her in the kitchen before the evening meal began. Mother told me she was Matthew's wife come back from Billericay." Sarah's mouth trembled. "But I knew her from before. I saw what she did to your poor mother."

Margery sat up and reached her hands out. Merryn moved aside and Sarah came and took them.

"I feared for you that day, Sarah. I was hiding in a secret passageway within the walls of the keep. I came back to protect Mother and could hear what went on. You were very brave and stood firm against that mob."

Sarah shuddered. "I was so afraid, my lady. I thought they might find you. I did what I could to put them off your trail."

"And I appreciated that." Margery turned to Ancel. "Where is your father?"

His hand clasped her shoulder and kneaded it gently. "Father is seeing to matters downstairs. He will determine if Matthew Cheyne or his son had anything to do with the rebellion."

"I doubt it," she said. "Matthew looked at Eua as if he didn't recognize her. The disbelief on his face told me he is innocent of any crime."

A light rap at the door sounded and Geoffrey de Montfort entered the bedchamber and crossed the room. Margery was touched by the concern for her on the nobleman's face.

"I have spoken to both the smithy and his boy," he said. "It's my belief that they had no knowledge of Eua's role in the uprising." Geoffrey paused. "Matthew is most upset but he wishes to speak with you, Margery. Are you willing to see him? He's waiting outside the door."

"Aye. Bring him to me." She pushed herself to a sitting position and steeled herself for the encounter.

Matthew Cheyne walked in, his head bowed as he shuffled toward the bed. As he raised his eyes to meet hers, Margery saw only pain and frustration.

"My lady, I am here to apologize to you. Eua . . . Eua did something unspeakable, acting against the laws of both God and man. 'Twas if she changed into a stranger before my very eyes tonight. I had no idea her heart had turned so black and such wickedness grew within her."

Fat tears began rolling down the blacksmith's face, spilling onto his faded tunic. "Lady Margery, I want you to know how sorry I am for

Eua's crimes against you and your mother. I realize nothing I can do or say can bring Lady Marian back to you." His voice quivered and his limbs trembled violently.

Margery's heart told her that she could not blame this man in any way for his wife's vile actions. "You have nothing to be sorry for, Matthew," she said simply.

"But my . . . my wife . . ." His voice trailed off.

"Matthew, I am sorry that you had to find out the way you did about Eua's role in the events that occurred at Highfield," Margery said. "In no way do I blame you—or John—for what she did. Eua's actions were her own. She alone is responsible and will one day stand in judgment for her sins."

"Thank you for being so understanding, my lady." He wiped his eyes with his sleeves, struggling to go on. "I come to tell you that John and I will leave tonight. You need never look upon us again and be reminded of what . . . of what Eua did. Highfield will be a better place with us gone."

Margery's heart told her that this man was blameless and it was for her to take the high road. If he and his son left Highfield, they might never become whole again.

"That would make me most unhappy, Matthew," Margery told him as she gripped Ancel's hand and used it to come to her feet. She went and stood before the broken laborer. "You and your son are good men and fine blacksmiths. We have a great need of your services at Highfield. I insist that you stay unless you feel you cannot."

Hope glimmered in his eyes. "You . . . you would not have us leave, my lady? You do not judge us or think ill of us?"

"Nay, Matthew." She gave him a sad smile. "You and I have both had to deal with unexpected loss. I want you to stay where you are wanted. Where you have friends. Where you can heal."

He bowed his head. "Thank you, my lady." His words were barely above a whisper. "I am most grateful for your mercy."

"And I am blessed to have you and John as a part of Highfield." Margery reached and took the blacksmith's hand in hers. She searched his eyes and saw this would be a man ever loyal to her. She pressed a kiss of forgiveness against the hardened knuckles and released his hand.

Matthew fell to his knees, great sobs coming from him.

"Come, Matthew," Geoffrey said. The earl led the smithy from the room.

"That was very generous of you, Margery," Ancel said. "But it was a wise decision."

She sighed. "I saw no need for the Cheynes to suffer more than they already have."

"You look tired," Merryn said. "We'll leave you so you can rest."

Margery gripped Ancel's hand. "Could you stay for a little while?" she asked.

"Of course."

Merryn and Sarah left the room. Margery held fast to Ancel's hand, feeling his warmth fill her. They sat in silence for some minutes before he told her he should go.

"We have the journey to Kinwick ahead of us if you're still willing to leave in the morning. You need to get some sleep."

"I am still eager to leave for Kinwick but don't go," she pleaded. "I have struggled some sleeping in this chamber since I gave up the solar for your parents to use. Seeing what Eua did to herself tonight has brought back all the horrible memories of what happened here."

"Would you like to move across the hall? You could sleep there and I in here," he offered.

"Nay. I want you to sleep here. With me."

Ancel's brows shot up.

"Hear me out," Margery said. "I don't want to be alone tonight. I need you with me." She paused. "I need your kiss, Ancel. Your touch. I want you to love me."

His hand cupped her cheek. "We are not married yet, sweetheart."

"I know. But we will be wed in less than a month's time. It's already the start of the third week in December, Ancel, and we will marry when the New Year comes."

"What if we make a babe tonight?"

She shrugged. "What if we do? Then he—or she—might come a few weeks early. I don't care." She gripped his hand. "I need you tonight. Don't deny me your company."

A slow grin spread across his face. "Your wish is my command, my lady."

Ancel pulled from her grasp and rose from the bed. He crossed the room and secured the latch on the door and then returned. Slowly, he removed every piece of clothing he wore until he stood before her, gloriously naked. Margery's mouth went dry as she gazed at him. The broad shoulders that seemed as wide as the bed itself. The mat of dark hair on his chest that ran down to a flat stomach. And his manhood itself, rising to stand at attention. Her eyes widened at its size and length. Although she had touched it once before, she really hadn't looked at it.

Curiosity had her reach out to finger it.

The head was smooth as silk. Margery ran the tips of her fingers over it before she grasped the firm shaft in her hand. Ancel groaned and pried her fingers from him.

"Not just yet, sweetheart. I need to see to you—and your needs."

She climbed off the bed and allowed Ancel to unwind her braid to free her hair and remove the layers of her clothing till she, too, stood naked before him. His eyes roamed her body.

"Perfection," he declared as he enfolded her in an embrace.

Her breasts pressed against the hard muscles in his chest. Margery couldn't help but glide her hand along it, smoothing the thick mat of hair.

"You are so very different from me," she proclaimed.

"Yet we will fit together as one. Soon," he promised.

He lowered his mouth to hers and parted her lips with his tongue. She didn't know how she had lived as many years as she had without his kiss. He deepened it, causing her to cling to his shoulders, digging her nails into his flesh. He pushed his fingers into her unbound hair and they massaged her scalp soothingly.

Then his hands glided down her neck and stroked her bare back up and down. A tingling began inside her, familiar yet new. Gradually, his hands went lower till they cupped her buttocks. His shaft pressed against her. She longed to touch it again and appease her curiosity about it but she would wait till he told her she could. Her breasts grew heavy and the nipples sensitive as they rubbed against his chest.

One of his hands remained cupped against her bottom, while the other roamed between them. He palmed one breast and Margery felt it swell to fit his hand. As he kneaded it, he kissed her neck, his lips moving to her ear. A shiver of delighted rushed through her. Ancel's teeth found her earlobe and tugged on it, bringing a wave of hot desire. Margery wrapped her arms around his neck and kissed him until she was breathless.

Ancel released her breast and his hand dragged between them, down her body, until he reached the apex of her legs. A drumming began inside her as she knew what to expect. He stroked the slit and Margery found her breathing became quick and shallow. Pushing a finger inside her, he captured her lips with his again. His finger knew exactly what to do to please her. Soon it was joined by a second, then a third, as she began writhing, grinding against him, whimpering in need.

Ancel slowly pulled his fingers from her and swept her into his arms. Carrying her to the bed, he set her down and pushed her back against the pillows. He hovered over her, his tongue touching her nipple, licking, teasing it. Lightning shot through Margery. Her arms went around him, holding his head hard against her. He played with one breast, then the other, tormenting her as the pounding inside her grew stronger.

Then his lips moved to her belly, kissing her softly. She wriggled under his touch, wanting more.

And he gave it to her.

His tongue glided down to her womanly parts and playfully darted in and out. Margery gasped at the contact between them, shocked—and maddened—by his touch. Ancel's tongue did even more than his fingers had. Suddenly, an immense heat rose within her and she bucked wildly against his mouth, riding out a wave of intense pleasure.

Finally, she stilled and thought her bones had melted into the mattress. She had no energy and couldn't even lift a hand to touch him.

He rose above her again, his mouth skimming her body till it reached her lips. His fingers toyed with her, rubbing that small nub that gave her so much pleasure.

Then they slid out and were replaced by his shaft. He thrust, once, hard into her. Margery gasped and nearly came off the bed but his body held her down even as he filled and stretched her.

"It's done," he said. "I've breeched your maidenhead. I know it hurt but it never will again."

Already, the pain had receded, replaced by a growing need for him.

"Fill me," she said. "Fill me with you and your love for me."

Ancel pressed a soft kiss against her brow.

Then he moved within her. Slowly, she became accustomed to the movement and caught his rhythm. A force built within her, screaming to get out, as he thrust harder and deeper. The buzzing and warmth from before filled her again and she cried out as he did. She felt his seed spill inside her, bringing an immense satisfaction.

He collapsed against her and quickly rolled to his side, pulling her with him. His shaft lingered inside her and Margery felt a contentment as never before.

Ancel gazed at her and said, "I love you, Margery Ormond. I cannot imagine what my life was like before you. There's only here. Now. And what's to come."

She laid her palm against his face, relishing his scent and feel and the way their bodies entwined as one.

"The past is gone," she agreed. "The future is ours to make. Together." Margery smiled. "I love you, Ancel de Montfort. I will till the end of time."

She snuggled against him as the world faded away and left only the two of them.

CHAPTER 20

MARGERY LOOKED ACROSS the great hall and thought how things had changed for the better in a short amount of time. Instead of the unease and fear that had existed with Lord Umfrey's presence, those breaking their fast this morning had smiles on their faces and engaged in conversation with their table mates. She enjoyed the new atmosphere at Highfield—and it was all due to the man at her side.

Ancel de Montfort was a natural leader and gained instant respect wherever he went. Moreover, this was a man who upheld his knightly code of honor. The changes at Highfield had occurred because of him.

And the change Ancel had brought to her life was only beginning.

Margery knew they would build a strong life together here—and at court—before they eventually took over the responsibilities at Kinwick one day in the far-off future. When she had worked on preparing Highfield for Christmastime twelve months ago, she could not have imagined how different her life would be a year later, and now she couldn't think of it without Ancel coming to mind. Last night had opened her eyes not only to what happened between a man and a woman physically but the depth and breadth of emotions within her let her know her life was only truly starting.

Did she look any different today after what she had experienced only a few hours ago? She didn't think so yet everything inside of her told a different story. Margery was surprised that happiness didn't bubble from her.

Ancel leaned close and said, "Father and I will go now and ready the horses and assemble the escort party to Kinwick."

"So we have soldiers from Highfield and Kinwick accompanying us to your home?"

"Aye. The road can be a dangerous place, my love. Sir Folcard will be in charge of the knights who go with us, while Sir Terryn will stay behind and keep things safe here until we return."

He took her hand and squeezed it. "Be ready to leave in a quarter hour."

Ancel signaled his father and both men left the dais.

Merryn turned to her. "Just think, the next meal you partake in under Highfield's roof will be as a wedded wife. You will be Margery de Montfort."

"I hadn't thought of that," she admitted. "I must thank you again for allowing us to marry at Kinwick."

"I love nothing more than for my family to gather, especially to celebrate the marriage of two people so deeply in love. Frankly, Margery, 'tis you I should thank for bringing such happiness to my eldest son. Because of events that occurred concerning Geoffrey when Ancel was a small boy, Ancel has always found it hard to trust, much less open up to others." Merryn paused. "But I see how he looks at you. There is trust—and love—in abundance."

"I feel fortunate to have Ancel in my life, Merryn. I've never known any couple in love but I see how you and Geoffrey are with one another and know Ancel has had that shining example his entire life."

"I know you already love my son, Margery, but I promise that your love will grow stronger each day you are wed. And when you have children together, it will multiply beyond your imagination."

Margery thought of their love play last night and wondered if Ancel's babe already grew within her.

"Excuse me, my lady. Will Artus requested your trunk be brought down," Christine said. "I took the liberty of placing your wedding kirtle and cotehardie into it before he carried it to the cart."

"Thank you," Margery told the seamstress. "You did an excellent job, Christine. I cannot wait for Ancel to see me in it."

"'Twas a pleasure to make it for you, my lady. I wish you and Sir Ancel much happiness." Christine excused herself.

Margery glanced back at Merryn. "I think we need to make our way to the bailey. We should be leaving soon." She reached for the small bundle which contained a change of clothing and her comb. Merryn had suggested she bring this and have Ancel tie it to his horse.

Several people came to tell her goodbye, including Sarah, who hugged her tightly. Her friend whispered in her ear, "The ways of a man and woman may surprise you, my lady, but my Harry has made me very happy. I know Sir Ancel will do the same for you."

Margery hid a smile, already knowing something about the physical pleasures of love. "I am glad you are so content with Harry," she told Sarah. "I cannot wait to wed Sir Ancel." She reached down and scooped up Whitefoot, handing him to Sarah for safekeeping while they were away.

Finally, she and Merryn left the manor house to join the men. Ancel awaited her next to Storm.

"Will left with your things a few minutes ago," he informed her. "We will arrive at Kinwick faster than he can since the cart will slow him down."

"That's not a problem," she said, handing him the parcel. "I have something else to wear inside this."

He took the bundle and attached it to Storm's saddle before he helped her on the horse's back. Joining her, Ancel said, "Mayhap we can continue our riding lessons at Kinwick. The stables have a variety of horses, so I know we can find a gentle one with a good temperament for you to practice on."

His arms went around her waist as he took up the reins. Margery leaned against his chest, content to be close to him for the three days it would take to reach Kinwick.

Sir Folcard motioned the escort party to ride out and they crossed the inner bailey. Margery waved to workers as they cantered by. They reached the outer bailey and picked up speed, heading for the open gates. Suddenly, Margery was confused. She watched Will drive the cart with her trunk through them. Why was he returning? Had he forgotten something?

The squire pulled up on the reins, a perplexed look on his features. As the horse came to a halt, Will stood, waving his arms wildly. Before he said a word, Margery knew. She held her breath, a wordless prayer on her lips. In that moment, her world came crashing down as Thurstan Vivers appeared on a midnight black horse, riding through the gates and coming straight toward them.

He yanked on the reins and stopped directly in front of Storm. Glaring at her, he said, "Where do you think you are going, Margery? And who are these people?" He pointed in Will's direction. "This boy said you were leaving for somewhere called Kinwick."

An icy chill ran through her as Ancel's arms tightened about her but she was not the Margery of old that Thurstan remembered. In her short time with Ancel, she had learned to speak up for herself.

"These people have helped keep Highfield going, Thurstan, at the king's command. You abandoned us," she accused. "You have no idea of the suffering that went on here in your absence."

"I had to leave, Margery," her stepbrother said, his irritation with her obvious. "Father sent me to London that day to bring back a horse he had purchased for Gervase. As I rode out, I saw the armed mob gathering. I raced past them in order to hold fast to my life. When I reached the city, chaos ruled. Fires spread everywhere. Noblemen were being massacred in the streets. I couldn't chance being caught and killed, especially since I knew the same thing was happening at Highfield."

"So you deliberately fled, knowing the mob would kill your family. And then stayed gone half a year, like a coward," Ancel said.

Thurstan sneered at the insult. "I assume you're one of the king's men. If you helped bring back order here or maintained the property, you have my thanks. But I've returned now and will care for things." He glanced around. "Especially since it is mine."

"So you know they murdered your father?" Ancel probed.

Thurstan shrugged. "I assumed the worst. I was lucky enough to make my way to the river and purchased passage to Calais. Unfortunately, I suffered an accident once I reached there and broke my leg. I couldn't walk, much less ride a horse, for several months. 'Tis why it has taken me so long to return and claim my title and inheritance."

"And you didn't worry in all this time about Lady Margery or what had happened here at Highfield?" Ancel asked. "You never thought to write and send word as to where you were?"

Margery sensed the contained anger in Ancel, both in his voice and body.

"They wouldn't have hurt women," Thurstan said coolly. "Margery and her mother were never in danger. I thought the rebels would bring harm to my father and brother, so I did what I had to do to protect myself. After all, I am the future of Highfield."

Margery snapped at his cavalier words and attitude. "My mother was murdered in her bed by that vicious mob. Her throat cut while she lay there, with no way—and no one—to defend her."

Her stepbrother's eyes widened. "I did not know." But no apology for her loss came from his lips and Margery's anger grew.

"I had to hide and when I came out, I discovered Lord Umfrey's body. They beheaded your father, Thurstan. Disemboweled him. Broke his legs and cut off his fingers. Gervase, too, suffered at their hands. You have no idea what it was like."

He pursed his lips a moment then calmly said, "'Tis unfortunate what occurred here, Margery, but I won't let anything happen to you. Don't worry, you are now under my protection."

"Nay," Ancel said firmly. "Lady Margery is under my protection now. I am Sir Ancel de Montfort, a member of the king's royal guard, and I plan to make the lady my wife. With me are my father and mother, Lord Geoffrey and Lady Merryn de Montfort. We journey now to Kinwick and will wed there come the New Year."

Thurstan studied Ancel a moment, appraising him and this new information. Margery's heart beat fast, knowing how devious her stepbrother could be.

"Do you have my permission to marry her, Sir Ancel?" he finally asked, his gaze steady. "I am her closest male relative and I have signed no betrothal contract with you. Are you betrothed, unbeknownst to me?"

"We are not," Ancel replied, "but the king knows we intend to wed. It was at his suggestion that we do so."

Margery wanted to wipe the smirk off her stepbrother's face as he reacted to Ancel's words.

"Get down from that horse, Margery," he told her. "I'll be the man to determine your future. Whether you stay here or leave. I may even take you to court to find you a husband."

"I have already been to court," she snapped, "and have met the king. Twice."

Thurstan's surprise was evident. Still, he recovered quickly and said, "With your beauty, I stand to gain a fortune. Men will battle for your hand. I'll simply sell you to the highest bidder. Now do as I say and get down off the horse. You are to come with me." He glanced around at the escort party. "I assume most of you men are soldiers sent by the king, so you may remain until he recalls you.

"As for you, Sir Ancel—and anyone with you—you are no longer needed nor welcomed at Highfield. I am the baron and my word here is law. I want you off my property. Now."

Margery turned and saw Ancel seethe at Thurstan's words as she told him, "You must let me go."

He dismounted from Storm and brought her to the ground. They stared into one another's eyes, a thousand unsaid words passing between them.

She couldn't let him leave without a final kiss goodbye. It didn't matter who was present. Margery reached up and pulled his face to hers. Their lips met in a final, searing kiss.

Ancel broke the kiss and said to Thurstan, "There is no need to take Lady Margery to court. I'll pay your bridal price. Name it."

Thurstan burst out in laughter. "You *love* her? You do. I can see it your eyes." He thought a moment. "But do you have access to such funds, Sir Ancel, for I would ask a high price. Do you own a large estate? I doubt it since you mentioned you are but a member of the king's royal guard and your own father looks hale and hearty."

"I'll provide the necessary funds," Geoffrey called out.

"No, Father," Ancel said firmly.

"'Tis part of your inheritance, Ancel. I don't mind parting with it in order to have Margery become your wife and a member of the de Montfort family."

"Keep your coin, Lord Geoffrey," Thurstan said. "I wouldn't sell Margery to your son if he were the last man left on earth." He shook his head. "I will ask you once again to leave my estate."

She shivered at Thurstan's callous, ungrateful tone and dropped her eyes to the ground. If she looked at Ancel again, she would burst into tears.

"Go back to the keep, Margery," Thurstan ordered, his tone harsh. "I am famished and have missed your cooking."

"Margery no longer cooks," Ancel declared. "Highfield now has its own cook and plenty of servants so that she is no longer run ragged. She should be treated as the lady she is and not your slave."

She raised her eyes to see how Thurstan would react. His face went blood-red in anger.

"Margery will do whatever I tell her to do. If I want her to lick my boots clean, then she will. If I decide she should remain at Highfield and serve me instead of marrying her off, 'tis my business, de Montfort. Not yours. Get off my estate." Thurstan wheeled his horse and headed for the stables.

Ancel grabbed her by the shoulders. "This is far from over, Margery." He looked to Will. "Stay here, Will. Keep your eyes and ears open and watch over Lady Margery." Glancing around the circle of Highfield soldiers, he said, "The same goes for the rest of you."

With that, Ancel leaped onto Storm's back and rode off. Geoffrey and Merryn gave her sorrowful looks that caused her heart to ache as they galloped after their son, the Kinwick men following suit.

Margery's new life ended before it had even begun.

CHAPTER 21

ANCEL RACED THROUGH the gates of Highfield, hatred for Thurstan Vivers causing the blood to pound in his ears. If he didn't ride away quickly, he might be tempted to kill Margery's pompous stepbrother. The scenery sped by in a blur as he pushed Storm.

His father's voice called out to him from behind. Ancel sensed the horses his parents rode gaining on him but he ignored them. Nothing would deter him from speaking to the king the moment he arrived in London.

"Ancel de Montfort! Stop your horse now!" shouted his mother.

At once, he pulled up on the reins and turned Storm to face her. Both de Montforts came to a halt in front of him. The soldiers from Kinwick remained at a respectful distance.

Ancel had grown up wanting to emulate his father in every way. Geoffrey de Montfort's skills as a knight were legendary. His patience in teaching other soldiers as well as his intelligence, courage, and generosity made him someone any man would look up to, especially his own son. But thanks to Ancel's early years without his father in his life, he'd formed a unique bond with his mother. During the years of her husband's imprisonment by the Earl of Winterbourne, Merryn de Montfort had ruled Kinwick with a strong, fair hand and been both father and mother to her young twins. Ancel's respect for his mother and her accomplishments made him stop now to listen to her. She'd always been the voice of reason, wise beyond her years. Hearing her out now might calm his rage.

She didn't mince words. "I know you want to run a sword through that bastard, Thurstan Vivers, and that's why you fled as you did. Going to the king now isn't wise, though."

Ancel's breathing slowed as he considered her words. "Why?"

"First, it might be days before you could gain an audience with him. Look how long it took you and Margery to see the king when you last went to London because of the politics involved. More importantly, think of the circumstances and the season. Richard may be a king but he's still a boy on the cusp of manhood. He has his newly-betrothed at court and will want to spend time with her, getting to know her. Even wooing her. Christmastime fast approaches and the king will want those around him in a celebratory mood, not blackened by anger and hatred."

She paused. "Our king has had nothing but trouble for the last six months. This uprising challenged not only the young monarch himself but our very system of government. It's taken months for him to regain control of England, thanks to men such as you, who armed themselves and rode out in the name of king and country. Richard is tired of conflict. Afraid of another challenge to his authority. He needs a brief respite of peace in his life—and time to get to know his future wife as they plan their royal wedding."

"Interrupting him now could have the opposite effect of what you might hope. Your problem is all-consuming to you but to the king, it matters little," his father added. "No matter the service you've given him or how many times you have risked your life on the battlefield for him. Let him enjoy this season of hope and goodwill before you approach him with your difficulties."

Ancel knew his parents presented a strong argument for having patience. Richard did show flashes of being temperamental. If anything, Ancel had never been an impetuous man, which the king appreciated. Ruining the king's mood with his problems would solve nothing and might even cause more conflict with Thurstan Vivers.

"Would you have me come to Kinwick with you?" he asked.

"Aye," his mother said, visibly relaxing. "We can talk through the matter and come up with a way to solve this dilemma."

"I worry for Margery, though," Ancel said. "Being left with that monster."

"Margery is a woman much like your mother," his father assured him. "Have faith in her—and in the love she has for you."

"I assume the first thing Vivers will do is notify the king that he has returned to Highfield," his mother said. "So young Richard's royal advisers will already know of the situation before you even approach him. They will have made null and void anything relating to you receiving Highfield and the title. But remember, Ancel, that the king has met Margery and knows how you feel about her. Though Vivers has control over her future at present, the king might persuade him to allow the two of you to wed."

"If we could only find her father, *he* would be able to supplant Vivers," Ancel blurted out.

"Her father?" Merryn asked, frowning. "Both her father and stepfather are dead."

"Lord Joseph Ormond may have wed Margery's mother but Lady Marian was already with child before they spoke their vows," Ancel revealed. "Margery doesn't know the name of her sire." Quickly, he explained what Margery had related to him and saw understanding dawn on his parents' faces.

"So the only clue she has is this silver pendant inlaid with garnets that she wears," Geoffrey noted. "I noticed it right away because it was so unusual."

"Aye. The pattern is odd and intricate. If I can discover her birth father's identity and he is still alive and chooses to acknowledge her, then Margery would be out from under Vivers' thumb."

"Then there is hope," Merryn said.

"I know where I must go," Ancel declared. "Margery once told me that besides the pendant from her true father, her mother gave her a ring and necklace moments before the revolting peasants arrived. Lady Marian had received these jewels as gifts from her father, the Earl of Waudum. I must journey to where Lady Marian grew up and see if I can uncover what man she might have been friendly with immediately before her marriage. I know there is a slim chance to unearth his identity so many years later but I must try."

"I met the Earl of Waudum years ago," his father revealed. "He had come on summer progress with the old king when Edward stopped at Kinwick one year. Waudum mentioned he was a widower but I remember him telling me that his lands lay just west of York."

"Then that is the place I will start," Ancel said, determination filling him.

His mother nudged her horse forward and brought it alongside Storm. She raised her palm to Ancel's cheek. "We will pray for you, my son. I wish for you to find success in this endeavor. I know how much you love Margery and hope you will be able to wed as planned."

Ancel raised his hand and covered hers. "Thank you, Mother. I'm sorry I cannot accompany you back to Kinwick and spend Christmas with the family."

His father approached his other side and placed a hand on Ancel's shoulder. "Do what you must, Son. When you have found your soul mate and become separated, you do whatever it takes to unite once more."

Ancel watched the tender smile his father gave his mother. Knowing that it was their great love that kept his father alive during seven long years of being locked away from the world gave Ancel new resolve.

"Tell everyone how much I love them," he said. "And that I plan to do whatever it takes to have Margery with us when we celebrate next Christmastime."

Ancel's knees urged Storm on. Now that he had a plan, he had hope.

ANCEL REACHED THE outskirts of York in just over four days. Storm was in bad need of rest after being pushed so hard for so great a distance. He found a place to care for the horse and rubbed Storm down himself since he knew the animal's temper would prove too much for a stranger to handle. He paid for Storm to stay three days and to be well fed, warning the owner to place the feed and water in their troughs and exit the stall quickly. He also paid for the use of another horse to see him around the area while Storm recuperated from the rough journey.

York proved to be noisy and crowded, with narrow lanes crammed full of houses. It smelled even worse than London did, with butchers' offal rotting in the ditches along the streets and privies built on the city moat. Like London, York was a place of great wealth and even greater poverty. The place left a bad taste in Ancel's mouth. After growing up in the country and spending time at Highfield recently, he found himself, like his father, with no appetite for city life.

Finding an inn, he bought a meal and rented a room for the night, letting the innkeeper know that he might wish to stay longer. After the hot meal filled his belly, Ancel shared the floor of a bedchamber with three other men. Even their snores didn't keep him awake as he fell into a dreamless sleep after his exhausting road trip.

Awakening early, he ate some bread and cheese in the public room below and then collected his horse and rode out west from the city. A brief conversation with the innkeeper this morning had given him a good idea where the Earl of Waudum's estate lay. After half an hour in the saddle at a steady canter, he saw a castle and steered his mount in its direction.

Minutes later, he arrived at the gate and gave the gatekeeper his name, being sure to inform the soldier on duty that he belonged to the king's royal guard. Granted entrance, Ancel rode to the keep and was met by a lanky fellow.

"Greetings," he called out as he dismounted. "I am Sir Ancel de Montfort, a member of King Richard's royal guard. I have urgent need to speak with the Earl of Waudum."

"Go to the stables, Sir Ancel. The earl is usually there this time of day. He's a great horseman and spends a good part of his day with the horses. 'Tis past the blacksmith's place and farther to your left."

Ancel thanked the man and rode to the stables. The head groom took his horse and sent him around the building to a fenced yard. A stout, balding man sat atop a fence as he watched a man try to mount a spirited horse.

"Lord Waudum?" Ancel asked.

"Aye." The nobleman gave Ancel a cursory glance and turned back to the enclosure. "Don't let him know you are afraid of him. He senses it. He can smell your fear. Try again."

After several attempts, the man managed to get on the horse's back and held on as the animal raced around the yard.

Waudum laughed and motioned the man off. "'Tis good enough for today. Leave him be. I'll care for him."

"You can have 'im, my lord," the stable hand said as he slipped between the bars in the fence.

Finally, Waudum turned back to Ancel after ignoring him. "What can I do for you?"

Ancel introduced himself and asked if Lady Marian had been his sister since the nobleman looked to be of an age similar to Ancel's parents.

"Nay, Lady Marian was my first cousin," he replied. "Her mother produced enough babes over the years but only Marian grew to maturity. I inherited the title from her father, my uncle. Why do you ask?"

Ancel stretched the truth some as he said, "The king has become interested in Lady Marian's daughter, Margery, and gave me permission to find out something of her and her mother's background."

"I see." Waudum said. "Frankly, I'm not sure what I could tell you. I last saw Marian when she left the north to marry." He frowned. "Can't remember who she wed. It's been too long. Someone down near Kent, I believe. They'd been betrothed for years."

"Lord Joseph Ormond," Ancel supplied.

Waudum nodded. "Aye, that's the name. I do remember when Marian's father died and I came to live here, I found two missives from her to the old earl. One told him of the birth of his granddaughter,

Margery. The other announced the death of her husband and that the king wanted Marian to wed a baron in Essex." Waudum shrugged. "I'm afraid that's all I can tell you."

"Do you know of anyone who fostered with your predecessor?" Ancel asked. "Someone who might have known Lady Marian?"

"Nay. By the time Waudum died, he was in ill health and hadn't taken anyone on in some years."

Ancel knew he would gain no more information from the nobleman. "Thank you for your time, my lord."

As he started to walk away, Waudum called out, "You might want to speak with our steward. He's been here many years and might be able to tell you more."

A sliver of hope rose within him. "I will do that. Thank you again, my lord."

Ancel walked back toward the keep and entered. He stopped a passing servant who took him to the room where the steward labored over a column of numbers. Once again, Ancel went through his story, ending with asking the man if he could remember any of the young men who fostered with the earl near the time Lady Marian left the estate to wed.

The steward scratched his head and stared into the distance. "I'm afraid names have started to escape my memory, my lord," he apologized. "That was near the time the old earl's health began to fail. Hmm. I can think of only two in service at that time and they were the last who fostered here. One was a page who left when Lady Marian did because the earl asked me to find another place for him."

"A boy would be too young. I am looking for someone older. Close to the age of one becoming a knight."

"There was one who did earn his spurs. Mayhap he accompanied Lady Marian south because he was from that area and ready to go home." The steward frowned. "I can see him but I cannot recollect his name. Just under six feet, with dark hair and brown eyes. He was a charmer, that one. Could make Lady Marian laugh like no one else. He was a great comfort to her after her mother passed."

A prickling teased Ancel's neck. Certainly, this knight was the man who had fathered Margery. Living here, being seen with her. Familiar enough with her to tease and make her laugh.

"And you don't recall his name?" Ancel asked.

"Nay, my lord. I do remember that he came from Kent because that was where Lady Marian headed in marriage to Lord Joseph." The steward brightened. "See, I do recall a few names every now and then."

"Thank you for your time. You have been most helpful." Ancel left the man and collected his horse from the stables.

At least he'd learned that her probable lover came from Kent. How ironic that the man lived in the very area where Lady Marian had gone when she left Waudum to wed. Ancel rode back to York, wondering if Kent should be his next stop. But with so little information, he didn't see what good it would do. Then it came to him.

The silver pendant.

Lady Marian had received the gift from her lover here, before her marriage. York, being a sizeable town, would be the logical place to purchase such an intricate necklace.

Ancel decided to visit every jeweler throughout the city to see if any of them remembered creating such an unusual piece—and the man who commissioned it. He urged the horse on, eager to begin his search.

CHAPTER 22

ANCEL ARRIVED BACK in York and decided to purchase parchment and ink in order to draw what he remembered about the pendant. It would be better to show the design to jewelers rather than try to describe it. He returned to the inn and dined on a meat pie and small round of cheese, washing it down with a decent ale. Remaining at the table after a serving wench cleared the meal, he made several poor attempts to replicate the necklace on his own and gave up in frustration. He pushed the parchment aside, mumbling under his breath.

"Having some trouble, my lord?" the innkeeper inquired.

"I am no artist," Ancel admitted, "yet I need to draw something important."

"Would you be willing to pay?"

"Of course. Do you know of someone who can draw?"

The innkeeper nodded. "Aye, Bartholomew. He's a bright lad. Comes in here often to eat. Let me bring you another cup of ale and I can watch for him."

Less than an hour later, a young man with hair more orange than red entered the public room. The innkeeper immediately spoke to him and then pointed out Ancel.

Approaching him, the newcomer said, "You have need of someone to capture something on paper for you, my lord? 'Tis what the innkeeper tells me."

"I do, Bartholomew, and would be willing to pay you for your time," Ancel said.

"Then let's get to it." Bartholomew seated himself across from Ancel and picked up the parchment. Studying it, he said, "Your sketches aren't bad but I think I can do better. Tell me what I need to draw. Describe it in as much detail as possible. In fact, close your eyes, my lord, and see it in your mind's eye."

Ancel did as requested and saw Margery wearing the necklace. As he explained what it looked like, he heard the scratching of a quill against the parchment. Deliberately keeping his eyes closed, he continued speaking until the sound ended.

Opening his eyes, Ancel gasped. "That's the pendant," he said excitedly. "Bartholomew, you have drawn it in great detail and you've never even seen it."

"What you said made it easy for me. You are familiar with the piece. Between looking at your attempts and hearing your words, it was easy to figure out what to draw."

Ancel slapped the freckled young man on the back. "I cannot thank you enough." He pulled out a gold coin from his purse and placed it on the table.

Bartholomew's eyes went round. "Nay, 'tis too much, my lord," he protested.

"Keep it," Ancel insisted. "You have done me a great favor."

"Thank you." The lad pocketed the coin and left and Ancel realized the task had taken up the entire afternoon. No shops would be open now.

He called over the innkeeper and asked him about any jewelers in the area. The man knew of two and a possible third one. Ancel would start early tomorrow and hope he would locate the man who had crafted the necklace.

After a restless night, he broke his fast and then visited the two jewelers the innkeeper had mentioned to him. Neither had seen a design remotely like the one he showed them. Once he awarded a coin to each, they had sent him to fellow jewelers nearby. By late afternoon, Ancel had almost exhausted his list. Only two men remained. He pushed away the rising anxiety and rode to the next shop.

Upon entering, a jovial man of two score greeted him with a wide smile.

"Welcome, my lord. What can I do for you this fine day? A bauble for a sweetheart? Or mayhap a ring for your wedding?"

"I have a design to show you," he said, coming to the counter the man stood behind and unfolding the parchment. "Might you know the man who crafted this piece?"

The jeweler looked at it a moment and nodded to himself. He lifted the page closer and nodded again, his eyes twinkling.

"I haven't seen this in many years but I am familiar with the design. I last saw it, oh, at least a score ago. Mayhap longer. 'Twas silver and inlaid with garnets."

Ancel's heart pounded rapidly. "Can you direct me to the jeweler who created it?"

"Of course. 'Twas my uncle who designed and crafted this pendant. My aunt had nothing but girls, so my uncle asked my father if I could apprentice with him. I had only been here a few weeks when a knight came in and told Uncle Oliver he needed a special piece made to give to a special lady."

"May I speak with your uncle now?" Ancel asked eagerly. "It's most important."

"Uncle Oliver's joints became inflamed a few years ago. The fingers on his hands are curled up and keep him in constant pain. 'Tis why he no longer owns this shop nor works at it."

"Where can I find him?"

"He lives at Saint Leonard's Hospital here in York. Besides nursing the sick and caring for those who have been orphaned, the Augustine canons also take in the elderly. You will find Uncle Oliver there."

Ancel asked for directions and hurried from the shop to his borrowed horse. The sun had begun to set when he arrived at the entrance to the hospital. After securing the horse, Ancel entered the building and was greeted by one of the canons who was passing by. He gave his name and then asked the priest about Oliver, regretting that, in his haste, he had forgotten to obtain the man's last name.

"We have only one Oliver here, my lord. Oliver Metcalfe. He is a good-hearted man. I can take you to him if you wish."

"Please, Father. I would be most grateful."

They wound their way through several corridors and arrived at a large room filled with dozens of cots. Men sat or lay on some of them, while others gathered around tables scattered about the room.

The canon said, "Oliver is the second man over there." He excused himself, saying he was needed to help finish preparing the evening meal for the residents.

Ancel took a calming breath and made his way over to the aging jeweler. "Oliver Metcalfe?" he asked.

The thin man with sparse white hair looked up. "I am Oliver Metcalfe, my lord." Gnarled hands rested atop the table. Ancel could see why Metcalfe could no longer practice his craft.

"I am Sir Ancel de Montfort. Might I speak to you for a few minutes?"

"Of course. I am glad for your company since my only visitors are my nephew and his family."

"I come from him. He is the one who told me that I could find you at Saint Leonard's."

"I am most curious, my lord. Please, continue."

Ancel set the parchment on the table and opened it. Pointing to the design Bartholomew had drawn, he asked, "Your nephew recognized this. He said you were the jeweler who designed this pendant many years ago."

Oliver broke out in a grin. "I most certainly am. 'Twas one of the most difficult pieces I ever crafted. The knight who sought out my services was most particular. In fact, not only did I produce the pendant for him but he wanted something of a comparable design for himself."

The jeweler's words triggered something in Ancel's memory. He remembered seeing something similar, made from silver and garnets, on a cloak of someone at court. The piece had stood out against the dark material. Ancel had only spotted it in passing and couldn't remember the name of the courtier sporting it or even if he had seen the man's face as he walked by.

But Oliver Metcalfe might know who wore the jeweled piece.

"Do you remember the name of this knight?" Ancel's voice sounded neutral to him but blood roared in his ears.

Metcalfe rubbed his hands together. "It's been many years, my lord."

"Take your time," Ancel urged.

The former jeweler closed his eyes. "I can see him. He was tall with dark hair. His brown eyes were surrounded with flecks of gold."

Ancel's heart quickened. *Those were Margery's eyes.* He sent a prayer up to the Blessed Christ for this man to remember the name.

Metcalfe opened his eyes. "The knight fostered with a nearby earl. I do remember that. Wait. It's on the tip of my tongue." He drew in a breath and expelled it slowly. "Sir Myles. That was his name. I cannot recall the rest, though I remember him telling me that he loved the lady very much."

Ancel finally had the answer. He knew immediately based upon the physical description and first name who Lady Marian's lover had been all those years ago. Sir Myles had come into his title a dozen years ago in Kent. Margery's father had become Lord Myles Peveril, the Earl of Mauntell, an adviser at the royal court.

And she had met the nobleman in passing when they gained their audience with the king a few weeks ago. Mauntell had accompanied Michael de la Pole and Sir Christopher Heron as the noblemen exited the royal chambers. The earl had been the third man in the trio who had helped to negotiate a bride for King Richard. The men had finished meeting with the king and spoke to him and Margery briefly.

Margery's father was alive. At court. Or had been. He might have returned to his home in Kent for the Christmas season but now Ancel knew his identity and could easily track him down.

"You have been very helpful to me," Ancel told the old man. "I do know Sir Myles."

Metcalfe wrung his misshapen hands together. "I am glad to have been of service to you, Sir Ancel."

"Is there anything I can do for you?" he asked.

"Nay, my lord. The good canons at Saint Leonard's take care of my needs."

"Could I provide a donation to the hospital in your name?"

Tears welled in Metcalfe's eyes. "That would be most kind of you, my lord. There are so many children here who have lost their parents. They always need clothes. And the priests could use money for more blankets or candles."

Ancel placed a hand on the jeweler's shoulder. "Consider it done." He rose. "Many thanks to you, Oliver. If I am ever in York again, I will stop by and see you and tell you how this tale ended."

"Happily, I hope, my lord."

"'Tis my greatest hope. Good evening."

Ancel left as one of the priests came in and announced it was time to eat. As the group began exiting the room, he caught up to the priest.

"Father, who is in charge of the hospital? I wish to make a donation."

"Father Cedric leads our group of Augustine canons. I can take you to him now."

Ancel met with the priest briefly and gave him almost every coin in his purse. The holy man thanked him profusely. With that, Ancel retrieved his horse and rode back to the inn. He would spend one more night under its roof before returning to search for Lord Myles Peveril, Earl of Mauntell.

ANCEL PONDERED ON where he should go—London or Kent? He wanted to find Margery's father as quickly as possible. He racked his brain as he rode south, trying to remember if Mauntell usually stayed at the royal court or returned to his home in Kent during the Christmas season. Ancel couldn't remember the nobleman being in London the past couple of years, so he decided to skirt the city and ride straightaway to Kent, hoping Mauntell would be at his estate. Ancel arrived early on the afternoon of Christmas Eve and easily gained entrance to the castle grounds once he identified himself.

He rode to the stables and asked if he could place Storm in a stall and have oats and water brought to the horse. The head groom brought a bucket of feed, which Storm gobbled greedily. Ancel rubbed the horse down and learned that the earl had returned from London two days ago.

"Good. My business is with Mauntell. I'll return for my horse shortly," he told the stable hand.

Ancel made his way to the keep, brimming with confidence. A servant admitted him and took him upstairs to the solar.

"Wait outside a moment, my lord," the servant instructed. He knocked and entered, closing the door behind him.

Ancel paced nervously in the hall until the man emerged.

"Lord Myles will see you now."

"Thank you." Ancel collected his thoughts and went into the solar.

Myles Peveril sat next to a blazing fire. "Good day to you, Sir Ancel. Your visit is a surprise to me. I hope the king is well?"

"I haven't been to London since I last saw you outside the king's chambers but I hope he is in good health."

Peveril frowned. "Then if you aren't from King Richard, what business do you have here?"

"Something that concerns you, my lord. And your daughter."

Peveril shook his head fiercely. "I have no daughter, Sir Ancel. You are mistaken. I have no children at all. No son. No daughter. Never a daughter," he protested.

"What of your daughter with Lady Marian?" Ancel boldly asked.

The color drained from the nobleman's face. "I haven't a clue what you speak of," he stuttered. "I know of no Lady Marian or any supposed daughter."

"What about—"

"I must ask you to leave, Sir Ancel, and never speak of such a rumor again."

"'Tis no rumor, my lord, but fact. You loved Lady Marian and she found herself with child."

"Nay. I deny this!" cried Peveril.

Ancel remained calm. "We are in the privacy of your solar, my lord. No one will know what passes between us except you and me. I know you fostered with Lady Marian's father, the Earl of Waudum. That you went to York and had Oliver Metcalfe, a talented jeweler, create a silver pendant garnished with garnets, for Lady Marian to remember you by. She was to give the necklace to her unborn child someday."

Peveril sank back in his chair, all the fight gone from him. He raised sad eyes. "How do you know all of this, Sir Ancel? I have spoken to no one of this. Ever."

"I am in love with Lady Margery Ormond, the daughter Lady Marian gave birth to after she wed Lord Joseph Ormond. No other children resulted in the marriage. When Margery was five, Lady Marian became a widow and married for a second time at the king's direction."

"To Umfrey Vivers." Peveril's words came out in a whisper.

"Aye. Vivers was murdered in the recent peasants' revolt, along with one of his sons. Lady Marian also perished at the mob's hands."

Peveril winced upon hearing those words but Ancel pressed on.

"The king ordered me to secure Highfield because of its close proximity to London. I did as he asked—and 'twas there I fell in love with Lady Margery. She shared with me that moments before her mother lost her life. Lady Marian gave her a silver pendant inlaid with garnets and told her daughter that it was from her true father. Not Ormond. She didn't name her lover but I have discovered that you are Margery's real father."

Tears streamed down Peveril's cheeks. "We loved one another, Marian and I. I came to foster with her father when I was seven and she was four. We grew up together. Became friends. Fell in love." He sighed. "I think I loved Marian from the first moment I saw her. We finally became lovers, despite the fact that we both had been betrothed to others at an early age."

Peveril wiped his cheeks with the back of his hands. "We couldn't help ourselves. We made love a handful of times shortly before we both left for Kent. Ormond's estate was there and I was returning home to Bexley after taking my knightly oath. Marian and I both knew we would marry others and have to bury our love and never speak of it to anyone. I had the silver pendant made up for her to remember me by and told her that if a child resulted from our times together, she should give the necklace to him or her when they came of age."

The nobleman pushed his hands through his hair. "I had a matching piece made to wear on my cloak. I wear it still and think of my beloved every time I see it. We never laid eyes on one another again. And here I am a widower and Marian lies in a cold grave."

He grew quiet and Ancel gave Peveril time to process what he'd just learned.

Finally, he looked up and asked, "Would she see me now? Lady Margery? Are you here to ask if I will attend your nuptial mass?"

Ancel answered, "There will be no marriage unless you intervene, my lord. We must unite, you and me, and rescue Margery from a dire situation."

CHAPTER 23

MARGERY HATED EVERYTHING about her life. For ten days, Ancel had been absent from Highfield and she had never been more miserable. Not only did she feel as if a part of her had gone missing but gloom and doom had descended all around the estate, worse than when Lord Umfrey was alive. No one smiled anymore. Everyone kept their eyes down and their tongues still during meals in the great hall. The spirit of renewal Ancel brought had withered and then perished on the vine.

If only Thurstan Vivers would drop dead.

Her stepbrother had dragged her to London the very day he'd ordered the de Montforts off his lands. Thurstan said she was already packed for a journey and they had little time to lose since the Christmas season approached and courtiers often returned to their estates at that time. He was eager to see what price she would bring to his coffers.

But first, he had made her bathe him.

Margery understood part of her role at Highfield was to assist guests with their baths and she had done so willingly in the past. She pointed out to Thurstan that he was no visitor and could wash himself.

Her stepbrother had slapped her so hard that she'd been knocked to her knees. He began dragging her by her braid up the stairs as she pleaded with him, hating herself for doing so. Finally, he'd released her and told her to have water brought to the solar. She did as he asked and meekly assisted him, tamping down her revulsion as she scrubbed his hairy back and chest. He'd stood in the wooden tub and then had her clean his manhood. His shaft began to swell as her cloth touched it. Thurstan laughed as her face flamed before he finally sat again, insisting she bathe his legs and feet.

Once she'd helped dress him, they rode to London, Will bringing her trunk in the cart that had been bound for Kinwick only hours earlier. For three days, Thurstan paraded her before various courtiers as they assessed her looks for themselves or their unmarried sons. Margery thought they studied her as they might horseflesh. The new Baron of Highfield emphasized her beauty and good breeding but some of Thurstan's remarks caused her cheeks to burn in embarrassment. He made it clear that he wanted a substantial financial arrangement that benefited him in order for some nobleman to claim her as his.

They returned to Highfield, where the new baron read through written offers he'd received for her in marriage. He'd done nothing but complain the past several days, first wishing the offers were larger in nature. Then he narrowed the choice down to four gentlemen and claimed he couldn't decide between them. Margery ignored his conversation as he spoke aloud, trying to think of ways to prevent a marriage between her and the nobleman Thurstan selected.

She now worked beside Maud in the kitchen to finish preparations for today's Christmas feast at midday. Once they'd returned from London, Thurstan ordered her trunk removed from the cart and taken to the solar, telling Margery she was to wear her clothes from before, as well as return to the cleaning and scrubbing she had performed inside the keep in the past. She saw the sorrowful looks pass between other servants as she labored in various rooms but felt no shame in the hard work she performed. She would rather do it and keep out of Thurstan's sight, for he still frightened her. Margery had caught him looking at her twice since he'd returned, naked desire obvious on his face.

He did allow her to dine next to him on the dais and she would need to join him in the next few minutes since it was time for the feast to commence. Quickly, she washed her hands and face and dried them. As she crossed the crowded great hall, her heart was heavy. This would be her first Christmas without her mother. Margery missed her more each day, never more so than after Ancel had been banished. She thought of the man she loved at Kinwick, surrounded by his parents and large, loving family, and fought back the tears that threatened to fall. She refused to let her stepbrother see any sign of weakness in her.

Thurstan awaited her on the dais and even offered her his hand as she stepped up onto it and took a seat next to him. Agnes brought a trencher for them to share and placed a large portion of goose atop it. Margery had coated the bird in butter and saffron to give it this golden appearance after roasting. Though it looked appealing, she doubted she could force a bite of the goose down.

Her stepbrother leaned close to her ear, his lips almost grazing it. Margery sat frozen as he said, "I am delighted to share today's special meal with you, Margery. Who knew this time last year 'twould be only the two of us left at Highfield?"

She kept her eyes lowered to the trencher and remained silent.

Course after course came out, some cooked by Maud and others prepared by Margery herself. Thurstan gorged himself on the mince pie, smacking his mouth while licking his fingers clean.

"Did you make this pie?"

"Aye." She pushed another bite into her mouth and chewed slowly, forcing herself to swallow.

Suddenly, his hand rested on her thigh, clasping it and then kneading it roughly. Margery leaped to her feet and hopped down to the floor.

"Margery!" Thurstan shouted. "Margery, come back here."

She ignored him and lifted her skirts, running across a silent great hall and out the doors of the manor house. Racing away, she heard Thurstan's boots as he chased her. In her rush, Margery tripped and pitched forward, landing on her hands and knees.

Strong hands lifted her from the ground. Thurstan's fingers curled around her upper arms. Anger gleamed in his eyes.

"You will never insult me again," he said, his voice low and deadly.

Margery no longer cared what happened to her. She had lost Ancel and her mother. Gone was the chance for lasting happiness. She spit in his face and took pleasure in the shocked look that appeared.

"I will never marry anyone you want me to," she declared. "I refuse to be the golden goose that you sell to the highest bidder. I will flee to a convent before I marry a man of your choice. You cannot force me, Thurstan."

Rage glittered in his eyes. "What a splendid idea, Margery," he said. "I should have thought of it myself. Aye, I do believe I will force myself upon you."

He had turned her words against her. Cold fear nipped at her.

"I will glide my hands up your silken thighs. Tangle my fingers in your long locks. Drive my shaft into you until you beg for mercy. I will do it over and over until I break your spirit like that of a wild horse. And after you have submitted to me, you will bring gold into my coffers." His smile turned evil. "Mayhap you will even go to your new husband with my babe in your belly."

She struggled against him but his fingers only dug deeper into her tender flesh, bruising her. Then he released her so suddenly, it shocked her. She became rooted to the spot and didn't move when he drew back his fist and struck her. Nausea flared within her as she crumpled to the ground.

Thurstan lifted her and tossed her over his shoulder. Each step he took jarred her, making her belly roil. Margery didn't know where he took her as she watched the ground sway beneath her. Then he threw a door open and crossed a room. By its length, she realized he'd brought her to the solar. He placed her in a chair. She clung to the chair's arms, trying to stop the wave of dizziness that overcame her.

Before long, Thurstan returned with one of her chemises in hand. Margery watched him rip the silk apart, tearing it into long pieces. It confused her why he did this. Then she understood as he pinned her arms behind her and wrapped a strip of the material around her wrists. She tried to get up and couldn't. He did the same to her ankles, bringing them together and tightly knotting the cloth strips around them. He left briefly and brought back one of her new cotehardies from her trunk that he'd had brought to his solar. Ripping it down the center, he wrapped it around her chest and waist several times, tying her to the chair.

Anger boiled within her as she wrestled against the restraints. "I'll kill you," she ground out.

Thurstan only laughed.

"I'll get free somehow and kill myself," she threatened.

"I don't think so, Margery. You aren't going anywhere."

He reached to the ground for another strip of her chemise and gagged her with it, then stepped back to study his handiwork.

"You always seem so assured and capable," Thurstan told her. "I rather like seeing you at my mercy." He sighed. "I have fantasized for years about all the things I wanted to do to you. Finally, fantasy will become reality." The back of his hand glided along her cheek and slid down her throat.

Her rage vanished instantly, being replaced by fear. Margery froze, growing still, no longer fighting to free herself.

Thurstan's lips replaced his hand, sending a wave of revulsion through her. Without warning, his hands dropped and squeezed her breasts, his fingers digging into the tender flesh as his teeth sank painfully into her throat. She cried out behind the gag. He placed his face close to hers, his breath hot against her cheek. His fingers brushed against her nipples and then began pinching and twisting them cruelly. Margery screamed, the sound muffled by the gag. Thurstan laughed low, his eyes gleaming as they raked up and down her.

His hands left her breasts and flattened, sliding slowly down her ribs. He pinched her belly, causing her to flinch each time he did so, which made him chuckle. They moved to her thighs. Margery locked her knees together.

"You think you can stop me from touching you where I wish, Margery?" Thurstan asked, his eyes heating. His hand grasped her throat, his fingers tightening. Gradually, the pressure grew stronger and stronger and she began bucking, trying to get away yet knowing she couldn't escape. Margery thought she might pass out and dreaded what he would do to her if she did. Finally, the pressure eased up. She went limp, nausea rising within her.

"I think I have decided whose offer I will accept," he told her. "I will pen a missive to Lord Goldwell and tell him to come fetch you. But first, I will finish my lovely Christmas meal that you helped prepare." His eyes gleamed. "And after I do, we will have plenty of time before Lord Goldwell arrives." His knuckles grazed her cheek. "You may even thank me, Margery, for initiating you into the marriage act. That way, when fat old Goldwell straddles you, at least you will have known what it is like to be with a real man."

She glared at him, loathing the sight and sound of him. Though she couldn't say the words, she knew her face told him what she thought.

"First lesson," he said softly. "You will keep your eyes averted. You will be docile." He slapped her, hard. Her head snapped to the side, wrenching her neck. Stars danced before her eyes as light and darkness played against one another. Her eyes watered fiercely.

"I'll be back soon. Then our fun can begin."

Thurstan left the room. In the stillness, Margery began to quake with fear.

What if she was already with child? Would what Thurstan did to her hurt Ancel's babe or cause her to lose it? More than anything, she had wished Ancel's seed did grow within her so she would always have a part of him. And what if her womb was empty now but Thurstan filled it? Would this Lord Goldwell, whom she couldn't even remember from the many suitors Thurstan had spoken with, know what had been done to her? What if this nobleman realized the babe she carried was not his? Would he beat her and reject the child?

Knowing the kind of man her stepbrother was, it frightened Margery what Thurstan would do to her when he returned. Hot tears poured down her cheeks.

Margery wished she was dead.

AS THEY DREW near Highfield, Ancel hoped the earl would stay true to his word and claim Margery as his daughter. After he explained how Thurstan Vivers had returned and put a halt to Ancel's plans to marry Margery since he was her closet living male relative, the nobleman still seemed reluctant to acknowledge his daughter outside the walls of his own solar. Ancel argued that Lord Myles no longer had a wife who might berate him for his youthful folly and that many men at court had fathered bastards. Ancel hated using such an ugly word to describe Margery but he needed for Peveril to understand how important it was to ride to Highfield immediately.

Finally, the man had acquiesced at Ancel's insistence and sent for his captain of the guard, who designated a dozen soldiers to accompany them. They had ridden all yesterday afternoon until the sun set and risen at daybreak to continue their journey from Kent into Essex. Ancel heard a few of the men grumbling about missing their Christmas dinner today but he knew they could not afford to waste any time. He'd been gone long enough for Vivers to have already betrothed Margery to another man, if not outright married her off for the money he so greedily wanted. Ancel prayed to the Living Christ that they weren't too late and he would find Margery free to leave with them.

They turned onto the familiar road to Highfield, one he had patrolled himself. Though Ancel would have enjoyed becoming lord of this large estate, the land and title meant nothing to him next to the woman he loved. With each hoof beat that sounded, he heard the name *Margery* echoed in it.

Reaching the gates, the soldier on duty greeted him by name before he could identify himself.

"Sir Ancel, you are a sight for sore eyes. Hold on a moment." The main signaled down below and the gates slowly swung open.

Ancel acknowledged the man with a wave and encouraged those in his party to follow him as he galloped through the outer bailey and into the inner one. Arriving at the manor house, he leaped from his horse and turned while Lord Myles did the same.

"Wait here," the nobleman instructed his knights. "I'll send if I have need of you."

The two men marched to the door and pushed it open, not bothering to wait for a servant to answer a knock. Ancel thought it odd that no noise came from the great hall. Surely, all of the people of Highfield would have gathered to celebrate the holy day of Christmas with a massive feast. He stepped toward the open doors to the room and saw every table full but no one said a word as they ate.

Before he could rush inside and confront Vivers, Margery's friend, Sarah, passed by, a pitcher in her hand. Ancel called out to her.

The servant turned, her eyes widening in surprise as she caught sight of him. She slipped from the room and took his arm, pulling him away from the doorway.

"Oh, Sir Ancel, you must find Lady Margery," she proclaimed, her eyes welling with unshed tears.

"Has something happened to her?" he demanded, as Lord Myles moved closer to them.

"Lord Thurstan is the Devil himself," Sarah said. "He's demanded that Lady Margery return to wearing rags and cleaning and cooking like a common serf. Something happened between them during the meal a few minutes ago. She ran from the room and the baron chased after her." She swallowed. "I saw him carrying her up the stairs, slung over his shoulder. She was limp. I fear he's struck her again."

"Again?" Ancel asked, rage exploding inside him.

Sarah nodded, misery evident on her face. "He's punished her a few times since he banished you and your parents from Highfield. Everything has changed for the worse, my lord. I am afraid he will kill her before he can marry her off."

"Return to the great hall," Ancel instructed. "Tell no one that you've seen us."

Sarah nodded and scurried inside the room.

"'Tis worse than I thought," Lord Myles murmured. "You were right to convince me to come. We must remove my daughter from this dangerous situation at once."

"Follow me."

Ancel rushed up the stairs and down the corridor to the solar, the only place Vivers would have taken Margery. He flung open the door and entered, looking around. Then he stopped abruptly, his eyes barely comprehending what he saw.

Margery. Shivering. Secured to a chair. Her face bruised. One eye swelling.

Ancel reined in the wrath that poured from every pore. He wouldn't direct his anger at her. She needed comfort and reassurance from him now. He approached her slowly and saw tears glistening on her cheeks.

Then he watched her eyes change from dull and lifeless. They filled with hope—with love—for him.

Ancel eased the gag from her mouth. His hands cupped her face as tears filled his own eyes. He tenderly pressed his lips against hers, wishing he could take away all the horrors she had experienced since they'd parted.

"Let me free you, love," he said gently.

Fresh tears cascaded down her porcelain cheeks. "Thank you for coming," she said, "but there is nothing you can do, Ancel."

"You're right about that, sweetheart. But *he* can." Ancel turned and motioned his companion forward.

Pain laced the nobleman's gaze as he said, "I am your father, Margery."

CHAPTER 24

MARGERY STARED BLANKLY at the stranger standing before her. Wait. Somehow, she remembered seeing him before yet she could not remember where. Then Ancel's words sank in.

This was her father.

The eyes that looked down on her in pity mirrored her own, warm brown rimmed in amber. Then she saw the pin fastened onto his cloak. The silver stood out against the black wool. Garnets studded the piece. Its unique designed resemble the one on her silver pendant.

"Father?" Her voice broke, thick with emotion. She continued to stare at him as Ancel used his blade to free her from the restraints Thurstan had placed around her limbs and body. Margery sucked in a quick breath as her hands and feet began throbbing painfully.

Ancel rubbed her bruised wrists with his strong fingers. "'Tis the blood rushing back and through your limbs, sweetheart. It won't hurt for long." He did the same to her ankles as her eyes never left those of the stranger who gazed down at her kindly.

Margery stood on shaky legs, with Ancel holding fast to her elbow to steady her.

But the nobleman—her father—pushed Ancel aside and wrapped Margery in a long embrace, swaying back and forth with her as he tenderly stroked her hair. Finally, he released her but captured her hands.

"I am Lord Myles Peveril, Earl of Mauntell," he told her. "Lady Marian, your mother, was the love of my life." He paused. "I am so sorry that she is gone."

"She gave me your necklace moments before she died," Margery said.

Her father lifted the pendant that hung around her neck, a smile playing about his lips. "I had this made for her shortly before we parted. Margery, you must know how very much we wished to wed but our parents had pledged us to others. I will tell you about the past later but 'tis imperative that we leave Highfield now."

"Not until I confront Vivers and what he has done," Ancel said.

"Nay. I don't want you to challenge him," Margery pleaded. "I only want to leave this place for good."

"But he—"

"He is a fiend. I know this. As dishonorable as any man can be." She placed her palm against his cheek. "But he isn't worthy of a moment of your time. Ignore him, Ancel. That will enrage him and be punishment enough. Please. Do this for me."

She saw him wrestling, wanting to bring justice to the man who had hurt her yet wanting to honor her wishes at the same time.

"Do as my daughter asks," her father urged. "Let us leave this place and never return."

Ancel's hand covered hers. "Only for you, my love. And if I see Thurstan Vivers outside the gates of Highfield, I make no promise of what might occur between us."

"Fair enough," she agreed.

"Do you have anything that you want to take with you?" he asked.

She had slipped into the hidden passageway when she cleaned the solar a few days ago, knowing Thurstan was out riding. Margery had reclaimed the necklace and ring her mother gave her that had been given to Marian by her father. She had kept both pieces inside a deep pocket, not wanting to wear them and have her stepbrother steal them away from her.

Then she remembered Whitefoot. Margery had left the dog with Sarah when they headed for Kinwick. Sarah let her know the pup was safe since her friend had kept Whitefoot out of Thurstan's sight.

"Could we stop by Sarah's and claim Whitefoot? She has been

hiding him from my stepbrother. If he knew what the dog meant to me, he would have killed him on the spot."

Ancel entwined his fingers with hers. "Of course."

They left the solar, her father trailing behind them. They hurried down the staircase and as they reached the bottom, she gripped his hand tightly.

Thurstan made his way toward them, his face red in anger.

"I told you to leave and never come back, de Montfort," he growled. "Release her. Margery, return to the solar at once."

Her father stepped forward. "You will no longer command my daughter to do as you please."

"Who are you?" Thurstan demanded, wariness lighting his eyes.

"I am the Earl of Mauntell—and Margery's father."

"You must be joking. Margery's father was Lord Joseph Ormond," countered Thurstan. "He died many years ago. Now step aside, old man."

Lord Myles held his ground. "You have no authority over Margery, Vivers. I legally claim her before all present as my natural child. Lady Marian carried Margery in her belly before she ever wed Ormond. As her father, I alone determine her destiny, not a stepbrother who has been so cruel to her. Now step aside, man, before I run my sword through you."

When Thurstan hesitated, her father continued. "I am not a man that you wish to make an enemy of, Vivers, for I have the king's ear. I have even negotiated with foreign governments to bring back a bride for King Richard and will attend the royal wedding as an honored guest. I advise you to let us pass."

Margery noticed many of Highfield's people had spilled out from the great hall and listened to the exchange between the two men. She caught sight of Sarah standing with her husband, crying, but wearing a smile. Their eyes met and then Margery knew she couldn't leave her friend behind.

Turning to Ancel, she asked, "Could Sarah and Harry come with us?"

Ancel nodded. "If they wish."

A look of defeat caused her stepbrother's shoulders to slump. Ancel led Margery toward the door, signaling to Sarah and Harry to join them as Lord Myles ushered them outside.

As they hurried away from the manor house, Ancel said to Harry, "Lady Margery wishes for you and Sarah—and Whitefoot—to leave Highfield and join us."

The carpenter beamed as he said, "I can have my tools packed up in the cart in no time, my lord." He looked to Sarah. "Is this what you want, Wife?"

Sarah threw her arms around her husband. "Aye!" she cried, covering his face in kisses.

They reached the spot where their guard waited. Ancel told the Bacons, "Gather your things and meet us at the juncture where Highfield's road crosses that of the one to London."

"Aye, my lord." Harry grabbed Sarah's hand and the couple ran toward his carpenter's shop.

As Ancel placed Margery atop Storm, she saw Thurstan had left the keep. He began to shout at them.

"You have ruined everything," he railed. "I cannot find where Father kept his fortune. I needed you to bring gold to me, Margery. I command you to remain at Highfield. You cannot do this to me. We took you in. Gave you a home. You owe it to me to stay."

She glared at him in return, taking delight that he hadn't remembered the hidden passageway containing his father's gold. "I will never set foot at Highfield again," she told him, her head high. "And I hope you rot in Hell, Thurstan Vivers—with your father and brother."

Ancel turned Storm and the group of soldiers, counting her father among them, galloped away. Margery relaxed against Ancel as they rode to the agreed meeting point and waited several minutes until Harry Bacon appeared in a cart with Sarah beside him. Her friend wore a huge smile and had Whitefoot sitting in her lap. It surprised Margery that Christine Morley and Clifton Walters sat in the back of the vehicle. She only wished everyone from Highfield could desert her stepbrother and come with them now.

As the cart approached, Christine called out, "Lady Margery will need a seamstress to produce new clothes for her." She grinned. "And something new made up for her wedding."

Clifton added, "My loyalties lie with you, Sir Ancel. If you are not to be the Baron of Highfield, then Thurstan Vivers will have to find himself a new steward. I hope it's all right that Christine and I chose to come with Harry and Sarah."

Ancel assured the pair that they were welcomed. Quickly, he and Lord Myles decided that half of the guard would accompany them back to Kinwick, while Lord Myles returned to his own estate. Her father promised that he would arrive at Kinwick in time for his daughter and Ancel's wedding.

The escort party broke in two, heading in opposite directions. As Ancel urged Storm on and Highfield fell from view, Margery truly believed she could leave her nightmares behind.

"WE ARE ALMOST home," Ancel said in Margery's ear.

Anticipation built inside her. She had heard so much about the de Montfort estate and was eager to finally see it in person. She wondered if any guests had come for Christmas Day and if any relatives remained behind since the feast day had come and gone. Their journey from Highfield took two days and they would be arriving close to the midday meal.

"There. Up ahead." Ancel's arm tightened about her waist as they came over the rise.

Kinwick took her breath away.

Rolling hills surrounded the estate, with the castle perched at the top of one. Margery had thought Highfield large but her former home seemed dwarfed compared to this place. Minutes later, the riding party approached the gates and they opened in recognition of Ancel so their horses didn't have to break stride. People everywhere called out friendly greetings to Ancel, which he returned. Pride swelled within her at how popular he seemed among the workers. Even soldiers in the training yard paused and waved as they rode by, headed for the keep.

As they drew near, Margery thought she saw double, for two Merryns stood side by side. As they came closer, she realized that one of them was much younger than Ancel's mother. Margery figured the woman to be Alys, Ancel's twin. Joy filled her face as she ran toward them.

"I knew you were coming," Alys proclaimed. "You can ask Kit. He'll vouch for me."

Ancel leaped from his horse and Alys fell into his arms in a happy reunion. Then he reached up and pulled Margery from Storm's back. Alys immediately kissed both of Margery's cheeks and held her tightly.

Pulling away, she said, "I told Mother that all would be well. That you and Ancel would soon arrive at Kinwick. 'Tis why I made Kit stay when he insisted that we leave for Brentwood this morning. I felt inside that you would show up today."

By this time, Geoffrey and Merryn strolled over to greet them. Both de Montforts embraced her and expressed how happy they were to see her.

"Come inside," Merryn said. "This brisk north wind has made it a very cold day. We want to hear everything."

"We have much to tell," Ancel said.

A handsome man with a warrior's build and green eyes threw an arm around Alys' shoulder. "You were right. As always." He laughed as he looked at Margery. "I am Kit Emory, Alys' husband and father to the terrible twins and a younger, much calmer son. I will warn you now that our twins can be a handful."

"Philippa and Wyatt are merely high-spirited five-year-olds," Alys confided to Margery. "The same as Ancel and I were at their age."

"Nay, Alys," Geoffrey interjected. "I'm afraid they are more like their uncle Hal with each passing day. I met you and Ancel when you were close to Philippa and Wyatt's age. You two were well behaved with only a bit of mischief in you."

"That's because Mother always had us well in hand," Alys said. "I may have inherited her gift of healing but I have trouble controlling my own children as she could with but a look. Mayhap, you should move to Brentwood and help me manage things, Mother."

Margery frowned, not because of what Alys teased about. It was Geoffrey's words about meeting Ancel and Alys that puzzled her. He had to be Ancel's father, for they were mirror images of one another, much as Merryn and Alys were.

Ancel slipped his arm about her waist. "I know you have questions. I see it on your face. It's all part of our family lore. Go inside with the others. I wish to rub Storm down to prevent him from nipping at anyone else, as well as see your father's men settled." He gave her a swift kiss. "I will be inside shortly."

She followed the others into the keep and then to the solar. Merryn had stopped a servant and told her they would take their noon meal upstairs. On the way, a tall young boy fell into step with them. Then Margery realized it was a girl who dressed as a boy.

"You must be Lady Margery," the girl said. "I am Nan, one of Ancel's sisters."

She should have guessed, for the younger de Montfort had her father's dark hair, worn in a single braid, and her mother's sapphire eyes. But the fact that Nan dressed as a young man gave Margery pause.

Then someone took her hand. Margery glanced down and saw a child with golden blond hair and the most unusual violet eyes looking up at her with curiosity.

"And who might you be?" she asked.

"I am Jessimond, my lady. I am five. But halfway to six," she said in a serious tone.

Margery bit her lip to hide a smile. "'Tis nice to meet you, Jessimond. Are you also a de Montfort?"

The young girl nodded eagerly. "I am the youngest de Montfort, though I came from somewhere else. But Nan found me, so I am sister to her and all the others. And I am an aunt to Alys' children, even though they are barely older than me," she said proudly—then giggled.

Margery found these de Montforts more intriguing by the minute. She wanted to learn where Nan found this golden-haired angel and how she came to be Ancel's youngest sister, as well as find out about the mystery behind Geoffrey's words.

"You are going to wed my brother?" Jessimond asked solemnly.

She nodded. "We will marry next month, early in the New Year."

"Good," Jessimond proclaimed, "because I like you." She released Margery's hand and skipped ahead to take her mother's instead.

They reached the solar, gathering around the large table within it. A servant named Tilda came and took Jessimond away to eat with her cousins, so that left seven of them around the table after Ancel arrived. As they ate, it took the better part of an hour for her and Ancel to describe the events that had occurred since Thurstan Vivers arrived at Highfield and separated Margery from Ancel and his parents.

She listened with great interest as Ancel described his journey to York and how he went to where her mother had grown up just west of the city. Then he recounted going from shop to shop, speaking with jewelers, trying to track down the origins of her silver pendant. At that point in the story, Margery had to show it to Alys, Kit, and Nan since they'd never seen it before.

What fascinated her most was hearing about Ancel traveling to Saint Leonard's Hospital and his revealing conversation with Oliver Metcalfe, the jeweler who had crafted her mother's necklace and her father's matching pin.

"I promised if I was ever north again, I would stop in and visit him." Ancel took Margery's hand in his and said, "I think we should go to York someday so Oliver can meet you and see why it was so important for me to find your father."

"But what next, Ancel?" Nan demanded. "How did you meet Margery's father?"

"That was the next portion of my travels, though I had actually met the man at court," he said, then he recounted his meeting with

Lord Myles at his country estate in Kent. "He told me that Margery's mother was the love of his life and we left on Christmas Eve to head to Margery's rescue at Highfield, which is in Essex."

Ancel squeezed Margery's hand as his gaze met hers. Margery knew he would skip over the details of how they had found her. So far, no one had asked about the swelling about her eye. She knew from how tender her cheek was that it must be bruised, as well.

As she expected, Ancel breezed through this part of his tale, though he did emphasize how bravely her father had confronted Thurstan and then how they marched from the keep as Thurstan ranted and raved and begged Margery to come back because he had no gold.

"And we have four others that came with us," Ancel concluded. "They are traveling by cart and will arrive in the next day or so."

"Who left the estate?" asked Alys.

"Sarah Bacon is one," Margery revealed. "She is my dearest friend and worked at the keep for many years. With her is her husband, Harry, who was the carpenter at Highfield."

"We can always use a good carpenter," Geoffrey said. "And Merryn will certainly find a place for Sarah. Who else?"

"Clifton Walters also deserted the baron," Margery said. "He revealed that his loyalty was only to Ancel. Since Ancel would not receive the estate from the king, thanks to my stepbrother's reappearance, Clifton wanted to return to Kinwick."

"But that's only three," Merryn pointed out. "Who is the fourth?"

"Christine, a seamstress that Ancel hired to come to Highfield," Margery said. "I left with no clothing. Thurstan would have had no use for her and Christine was smart enough to realize that I would need new clothes."

"And something to wear for our wedding," added Ancel. "Besides, I think Clifton may be sweet on Christine."

"Oh, I forgot something most important. My dog, Whitefoot, is with Sarah in the cart. Ancel brought me a puppy as a companion a few months ago. He follows me about wherever I go."

"He's a water spaniel and very smart," Ancel said. "We couldn't leave poor Whitefoot behind."

They continued talking the rest of the afternoon. Merryn said that they must decide when the wedding would take place because she would need to send messengers to various estates to invite their guests.

"Ancel's cousins, Elysande and Avelyn, will expect to attend," Merryn said. "And their husbands, Michael and Kenric, will accompany them, as well as their children." She turned to Margery. "My brother and his wife live at Wellbury, my former home. Their estate adjoins ours. And, of course, Hardie and Johamma must come, too. Our sons, Hal and Edward, foster with them."

"Don't forget Raynor and Beatrice," Geoffrey said. "Raynor was the first man to put a sword in Ancel's hand and had a huge part in raising him and Alys."

Another cryptic statement which Margery would question Ancel about when they were alone. But for now, she added, "And don't forget my father. Lord Myles returned to his estate after helping rescue me but agreed to come to Kinwick for our wedding."

Alys looked at her brother. "Let's talk about important things. Are you going to send to London for material for Margery's new wardrobe?"

Everyone laughed heartily. In their laughter, Margery knew she'd found a place where she belonged.

CHAPTER 25

ONCE THEY HAD eaten the evening meal, Geoffrey took Ancel aside and said, "You have had a busy time since we last saw you. I am happy that you found Margery's father and that Lord Myles stepped up and claimed her as his offspring."

"I worried whether he would or not," Ancel confided. "It took some convincing on my part. That he did will keep me forever in his debt."

"Margery suffered at Vivers' hand," his father stated, a sympathetic look in his eyes.

"Aye. 'Twas a bad situation, Father."

"You two have not spent a moment alone in some time," his father pointed out. "Why don't you take Margery up to the solar now for some privacy? After that, I'm sure your mother and Alys will discreetly tend to her bruising."

"Thank you, Father." Ancel turned and saw Margery deep in conversation with Alys. The two women had spoken nonstop during tonight's meal. It made him happy that Margery had taken to his twin so well. Alys was, and always had been, his other half. The bond between them might be invisible but it bound them together inexplicably.

He walked over to where they sat conversing by the fire. "Pardon me for interrupting, but I would like to spend a little time alone with my future wife."

Alys stood. "You have chosen well, Brother. Margery is the one for you." She kissed his cheek. "Kit and I and the children will return to

Brentwood in the morning to tend to a few matters but we will come back in plenty of time for your wedding."

His sister looked to Margery. "Come by our bedchamber for the salve I spoke of. After you use it for a few days, you will look like your old self again."

"I will," Margery promised as she rose. "I am so glad we finally met, Alys."

The women embraced. "I am happy to have another sister," Alys declared. "We must visit each other often." Alys returned to Kit's side, where he played on the floor with their children.

Ancel tucked Margery's hand into the crook of his arm and led her from the great hall.

"Where are we going?" she asked.

"Father suggested we go to the solar and relax for a while since we haven't been alone in some time."

A fire greeted them inside the room. Ancel poured wine for them and sat in the chair his father usually claimed. He pulled Margery onto his lap, not wanting her far from him. One arm went around her waist as he entwined their fingers together. She gave out a contented sigh and rested her head against his shoulder.

"I want to answer some of the questions I believe you have."

"Only if you wish," she murmured, relishing his nearness.

"Oh, so you would marry me despite being curious about my family's history?"

Margery lifted her head. "I would wed you tonight if we could." She placed her head back.

"Still, I would have you know a few things." He paused. "I haven't spoken of this since I was a small boy." His fingers tightened on hers. Ancel took a deep breath and made himself relax as the memories whirled inside his mind.

"My father disappeared the day after he wed Mother. He was gone several years. She gave birth to Alys and me. Our cousin, Raynor, helped her as best he could with both the estate and us. For the most part, though, Mother ran Kinwick on her own and did a wonderful job raising two children without a father."

Then the story poured out from him. He told Margery of Geoffrey de Montfort's imprisonment by a wicked earl seeking vengeance and how the earl's son released Geoffrey upon his father's death. He explained how another knight, who almost wed his mother before his father reappeared, carried his jealousy to the extreme and imprisoned Geoffrey in his own dungeon, hoping to win Merryn and Kinwick.

"I was young. Barely older than Alys' twins are now. I had no idea that a knight could act dishonorably and break his word of honor. Fortunately, we found Father and he sought justice against Symond Benedict from King Edward. It took time for my father to heal, both physically and spiritually. But his great love for Mother had always given him hope during the years they spent apart. Together again, they found their love could conquer all the wrongs."

Ancel swallowed. "I have never talked to another soul about this but I wanted you to know, for their story is a part of my own."

Margery pressed a soft kiss against his jaw but remained silent.

He waited and then said, "You will meet Raynor at the wedding. He acted like a father to Alys and me. Raynor will always hold a special place in my heart. I think you will adore his wife, Beatrice. She is the tiniest thing, with a will of iron and a heart full of kindness. Their two boys foster with my uncle Hugh, while Cecily, their only daughter, has recently returned home from fostering at Wellbury."

"I look forward to meeting them and all of your relatives."

"As for Jessimond? Nan and Father stumbled upon her. She'd been placed in a basket and left on Kinwick lands, practically a newborn. Though we tried to find them, her parents were never located. Mother loves nothing more than a small babe, so she and Father embraced Jessimond as their own. She is the youngest de Montfort, loved as much by them as any of their other children."

Margery raised her head and gazed into Ancel's eyes. "Thank you for sharing all of this with me. It makes me love you—and your family—even more. You come from loving, generous parents. I feel privileged to be marrying into the de Montfort family and will be proud to carry your name."

With that, her lips touched his. The kiss started gently and then heated up. Ancel's tongue slipped into Margery's mouth and drank in her sweetness. His hand caressed her neck and dipped to her breast, fondling it, teasing the nipple till it stood at attention. His mouth trailed downward, kissing the top of her perfect globes, wishing he could do more. Much more.

He lifted his head and took a deep breath, trying to gain control of his emotions. "I don't think it would be wise to continue this further. Father may have offered us the solar for some privacy but I don't think that extended to finding us naked in his and Mother's bed," he teased.

"We will be together soon," Margery promised.

He thought a moment. "Are you—do you know—if you are with child from our previous coupling?"

"'Tis too early to tell." She smiled. "If I am, I hope you will be pleased."

Ancel smiled. "I will always be pleased with you, Margery. Forever and ever." His mouth returned to hers and they kissed until a discreet knock sounded at the solar's door.

He stood and placed Margery in a nearby chair and went to answer it. His mother swept in, a basket on her arm.

She gave them a knowing smile but merely said, "Let me look at your face, Margery. I have something that will help heal it quickly."

Ancel excused himself and left the room, his step light—and his heart even lighter.

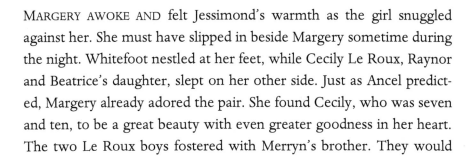

MARGERY AWOKE AND felt Jessimond's warmth as the girl snuggled against her. She must have slipped in beside Margery sometime during the night. Whitefoot nestled at her feet, while Cecily Le Roux, Raynor and Beatrice's daughter, slept on her other side. Just as Ancel predicted, Margery already adored the pair. She found Cecily, who was seven and ten, to be a great beauty with even greater goodness in her heart. The two Le Roux boys fostered with Merryn's brother. They would arrive today with Hugh and Milla Mantel in time for the wedding, as would Lord Hardwin and Lady Johamma, who would bring Ancel's brothers, Hal and Edward.

She lay in bed, happiness spilling from her. Alys and Kit had returned as promised, bringing their three children. Ancel's cousin, Elysande, came three days ago with her husband and their three children. Elysande's sister, Avelyn, arrived a day after with her husband and their two children. The keep had been full of noise and laughter as Margery got to know Ancel's extended family.

It was a bit overwhelming, though, and she was grateful when Elysande took her to the quiet of the stables. Ancel had told Margery that Elysande knew more about horses than anyone in all of England, male or female. She had given Margery a riding lesson and made small adjustments in the way Margery held the reins and sat on her horse. They had ridden together again yesterday in the meadow and now Margery bloomed with confidence. She hoped when she next rode out from Kinwick that it might be on her own horse. More than anything, she wanted Ancel to be proud of her.

A knock sounded at the door and Merryn entered, bearing a tray. Alys and Beatrice followed closely behind.

"Wake up, everyone," Merryn called out. "Margery needs to break her fast quickly since hot water for her bath will soon arrive."

Nan grumbled from the other bed as she sat up, complaining about what Merryn insisted she wear for the wedding.

"Christine worked hard on your new cotehardie, Nan, and you look wonderful in it," her mother said firmly. "You may not appreciate it but you will wear it."

Nan remained silent but Margery knew the girl would please her mother and wear her new clothing. At least for today.

Alys shrugged as she told Margery, "I could say the same thing to Philippa and she would argue with me all the day long. Mother has the magic touch when it comes to children."

Margery shared her meal with Jessimond, but the small child ate more than she did. Her excitement kept her from eating much. Then

Elysande and Avelyn arrived to help her with her bath. Avelyn washed her hair, while Elysande laid out her clothes. Ancel's cousins helped dry and dress her, then Cecily combed out her hair as Margery sat by the fire in order for it to dry more quickly.

Suddenly, Philippa burst into the room and ran to her mother, tears spilling down her cheeks.

"What's wrong?" Alys asked as she pulled her daughter into her lap.

"Raynor is mean," Philippa declared.

"Why do you say that?" her mother asked.

"He won't make a sword for Wyatt and me. He made one for you and Uncle Ancel, Mother. He should make one for us."

"Did Raynor give you a reason, Philippa?" Beatrice asked.

The girl's bottom lip stuck out. "He said we weren't old enough. That we had to be six."

"Well, that is when he made wooden swords for Ancel and me," Alys said. "You and Wyatt are only five, Philippa. When you turn six, you will be taller and stronger and more capable of holding your wooden sword and learning how to use it."

"But that's too long," complained Philippa.

"Nay, little love. The two of you will be six come March. 'Tis only two months away."

"So Raynor will make us a sword then?"

"I will make sure he does," Beatrice assured Philippa.

The child beamed as she climbed off her mother's lap. She took Jessimond's hand. "Let's play." The two girls skipped out of the room, Whitefoot wagging his tail merrily as he followed them.

"See what you have to look forward to, Margery?" asked Alys.

"I cannot wait." Margery grinned. "Even if I have terrible twins."

With her hair combed and dry, Avelyn arranged it in an artful style. Merryn gave Margery a hand mirror to see the results. Her reflection pleased her. Not only had Avelyn done a worthy job, but the salve Margery had used on her face had rid her of any swelling and bruises. She would go to Ancel looking her best, wearing her new chemise, kirtle, and cotehardie that Christine had created from material brought back from London.

"I cannot imagine a more beautiful bride," Merryn said as she kissed Margery's cheek.

"The russet and blue make for a lovely combination," Cecily agreed. "I hope I will marry in finery like this."

"I will be happy to lend Christine and her talents to you, Cecily, when your time comes," Margery promised.

A loud rap drew the attention of all the women packed inside the bedchamber. Geoffrey stuck his head in and said, "It's time."

Everyone filed from the room, leaving only Margery and Merryn. Geoffrey stepped inside and took Margery's hands.

"Merryn and I already look upon you as a daughter, Margery. The joy we see on Ancel's face tells us of the great love he has for you." He bent and kissed her cheek. "Your father awaits you. Let me escort you to him."

They left the room. At the end of the corridor, at the top of the stairs, Margery saw Lord Myles. It still amazed her that Ancel had found this nobleman and that he'd acknowledged her as his offspring.

Geoffrey and Merryn preceded them down the staircase. Her father lifted her hand and brushed a kiss against her knuckles.

"You are a vision of loveliness, my dear. You resemble your mother in so very many ways. I only wish she could be here to share this day with you."

She saw the wistful look in his eyes and ached for him. He had been forced to let go of the woman he loved and spent a lifetime apart from her.

"I believe she is watching over us, Father, and that she is happy we have found one another."

"I think so, too," he agreed. "But come, Daughter. You have a man who loves you dearly. He is impatiently waiting for you outside the Kinwick chapel."

Her father led them from the keep and across the bailey to where a large group gathered in the cold, though it pleased her that the day proved to be a sunny one. Margery saw many of the relatives she had recently met, as well as others who worked the land or served the de Montforts in different capacities. Sarah gave her a wave and smile, while Harry winked at her.

Then suddenly, Margery stood before Ancel, resplendent in midnight blue and gold. The chill of the winter day dissipated when she saw the heat in his hazel eyes. He took her hand in his and drew her near. Warmth enveloped her.

They spoke their vows in front of the crowd but they only had eyes for one another. Minutes later, the priest called for Ancel to produce the wedding ring. He turned to Hal, his brother, who acted as the best man. A grinning Hal handed the ring to Ancel, who faced Margery and slipped it onto her thumb. She chose to look into his eyes as he spoke his vows to her.

"In the name of the Father." He withdrew the ring and placed it on her first finger. "And of the Son." He changed it again to the next finger. "And of the Holy Spirit. Amen."

Once more, Margery felt Ancel pull the ring away before he slid it onto the finger where it would rest from now on.

"With this ring, I thee wed. This gold and silver, I thee give. With my body, I thee worship and with this dowry, I thee endow."

She tore her gaze from him to finally look at the ring that would forever be a part of her—and gasped. The ring wasn't the silver band they had chosen in London. Instead, it was an intricate pattern of garnets inlaid within a silver band. It closely resembled her pendant and her father's pin.

Tears sprang to Margery's eyes. "Nothing could have pleased me more," she whispered. "I will cherish it always."

Ancel smiled. "This wedding ring is a symbol of your past, the present, and our future. May we share a life full of joyful days." He leaned in and whispered into her ear, "And may our nights be full of unbridled passion."

As her new husband kissed her, Margery felt whole, enveloped in Ancel's love.

EPILOGUE

ANCEL LED MARGERY down the road that ran alongside Westminster Abbey. The streets teemed with people hoping to see the newly-wedded royal couple emerge after the ceremony took place. He had brought her to see the church when they last visited London but this would be the first time she had entered it.

"Every English king has been crowned here for over seventy years," he told her. "At the moment of their crowning, they are seated upon a throne called Saint Edward's Chair. And this will be the sixth time a royal wedding has taken place here, though the last one was almost a hundred years ago."

He seated her and gave her a swift kiss. "I'm sorry I have to leave you alone, my love, but duty calls. I will be allowed to sit with you at the wedding feast, though." Ancel kissed her again, bringing a rush of powerful feelings that occurred inside her every time he did so.

Margery blew him a kiss as he hurried off, looking splendid and so broad and tall. He would be in the group of royal guardsmen that escorted the king into the church. She bided her time, studying the architecture of the abbey and listening to conversations around her.

"I hear she's quite plain."

"What do you expect from someone from *Bohemia?*"

"Did the king truly have to pay to wed her instead of receiving a dowry?"

"Aye, he gave it to her brother, Wenceslas, the King of Bohemia. Though Anne is supposedly cultured and connected to royalty throughout Europe, she is quite poor."

"I hear he's smitten with her already."

"She brought an escort of many Bohemian ladies and gentlemen with her. The king supposedly will grant annuities to many of them."

"That won't go over well at court. I hear much criticism regarding her."

"There is always criticism when a new queen arrives in England."

Margery felt sorry for Lady Anne. She had enjoyed meeting her and hated all the cruel remarks being made about England's future queen.

With much fanfare, King Richard entered the church and made his way to the front. Margery thrilled to see Ancel close to the king. It still amazed her that a boy of four and ten ruled their country and that Lady Anne was less than a year older than her husband-to-be.

A buzz ran across the church as the bride came down the aisle, wearing purple silk with shoots of gold in the skirts and a jeweled collar bearing one of her badges, the ostrich. Rubies studded the entire bird, which was surrounded by a field of large pearls. Lady Anne looked quite small as she was led to where the Bishop of London stood with the king.

But what warmed Margery's heart was the smile the king gave his bride as she joined him at the altar. It spoke of true affection—even intimacy—between them. For a royal marriage to begin in love was unheard of, yet Margery knew what love was like and sensed this young couple possessed it and would cherish one another just as she and Ancel did.

After their vows, the bishop gave a short homily. She spent her time admiring her husband instead of listening. Then the newly-married couple sealed their union with a kiss and the royal guard surrounded them. The knights accompanied them back up the aisle and outside. Margery heard the cheers from the crowds gathered in front of the church.

She waited patiently since Ancel said he would return for her as soon as he could. When he did, most of the wedding guests had vacated the abbey.

Her husband took her hand and brought her into the wintry day. They struggled against the mass of people teeming in the streets as they made their way toward the palace. Almost an hour later, they arrived. Margery thought they would be late but Ancel assured her that the feasting hadn't begun yet. He brought her through a maze of corridors, confusing her to no end but then she spotted a few familiar items in the halls and knew she'd been this way before.

"We are going to the king's rooms?" she asked.

"Aye. He asked to speak with us briefly before the feasting begins. I know not what he wants."

They gained immediate entrance and found the king with a single servant who removed the heavy crown that he'd worn during the nuptial mass. The king dismissed the man and faced them.

"Ah, my favorite knight and his new wife. 'Tis good to see you."

Margery dipped into a deep curtsey as Ancel bowed next to her.

"Rise. I haven't much time."

They did as commanded. The king sat and sighed. "I am hosting a tournament for a few days to celebrate my marriage. I would like for you to enter it, Ancel, as my personal representative."

"Of course, your highness. What events would you have me compete in?"

The king told him and then said, "My new queen will be crowned in two days by Archbishop Courteney in Westminster Abbey. She would like Lady Margery to be present as one of her ladies-in-waiting." He frowned. "She brought far too many Bohemian women with her for my taste. I want her to work on her English, my lady. She likes you. Trusts you. If you are willing to serve her, I will grant you apartments here at court."

Margery looked to Ancel and he nodded. "We both will serve you in whatever capacity you ask, sire."

"Good, because I want you at court a majority of the time. I need you here, Ancel, no matter what Mauntell says. He thinks the two of you should stay at his Kent estate for the foreseeable future."

"We have been invited to visit my father so I can get to know him better," Margery said. "But there's been no talk of us living at Bexley."

The king thought a moment. "Oh, 'tis the first I have seen you since Lord Myles and I spoke. Peveril has no issue, other than Lady Margery. He has petitioned me for his title and estate to go to Sir Ancel upon his death instead of reverting to the Crown." A look of pure boyish mischief crossed the king's face. "A better title and an even larger estate than Highfield—and Lady Margery as your wife. What do you say to that, my friend?"

Ancel smiled broadly. "I would say that whatever pleases your majesty will please my wife and me."

Richard burst out laughing. "Then the queen and I reserve the rights to you for now. You can have Bexley—and Kinwick—down the line."

"Your majesty, it's time," a servant said from the doorway.

The king rose. "Shall we go celebrate my marriage?" He strode from the room and Margery and Ancel fell in behind him.

They reached the banqueting hall and Ancel led her to a table filled with his fellow knights and their ladies. After many toasts to the good health of the king and queen, her husband turned and held his cup up to her. Margery brought hers up, as well.

"To us, my love, my dearest love," Ancel proclaimed. "And to you, my wife, my life. Margery de Montfort, I am forever—and always—yours."

Ancel kissed her amidst all the noise that surrounding them but, in that moment, Margery felt as if they were alone. As he deepened the kiss, she knew their love would stand the test of time.

The End

About the Author

As a child, Alexa Aston gathered her neighborhood friends together and made up stories for them to act out, her first venture into creating memorable characters. Following her passion for history and love of learning, she became a teacher who began writing on the side to maintain her sanity in a sea of teenage hormones.

Alexa's historical romances use history as a backdrop to place her characters in extraordinary circumstances, where their intense desire for one another grows into the treasured gift of love.

She is the author of *The Knights of Honor*, a medieval romance series that takes place in 14th century England during the reign of Edward III and centers on the de Montfort family. Each romance focuses on the code of chivalry that bound knights of this era.

A native Texan, Alexa lives with her husband in a Dallas suburb, where she eats her fair share of dark chocolate and plots out stories while she walks every morning. She enjoys reading, watching movies and sports, and can't get enough of *Fixer Upper* or *Game of Thrones*. Alexa also writes romantic suspense, western historicals, and standalone medieval novels as Lauren Linwood.

Alexa loves to hear from her readers. You can connect with her through FB, Twitter, and her website: alexaaston.com.

Facebook:

facebook.com/authoralexaaston

Twitter:

twitter.com/AlexaAston

Newsletter sign-up:

madmimi.com/signups/422152/join

Amazon Page:

amazon.com/author/alexaaston

Made in the USA
Middletown, DE
02 September 2018